I CONTAIN MULTITUDES

A NOVEL

CHRISTOPHER HAWKINS

Published by Coronis Publishing.

www.coronispublishing.com
www.christopher-hawkins.com

Science Fiction/Fiction
Thrillers/Fiction

Print ISBN: 978-1-937346-17-1 Ebook ISBN: 978-1-937346-18-8

Also by Christopher Hawkins

Suburban Monsters
Downpour

For Erin

1

They slowed the car down just enough that Trina didn't break anything when she hit the pavement. Lights flared red as the car screeched to a halt. She dusted herself off, wondering if the kids inside might throw the thing in reverse and come back at her. They didn't. They only sat with the passenger door open, revving the engine, daring her to follow them until they were sure that she wouldn't. Tires spun dirt at her and she kicked it back as the car lurched forward and the door swung closed. Trina shouldered her backpack and watched them go until the lights were gone, leaving her dirty and sore at the edge of the cracked blacktop.

The road stretched out ahead and behind without a break or a bend in sight, like a string pulled taut across the sandy earth. Those kids couldn't have picked a worse place to leave her if they'd tried, with the sky growing dark and the low hills of the desert rising up on all sides. If she was caught out here, there'd be nowhere to hide, no water to cross. None to drink either, though she figured she'd be able to make do until the next Turning. If she was going to get caught, chances were it would have happened by now. Either way, there was no turning back, no sense going anywhere but forward.

She imagined it was possible that she'd run across the car and the kids again at some stop somewhere up the road. There'd been three of them, two girls and a painfully skinny guy whose names she hadn't bothered to register. They were younger than she was, barely out of their teens, and Trina had been desperate enough to say yes when they offered her a ride. They hadn't gone more than three miles before the blonde with the pixie-cut hair started eyeing her up like they were going to rob her. Or worse. Trina told them to stop the car, and after another mile they almost did. It was good enough. Those kids wouldn't last, but the ache in her shoulder would stay. Maybe that would be enough to keep her from taking any more reckless chances.

Trina walked for more than an hour before she saw the distant light of the sign bleeding up into the starry sky, and almost an hour more before she was finally close enough to stand beneath it. It was one of those old-fashioned neon jobs with the letters spelled out in loops of dusty glass tubes. Next to it crouched a single-story building with a flat roof and a handful of doors that opened directly onto the parking lot. The kids' car wasn't in that parking lot, but it wouldn't have made a difference if it had been. It didn't matter that the place made her itch just looking at it. She was tired and there was nowhere else for miles, and the word VACANCY still meant what it always had. It blinked at her in blue, the electric buzz of the thing drawing her in like a bug zapper drew in flies.

The manager's office was a grim cubicle lined with peeling wallpaper and cloudy windows. A ceiling fan turned lazily, stirring the musty air, and a bug trap in the corner of the floor turned the itch into something more like crawling. Still, it was better than going back to the road. She leaned against the chipped Formica countertop and was just about to ring the bell when a door opened and a squat man lumbered in, leaving the sound of a flushing toilet behind him.

"Forty-five," he said, not bothering to wait for her to ask, not bothering to meet her eye. She pulled a wad of brightly-colored bills out of her pocket. It took her a while to find the right ones. The man counted them against the mound of his stomach and let out a little grunt to let her know she'd gotten it right. He wore a faded short-sleeve shirt, its buttons straining, and he had a tattoo on one forearm in the shape of a lightning bolt. He slid the guest book toward her and slapped a key down on top of it. She took the key and signed her name like it still meant something.

"Ice machine's busted," he said. "Checkout's at noon or I charge you for another night. No guests, no funny business, yeah?"

She nodded, but the man had already turned away.

···•··•···

The room was no better than the front office had led her to expect, with wood-paneled walls and shag carpet and a lamp with a bulb she had to fiddle with before it would light up. The sheets were old and had cigarette burns on their edges, but they smelled like they'd been washed recently, and after the road even a lumpy mattress seemed like a luxury.

She rinsed her face in the slow trickle of water from the bathroom faucet. The mirror was cracked, but she had no use for it anyway, and the shower looked like it was held together with sloppy ropes of caulk that had long since crusted over with mildew. She could smell herself through her clothes, but getting clean could wait until morning. If she waited until morning, there might even be soap.

She kept her jacket on, afraid to lose it, and flopped down on top of the bedspread. Ancient springs groaned beneath her and she took comfort from the sound, from the squeaky insistence of it, the very *realness* of it. She pulled her backpack close and curled herself around it, as if it were an egg, just ready to hatch. As the sound of the springs gave way to the steady rhythm of her breathing, her last thoughts were of flowers, and of wrinkled hands closing over her own. She smiled, because she could see the flowers in her mind as clear as if they were right in front of her, fat peonies, each one with petals like a burst of fireworks. She smiled, because in her mind the flowers were blue.

·········

When she awoke, the angle of the sun through the window blinds told her that she'd slept through most of the morning. She remembered the manager's warning about checkout time, but she knew at once that the manager wasn't there anymore. The mattress didn't groan as she stood up. She pushed down to test it and found that the lumps were gone, the sheets no longer thin and full of holes. In the sunlight, the room was bright, with white-painted walls and an abstract painting in a silvery frame hanging across from the bed. Better than that, it was clean and new, and she wasted no time taking off her shoes to feel the carpet beneath her bare feet.

When she turned the bathroom tap, the water came out strong and cold. She cupped her hands beneath it and drank until her stomach hurt. This time there were towels that looked fluffy and unused, and there *were* soaps—little triangles wrapped in paper—sitting on top of them. She pulled some cleanish clothes from her backpack and kept them perched on top of the toilet lid, watching them warily as the grime and weeks of road dust spiraled down the drain between her feet.

As she scrubbed, she thought of the kids who'd booted her from the car and wondered if they were still out there, somewhere. She wondered if she had ever been that young. If time still had any meaning, she'd lost it long ago. Her fingertips found the raised ridges on her skin, little scars on her arm, on her stomach, but she had long since stopped wondering how she had gotten them.

There was a diner across the road from the motel that hadn't been there when she'd checked in. It sat in the middle of a row of aging brick buildings, all of them crowding up against the wide sidewalks. Shining cars with high tailfins wrapped in chrome crept by in the street as sharp-suited men wound their way between them. On the far side of the street, a woman in sunglasses and a wide-brimmed hat was being pulled along by a terrier on a leash. It was all so bright that Trina had to squint to look at them, but her eyes kept returning to that diner, to the white and orange striped awnings over its windows. Her stomach gave a little turn as the smell of frying bacon came to her on the breeze, and she decided that she could afford to linger here, if only for a little while.

The place had hand-lettered signs in the windows and a little bell that tinkled as she opened the door. She found a booth away from the windows where she could see the entrance and tried to lose herself in the cushions. The waitress poured her coffee without asking. She had red hair that was pulled back tight and wore a white apron over a lime-green uniform that might have gone out of style forty years ago in some other world, but she seemed perfectly at home in this place, among the vinyl-backed seats and metal barstools.

"Is there a bus stop, or a train station somewhere around here?" Trina asked.

"I suppose that depends on which way you're headed," the waitress said.

"I don't know yet."

"Well, it's like they say, if you don't know which way you're going, any road'll get you there."

Trina brought the coffee mug to her lips and stared at the waitress over the rim. The waitress' smile didn't waver.

"But if you go south on Main Street here, there's a bus depot that'll give you some options. If you've got a mind to stay though, we've got a mean pot pie on the dinner menu tonight. Fresh mushrooms. Cook brings 'em in special."

The waitress took her order, punching holes into a strip of paper with a metal stylus, and walked away, red ponytail swaying against her back. Trina wondered if the waitress had gone to bed the same way she had last night. Was this just another day to her? Just one in a series of days, each one so much like the last that they blurred together in her memory, familiar but indistinguishable? Would her tomorrow be the same?

A little girl peeked at her over the back of the next booth. Dark ringlets of unruly hair hung down over bright eyes that were gone as quickly as they'd appeared. Trina scanned the other tables, trying to see what they used here for money. There was a crumpled collection of paper strips in her jacket pocket, probably what was left over after she'd paid for the room last night. None of them had denominations on them, but she had a feeling they wouldn't be enough.

When her food came, she pulled the plate close and hunched over it with her fork in her fist. There were potatoes and bacon, with a whole plate of pancakes and eggs that still tasted like eggs. They made a dense little ball in her stomach, but she kept going anyway. She couldn't remember the last time she'd eaten, and didn't know when she'd be able to again. She caught a man looking down his glasses at her from two tables over, but she paid him no mind. In a few hours he'd be gone anyway, gone with all the rest of it.

When she reached for the water glass, she saw that the little girl was there again. Her eyes were a pale blue and her face was smeared with jelly. She smiled down at Trina, and her smile made it seem as if someone had turned on a light in a dark room. Trina put her hands over her eyes and the girl ducked back down, giggling. When she took her hands away, the girl popped up, bouncing with excitement, the tight curls of her hair dancing around her face. Trina smiled back, watching until the girl disappeared again, tugged down by a mother who didn't even bother to turn around.

Trina pulled the paper placemat out from under her plate and found a map on the other side. It was made for kids to color in crayon, with big block lettering and a cartoon truck driver waving out of the window of his cab. But apart from the little-kid trappings, it was nearly the same map she had seen three weeks ago on the wall of a train terminal. Some of the roads were different, but the basic layout was the same. She found the familiar spot near the north edge where two of the larger roads merged into one and rubbed an X into it with the edge of her fingernail.

The little girl came up again, moving slow with mischief in her eyes, making the two of them co-conspirators. Trina laid a finger across her lips, and the little girl bit back a giggle as her whole body started to tremble. Trina tried to smile back, but couldn't quite manage it this time, not before the little girl's mother spun her around and sat her back down again.

Should she tell them, she wondered? Should she take the mother aside and whisper the truth into her ear, that she should hug her daughter and hold her tight while she still could? Would it make one difference either way, when the change came, when this diner and the waitress in her uniform and the curls in the little girl's hair blew away on the wind as if they'd never been there at all?

Trina turned back to the map, and kept her head down as she tried to work out the distances. There was a wide arrow in the center of the paper with a drawing of the diner sitting beside it. The road she needed to take wasn't the same one as the night before, but the distance seemed mostly the same. If she started out now, if she could get to the bus depot and find one going that way without any stops, she might just make it this time.

She looked up, hoping to see the little girl, but the little girl wasn't there. She and her mother were gone, and they had left a little stack of the paper strips behind among the dirty plates. Trina thrust them into her pocket when no one was looking and hurried out the door.

··········

There was a little bookshop across the street with fading hardcovers in the window and green paint peeling away from the door. A little cart with a taped-on sign advertised the books it held as *One for a Tad, Three for a Shred*. She felt the wad of papers in her pocket, and thought for a moment about buying one. She didn't have time to waste, though, and needed all she had for the road ahead. Still, something kept her lingering in that doorway, a nagging tingle at the base of her skull that she had long since learned to trust.

She saw the thing a moment later, a tall silhouette with long, spindly limbs and a wide-brimmed hat. It stood beneath a tree at the edge of the town square, a figure not clad in black, but made of black, as if someone had cut a hole out of the world in the shape of a man. It stared out at the crowded street, its outline shifting and shimmering like heat rising from a desert road.

Trina ducked back in the doorway and watched the Shadow as its head tracked from side to side, eyeless but still searching. Searching for her. It was The Tall Man. He was alone this time, but where there was one of them, the others were never too far behind. It hadn't found her yet, but it would. It was only a matter of time.

She waited as a group of people passed and fell in behind them, keeping pace, letting them shield her from the thing's view. It seemed to sense her movement and set off in her direction, advancing with deliberate strides. It stepped through the fence without slowing. The iron rails bent around it like taffy and snapped back into place in its wake. No one on the street reacted to its presence, but they still altered their paths, as if by instinct, to stay out of its way. It passed them by inches, but they didn't seem to know it was even there.

Trina turned the corner, and when she was sure the thing couldn't see her, she broke into a run. There was no one here to hide behind, but she could see an alleyway up ahead. If she could make it there without being seen, she figured she might just have a chance. A pickup truck trundled out from that alleyway and paused before it turned onto the street. She hopped into the back and flattened herself down against the tailgate. By the time The Tall Man reached the corner, she was already halfway down the road.

···•·•····

The back of the truck had been stacked with boxes, so the driver didn't notice her until they were the better part of a mile out of town. She muttered an apology when he pulled the truck over, but he waved it away and asked her which way she was headed. When she pointed east, he smiled and said that he could take her as far as Midlington. She checked the map and told him that would be okay.

The guy looked older than she was by more than a few years, but he was handsome behind the black stubble on his chin and he seemed harmless enough. He had a nice smile and when he asked her where she had come from, he listened, even though she could tell that he knew she was making it all up. There was something in the way he looked at her, not just looking but really seeing. She hadn't been seen like that in a long time.

When she left him later that night, snoring softly on the narrow bed in his one-room apartment, she dressed in the dark without looking back. She couldn't risk seeing that his face wasn't the same one that had smiled at her just a few hours before. She couldn't risk learning that the man in the bed didn't remember her at all.

2

The Shadows had almost caught up with her six Turnings ago. Or was it five? She'd been picking her way across a bombed-out town, abandoned barricades blocking the roads, no way through but on foot. It had been The Cheerleader that time, skipping through the ruins of an old farmhouse on a distant hill, her high ponytail bouncing as she bent her way through the crumbling walls. She'd brought The Burnout with her, and it was The Burnout that had seen her first, slouching his way in her direction, drifting faster than she could run.

She'd lost both of them at the river, where she'd pushed off from the bank in a rusty old barge to leave them staring after her at the edge of the water. She'd hidden beneath a tarp, letting the current take her where it would while she waited for the morning. When morning came, the barge was full of gravel and moored against a concrete quay in the middle of some new city. Towers of metal and glass loomed, their faces reflected in the dirty river, but the Shadows were gone.

Now she was on a bus, crossing another river, maybe even that same river, for all she knew. She had dozed off, and upon waking she'd been surprised to find her surroundings exactly as she'd left them, from the red and blue checkerboard of the upholstery to the man in the green baseball cap snoring softly three rows away. She'd been dreaming of her grandfather, and in the dream, she could feel his hands cupping her own, wrinkled skin beneath a child's fingers, stretched over knobs of tendon and bone. In the dream she couldn't see his face, but she knew, even after waking, that he had been smiling at her.

The night was moonless, but she could still see the wide, dark water flowing lazily beneath her. She watched it through her reflection in the window and wondered how many times she had passed over a river just like it. A dozen? More? She'd lost count of all the crossings, of all the times she'd had to dive underwater to hide, of the nights spent shivering beneath bridges and docks. She'd even waded across one once, at a narrow place where the river had dried shallow. The flow had been little more than a trickle, but it had been enough to make her shoes muddy. The mud had stayed with her all through the next day, long after the place it had come from was gone.

She got off the bus when they pulled into a truck stop for a bathroom break. Her ticket was good for another eighty miles north, but she knew she wouldn't make it that far. The sun was starting to peek up over the soybean fields and she could feel the Turning coming on, a low vibration at the base of her spine, like a guitar string being tuned.

There was a coffee shop across the road, tucked into a strip of stores on the outskirts of a mall parking lot. It had a row of little wrought-iron tables on the sidewalk outside that looked just perfect for watching the sunrise. She left the bus for lost and picked her way across the empty two-lane highway, down the drainage ditch and up again. By the time she sat down with the tall, ceramic mug warming her fingers, the thin clouds on the horizon had become a riot of orange and pink, layered like colored sand in a jar.

She closed her eyes and brought the cup to her face. The coffee still tasted like coffee in this place, and its warmth drove some of the chill from the air. She was reminded at once of the beach, the way the sand still held the heat of the sun even after the evening air had begun to cool. Had she ever even been to the beach? She thought that she had to have been, even though that beach was surely long gone by now. When she breathed deep, she could almost feel the sand beneath her toes.

A nearby rustling sound broke her out of her thoughts and made her open her eyes. The cup in her hands had cooled and the sky in the east had brightened. How long had she been sitting there, thinking of the beach that she might never see again? How long had the old man been sitting at the next table, with a pen and a folded-back newspaper in his hands?

He was thin, in a button-down shirt with the sleeves rolled up past his elbows. He sat with his legs crossed at the knees, pants pressed to a crease, his brown leather shoes shined to mirrors. His salt-and-pepper hair was swept back and in need of a trim, his glasses round and perched at the tip of his nose. When he set his pen down on the table to trade it for the coffee cup, his eyes never left the paper.

"Word search or crossword?"

He turned his head, looked down at her over his glasses. "I'm sorry?"

"I see someone with a pen in a newspaper, I figure there's only two choices, right? Word search or crossword."

He seemed to consider this for a moment, smiled politely and turned back to his paper, no longer looking at it, but over it, across the road.

"You're missing your bus," he said.

She watched the big thing pull away from the terminal and trundle onto the highway, chrome gleaming in the early morning light. She took another sip from the cup. "It's fine," she said. "There'll be another one."

The pink bands of clouds were breaking apart, and the ones that were left had lost their color. The sun was just peeking up over the horizon now, like a secret waiting to be told. The Turning was coming. The air was thick with it, and it wouldn't be long now.

"Wait," she said. "How'd you know it was my bus?"

He folded the paper closed and looked her up and down, as if he wasn't quite sure of the answer. "Well, the backpack's a bit of a giveaway," he said. "Your jacket looks like it's seen a few miles. So do your shoes, in fact. Also, there's only one bus, and seeing as how you're not on it..."

He smiled, and she smiled back at him. It surprised her how easy it was to smile back at him. They were two people having a conversation outside a coffee shop, almost like real life.

"Besides," he said, "if you don't mind me saying so, you have the look of someone who doesn't like to stay in one place for too long."

She nodded, impressed. "Crossword, then."

"How do you figure?"

"Well, word search people just want to see the thing that's right in front of them, yeah? The answers are already right there. They know what they're looking for. They just want to feel good about finding it. Crossword people, they like clues, figuring things out. Look at the spaces, see what fits. It's like the difference between checkers and chess. Most people are one or the other."

"And the crossword is chess?"

"Yep."

"Then I will take it as a compliment."

He held out his hand to her and she took it. It was warm and solid and at least as real as anything else in this world. "Colin Wilson," he said.

For now, she thought. *Maybe only for another minute longer.*

"Trina Bell," she said, giving her name without hesitating but not quite knowing why. "So, you live here, yeah?"

"I do."

"What's that like?"

Colin shrugged, surprised by the question. "Well, it's a nice enough place, I suppose."

Trina shook her head. "No, I mean what's it *like*? Do you have a job? Do you have people? Like, people who know you?"

"Um. Well, of course I do."

"Have you known them forever? Like, they've always been there? The same people? The same places? Or is it all brand new, like the day is just one surprise after another?"

He was turned around in his seat now, and she felt a little thrill as he looked at her, at the way the wrinkles around his blue eyes scrunched as he tried to figure out what she meant. He was looking at her, really looking at her like no one had looked at her since the guy with the pickup truck. But this look was different. It was open and unguarded, no guile, no agenda. There was only curiosity, pure and disarming, without any expectations.

"I'm afraid I don't catch your meaning," he said.

She slumped back in her chair. "No, I don't suppose you do."

The sun was a little knife of gold on the horizon now, bright enough that she had to squint against it. She wondered if she could stare at it long enough for it to burn itself onto her retinas, long enough for her to carry it with her into the next world, and the next and the next, to have some proof that it had been here, when there was nothing left of this place but a memory.

"How long have you been on the road?"

She smiled a little at this. "You're the crossword person. You tell me."

"If I had to guess, I'd say quite a while."

She took a sip of her coffee. It was down to the dregs and all she could taste was the bitter.

"This isn't a bad place," he said, "if you're looking to put down roots for a while. There's a diner over on maple street makes a mean rhubarb pie, and it's just about a guarantee you can find a room for rent if you need one. And we have a good library. You can tell a lot about a place by the quality of its library. Of course, that's where I work, so I have to admit to a bit of bias."

There was a sort of rapid-fire eagerness in his voice as he spoke, and Trina couldn't help but lean into it.

"Not too exciting, I know," he said, "but it might grow on you."

There was a tightness in the air, like a rubber band ready to snap, and it made Trina realize how much she was enjoying this moment, and how much she would miss it when it all went away. "No," she said. "It doesn't sound exciting at all. In fact, it sounds just about perfect. But I can't stay."

"Where are you headed, then? If it's all right to ask?"

She took a good, long look into the older man's eyes and tried to gauge his intentions. His interest was sincere, and he seemed harmless enough. He might be a stranger, but everyone was a stranger. She couldn't hold that against him.

"Can you keep a secret?"

He seemed to think it over for a second, then nodded that he could. They had a minute more, maybe two. After that, it wouldn't matter either way.

"There's a particle accelerator," she said at last. "Up north about two hundred miles from here. I think it's in Wilmont this time. Or is it Beaumont? The names are always different and sometimes the places just aren't there at all. I made it as far as the city limits once, but by the time I got there the whole city was cordoned off and all the soldiers were wearing gas masks. I never did find out what happened because I fell asleep at the intake center and when I woke up, I was in a hospital waiting room a thousand miles away, curled up on one of the couches."

She watched him over the rim of the coffee mug, holding it up like a shield. She'd told her story before, back in the early times, when she'd still thought that telling might make a difference. She couldn't remember how long ago that had been.

"When I looked at a map, all the places had changed, but I was pretty much right back where I started. But I have to get to that accelerator, because whatever's happening to me, whatever sci-fi crap is causing this, it has to be coming from there, right? Or at least they have to know how to make it stop. So, I either sit still or I try again. So, I try again. And again. And again. And it doesn't matter if I'm running or standing still, because this world keeps changing around me, and I have no idea what it's even going to be from one day to the next. I'm just...stuck."

She watched his face, and felt an odd sense of satisfaction at the thought that she might manage to push this man away before the Turning came, because she had found herself drawn to him, maybe even liking him. But he didn't turn away from her or even roll his eyes. He only watched her as she talked, silent, smiling.

"This is the part where you tell me I'm crazy," she said. "Go ahead. I've heard it before."

He set his mug on the little table and laid the paper alongside it. He picked the lint off his pants as he considered. "No, young lady," he said, measuring his words. "I don't think you're crazy. I do, however, think that you're having a joke at an old man's expense, and I'm sure you'll forgive me if I don't find it quite as funny as you do."

She looked away then, because she could see in his eyes that she had wounded him after all. Even though he wouldn't remember it, even though he wouldn't even exist beyond this moment, she would remember, and the memory would not be kind.

"You're right," she said, and stared into her cup. "It wasn't funny. It's not funny at all."

She felt the tug again at the base of her spine, insistent this time, inevitable. Her body tensed, and she had to close her eyes, as if she were fighting back a sneeze. Her hair stirred with a rush of wind, like standing on a subway platform when the train goes by. At once the air was filled with raised voices and the sound of rushing cars. Her balance faltered, and she was glad to be sitting down as a wave of nausea came quickly over her and just as quickly subsided.

When she opened her eyes, the highway and the drainage ditch and the truck stop were gone. In their place was a city street lined with stately brownstones and glass storefronts raised off the ground with little steps beneath their doorways. The coffee shop had become a little sidewalk café. The tables were still wrought iron, but now there were more of them and every one was filled. The cup in her hands was still the same brown coffee mug. The people at the other tables had wine.

"Well, if you'll excuse me," Colin said, setting down the folded newspaper, made of shinier paper now than it had been before, "Work calls and I don't want to risk being late." He gave a shrug and fastened the button of his suit jacket. He hadn't been wearing one before, and the weave of the fabric seemed almost iridescent, changing color as it caught the light.

He turned back and regarded her with a thin smile and a tilt of his head. "Thank you for a *very* interesting conversation, Trina Bell. I hope you find your way to wherever you may be going."

She stared at him as he wove his way between the tables, and as she did, her heartbeat rose in her throat. He waved down a cab, and as he disappeared beneath its gull-wing door she bolted to her feet.

He had remembered her. He had remembered their conversation, all of it. And he had remembered her name.

She snatched the paper off the table, and saw the marks he had made in the half-finished sudoku puzzle that was printed there. He had remembered her. Everyone else had forgotten her, but he had remembered.

3

"Can you follow that car?"

Trina ducked into the back seat of the cab and watched over the driver's shoulder as Colin Wilson's taxi began to pull away. The driver barely glanced back at her. "Credplate."

"Wait. What?"

"Credplate." He spoke impatiently and pointed over his shoulder at the key slot on the wall of the passenger compartment. "Need credplate or I cannot go."

"Oh. Okay." She patted down the pocket where she'd put the change from her bus fare and came away with an oblong black wafer the length of her finger. She swiped it through the key slot once, then turned it around and did it again until a light flashed green and the little viewscreen beside it came to life.

The driver let out a little grunt of approval, pushed a lever and pulled back on the wheel. Trina's stomach gave a lurch as the car tilted and began to rise into the air. "All right, miss. Where we goin'?"

She crept to the window and watched the ground fall away beneath them. They were flying. That was a first in as many Turnings as she could remember, and it worried her. The sky was full of distant shapes, vehicles jockeying for position, moving together like a flock of birds. If Colin's cab was among them, she couldn't tell it apart from the others. She sank back against the seat. The leather creaked beneath her, mocking. "Forget it," she said. "He's gone."

"Is no problem," the driver said.

She sat forward, waiting for him to say more. His eyes were focused on the sky in front of him.

"Is no problem. Cab number eight-two-seven, yes?"

Was that the number? Had she even seen the number? She couldn't remember, but it was still something where an instant ago she had had nothing. "Um, yeah?"

"Is no problem. I can follow signal. Transponder. No problem."

She felt her insides unclench as she fell back against the seat. Relief washed over her in a wave, and yet, the cab was not turning.

"Still, is not very legal. Could be big trouble for me if I get caught, yeah?"

She found a slider marked TIP on the little viewscreen, and turned it all the way up.

"I won't tell anyone if you don't."

·········

The cab touched down and wove the last few blocks through crowded, one-way streets to stop at a corner in front of a tall limestone building. Unlike the narrow buildings that lined the streets like high walls, this one was large and set apart, with a small lawn crisscrossed with bare paths worn down by time and the passage of many feet. Glass doors were set in the building's face beneath a stone arch, and a circular stone turret jutted from its side like something from an old medieval castle.

"Are you sure this is the right place?" Trina turned to ask the driver, but the door had swung closed and the cab was already pulling away. On the other side of the street was a grassy expanse of park land bordered by a wide canal. Beyond it, Trina could see the silhouettes of a distant city, its impossible, tapered spires stabbing up past the clouds as the black dots of vehicles swirled around them, orbiting as if they were tied with invisible strings.

Trina kept to the sidewalk and tried not to be obvious about watching a cluster of boys as they negotiated the entryway. The one in the lead had an identification card on a lanyard around his neck, and when he held it up to a reader, the door popped open. A few moments later, when a group of girls did the same, she fell in behind them and slid past the door before it had a chance to close.

Inside was a small lobby with a little metal desk that Trina barely noticed for all the rows of bookshelves that fanned out beyond it. They stretched from floor to ceiling, with barely enough room in the aisles for a person to squeeze through. More books lined the curved walls of the building's high turret. Students floated among them on rounded platforms that carried them up to the high shelves.

Yeah, miss, she imagined the driver telling her, *this is definitely the place.*

A woman with close-cropped hair sat behind the desk. It took Trina a moment before she could remember the old man's name. Colin. It felt strangely familiar on her tongue as she asked for him. The woman smiled and directed Trina to a stairwell tucked away at the far end of one of the rows. Trina clung close to the rail as she mounted the steps and watched the students as they passed. No one spoke to her. No one seemed to even notice that she was there at all.

It didn't take her long to find the name on a little plaque outside the open door of a third-floor office. A too-big desk was wedged inside, with neat stacks of books and papers pushed out to its corners. The old man was there, sitting behind the desk with his chair turned and his back to the door. Trina raised an unsteady hand to rap against the door frame, but the sound it made was so faint that he didn't hear.

She cleared her throat, and almost managed to say his name again before he turned around. There was a book in his hands, and the look on his face was pleasant, almost eager. But when he saw Trina in the doorway, the eagerness fell away, and the eyes behind his glasses lost some of their light.

"Did you follow me here?"

Trina had been so focused on finding the old man that she hadn't had time to think about what she was going to say to him. All at once, she was afraid of saying the wrong thing. "I...well, yeah, I did. But—"

He gently closed the book and laid it aside, squaring its corners against the edge of the desk. "I see. It's not enough to poke fun at a lonely old man in a café. You have to harass him at his place of work as well?"

"Harass? No." She shrugged her backpack higher up on her shoulder and realized she was crushing the strap in her fist. "It's not like that. I just—"

"Young lady. Miss Bell, was it?"

The sound of him saying her name stopped her cold. It seemed so impossible, but he remembered her. He had met her in that coffee shop in that other world and he still remembered her now. There was so much that she wanted to say to him, so much she wanted to ask him, but her brain was like a record where the needle had skipped, and all she could do was nod.

"Miss Bell, I'm sure this is all quite amusing for you, but it is not at all amusing for me. I don't know what it was that made you decide to make me the subject of your attentions, but you've had your joke, and now I would appreciate it very much if you'd leave me in peace."

She closed her eyes, took a deep breath. When she opened them again, he was on his feet, gesturing toward the door. "Look," she said, "could you just give me a minute? I just need one minute, all right?"

He folded his arms across his chest and looked down his glasses at her. At once she was aware of how tall he was, of how small she felt standing in front of him.

She took another steadying breath. "I'm not making fun of you, okay? And this isn't a joke. Everything I told you, back in that coffee shop? It's all true. All of it. Every word. I swear."

He shook his head, an almost parental gesture of disappointment. "Yes, I remember what you told me in the *café*." He leaned into this last word, said it so sharply that it might have been a dagger. "It wasn't funny then, and I'm afraid that it is not funny now."

Something in Trina's insides went wobbly and she felt her cheeks start to grow hot. "Look, I know it sounds ridiculous." Each word was like a rock in her throat, and as they came loose they threatened to bring a torrent of angry tears with them. "It is ridiculous. I know it is. But that doesn't mean it's not happening. And I know you think I'm crazy, or full of shit, or whatever, but when everything changed, you still remembered me. And that has *never* happened. No one's ever remembered me before. Not once. But you did. You even remembered my name."

He squeezed past her through the doorway, but she got in front of him again, walking backwards.

"Look, I don't know what it means, and I don't know if there's anything you can do to help me get out of this...whatever it is, but I do know that I'm not letting you out of my sight again until you just...talk to me."

He stopped walking and sighed. They were near the stairwell now, and people were starting to turn curious looks their way. His mouth curled into a smile that hovered somewhere between compassion and pity as he looked down at her over the tops of his glasses. "Young lady," he said, "Perhaps the help you're looking for isn't the kind that I'm equipped to give."

He took a step to get around her, but she wouldn't let him by. "Oh nonono. I mean, I know how this sounds, and I get it. I do. But I've been through all of this more times than I can count, and I can prove it. I just need you to listen to me. Five minutes. That's all I'm asking."

He was looking at her, really looking at her, maybe for the first time since before the little coffee shop had turned into a café. More than looking at her, he was studying her. His lips were pressed to a thin line, and she couldn't tell if she was getting through to him. She wasn't about to beg, but she was ready to tackle him to the ground if he tried to walk away again.

Colin opened his mouth as if to say something, but stopped himself. His brows furrowed the way they had when she first saw him working at the puzzle in the newspaper, and he seemed to forget that she was there. All his attention turned toward the stairwell, which had grown dark and suddenly empty.

A sinking feeling worked its way toward the pit of Trina's stomach, one that told her that staying here was a bad idea. One look down the stairwell and the sinking feeling twisted into a pang of alarm. She leaned out over the railing until she could see to the bottom, two stories below. Darkness cloaked the stairwell, and the darkness was moving. It crept its way up the stairs, halting and searching as it went. Where the Shadow fell, the air around it seemed to shimmer, like waves of heat rising from a desert road.

"Shit." Trina tugged back on Colin's elbow. "Come on. We've gotta go."

Colin didn't move. He stood staring, his eyes widening as the stairs seemed to bulge and swell, warping beneath the Shadow as it moved. Trina tried his arm again, but she could not tear him away.

"Colin!"

At the sound of his name, he snapped his head around. His face was stricken, his eyes confused, like a child waiting for a parent to tell him what to do.

"Is there another way down from here?"

He nodded, and she could see his throat move as he swallowed hard, collecting himself. "The rotunda." He pointed toward a bend in the hallway and when she ran for it, Colin followed. The Shadow in the stairwell was close now. She could almost feel it, like a magnet with the poles reversed, pushing the world away.

They turned the corner at a run, and drew confused stares from a cluster of students as they passed. There was a silver railing at the end of the hallway. Beyond it was the wide-open shaft of the circular turret, its bookshelves winding along its walls and down through the floors below. There were gaps in the rail where the floating platforms were parked, each of them a tiny balcony that jutted out over the chasm.

Trina glanced back over her shoulder. The thing was with them in the hallway now. She could see its dark outline shimmer as it turned the corner, padding toward them on all fours. Its head swung from side to side, hunched low and searching, like a wild boar rooting for food.

The cluster of students drifted toward the wall, but they were still looking back at Trina. They didn't see the Shadow pass, even when it was right alongside them. The thing paused and crouched low, settling itself back on its haunches. Trina's throat clenched into an icy knot. It hadn't found them yet, but it would. It just needed time.

Colin was at the railing now, fiddling with a set of controls on one of the platforms. There were buttons and a thumb-control joystick on its handlebars, and recessed spots on the base that showed where to stand. Trina found her own platform and tried to follow his movements, but he was working too fast. The Shadow inched closer, sniffing as it grew taut, getting ready to pounce.

Colin's platform detached from the balcony with a mechanical click and carried him out into the open air. Trina stabbed her finger at the buttons of her platform, but none of them seemed to do anything. The hulking, canine shape was closer now. The floor yielded beneath its weight, warping around its enormous paws with every step. It made no sound as it tensed to leap, its eyeless head slung low, its black mouth gaping.

The mosaic floor was three stories below her, too far to jump, but only if she was aiming for the ground. Colin and his platform drifted out into the air. When he looked back at Trina, he must have seen the intent in her eyes because he started to shake his head, but Trina already had one leg over the railing.

The Shadow leapt for her. Her legs were shaking, but she forced them to push her off from the rail, and at once she was falling. She reached out for Colin, collided with him and bounced. He caught hold of her with one arm, and her feet slipped against his platform as the world around them began to spin.

Together they fell, spiraling down like a dandelion seed on the wind. Someone screamed as they crashed into the curving wall, knocking one of the shelves loose and sending a rain of books fluttering to the floor. They were spinning faster now, and Colin's grip around her middle began to slip. She grabbed at his arm, trying to hold on, but it was no use. The platform spun again and it threw her, flailing, into the air.

She hit the floor hard on her shoulder and skidded along a carpet of loose pages into the wall. Colin followed a moment later as his platform crashed down onto the tile. Far above, at the silver railing, the Hound stared down at them, as if unsure what to do. Then, without a sound, it turned and bounded back toward the stairwell, its head bending through the bars as it retreated, as if the railing hadn't been there at all.

Trina fought to her feet. Her arm was bruised, but it wasn't broken. The strap of her backpack was still hooked around her elbow. She winced and shrugged it up onto her shoulder as she helped Colin up off the floor. His glasses were askew, and there was a question on his face that she didn't have time to answer. The Hound was quick, she knew, so quick that it was probably already down the stairs. That meant they had to move.

She grabbed Colin by the hand and pulled him along, scrambling through the torn pages. A crowd had begun to gather in twos and threes. The short-haired woman at the desk was on her feet, her hands pressed to her cheeks, her mouth rounded into a shocked little O. They were coming to help, but didn't know they were only in her way. There were already too many of them between her and the door.

Colin pulled back on her arm to slow them down. He had regained enough composure to straighten his glasses, but his fear was plain. "What...what was that?"

Her words died in her throat, because as she turned, she saw another Shadow approaching them, a dark nothing in the shape of an old woman. It moved between the bookshelves at the far end of a long aisle, pulling itself forward with its spindly arms, arms that seemed too long for its bent and narrow body.

Colin saw it too, because now he was tugging at Trina's arm, the sleeve of her jacket crumpled tight in his fist. Together, they ran for the door, but when Trina tried to shoulder it aside, it wouldn't budge.

Colin swore under his breath and fumbled in his pocket for the keycard. The Shadow was closer now. As it moved, Trina could see what passed for a tight bun of hair bobbing loose at the back of its head. A teenage girl stood in its way, head down and book open, oblivious. The Shadow passed through her, and as it did, it twisted the girl's body like taffy, her face contorting, her limbs elongating into grotesque shapes, only to snap back once the thing was through.

Colin let out a sound of triumph that was halfway between a laugh and a squeal and slapped a card to the flat glass plate. The door disengaged with a little click, and Trina shoved it open with both hands. Amid a sea of confused stares, they set off running.

They were almost to the street when the Shadow burst through the door, bending it aside as if it wasn't even there, not bothering to slow down. The Hound followed a moment later, pushing through a hole in the window-glass that closed behind it with a rubbery snap. It started toward them, padding, barely at a run but closing fast, with the hunched old woman close on its heels.

Colin lagged behind as he searched the other buildings for a safe place, but Trina pulled him along. Their only chance was the canal. She could see its concrete bank looming just beyond the edge of the vacant lot. They could get there if they were fast enough, but it would still be close. She only hoped the canal wasn't dry. If it was dry, then it wouldn't matter how fast they ran.

"We'll have to jump."

"Jump?" Colin was almost alongside her now, his long strides making up for his hesitation. Trina chanced a look over her shoulder. The Shadow-woman was there, its arms outstretched. Its long fingers brushed her arm and she cried out. Its touch was so cold that it burned her skin like liquid fire.

Somewhere in those last steps, his hand found hers. He did not hesitate, did not slow as they reached the edge. The Hound was just a few feet away, then only inches. Together, they leapt out into the open air, Trina closed her eyes, and hoped that the water would catch them.

4

Trina lost hold of Colin's hand somewhere during the fall. As the silty water closed over her head, the whole world seemed to go dark. She lost all sense of where was up and where was down. Weightless, she had the panicked thought that the Turning had come again, that when she found the surface and broke through, the old man would be gone.

She found the light and kicked toward it, fighting the strange vertigo that told her she was swimming in the wrong direction. She broke through, sputtering, as a strong hand grabbed her by the back of her shirt and pulled her toward the shore. Her backpack hadn't followed her down. She hooked it with her arm as it floated by. When she reached the sloping concrete bank, Colin hauled her the rest of the way out of the water. Dripping, they fell against the incline, gasping for breath.

"What...what are those things?"

The two Shadows stood at the edge of the retaining wall on the opposite shore. Their outlines still writhed, but they seemed frozen in place, pinned to the edge of the precipice, high above the slow-moving water.

Trina shrugged her way out of her sodden jacket. "You see them too?"

"Of course I see them," Colin said, his voice rising. "They're right there!"

A crowd was forming at the edge of the retaining wall, curious students and onlookers arriving in one and twos. They whispered to each other, and stared across the water at Trina and Colin as they shook out their clothes. A few called out to help. They paid no attention to the Shadows, even when they were close enough to touch them.

"They can't see them at all, can they?" There was wonder in Colin's voice, and no small amount of fear.

"Right." Trina rubbed at her arm where the thing had touched her, wincing at the frigid pins-and-needles feeling that seemed to go all the way to the bone. "I'm guessing you haven't seen one before?"

Colin shook his head, but wouldn't take his eyes off the shimmering silhouettes. The Hound was frozen in mid-stride, its tail stiff and pointed. The old woman had her hand outstretched, as if she was beckoning to them across the water.

"Well, don't worry. They're not going to come after us. They're stuck there until the next Turning."

Colin didn't seem to hear her. He only stared with his mouth open at the empty shapes across the canal. "What are they?"

Trina stopped inspecting her backpack long enough to point across the water. "That one's the Hound. At least, I call it the Hound. Not very imaginative, I know. And that one? That's the Crone. She's bad, but at least she's slow. I think we got lucky. The Tall Man would have caught us for sure."

"No, I mean...what are they?"

She looked back at the shimmering outlines, their surfaces so dark that it was like looking through a window into another world. "Honestly," she said, "I was hoping you could tell me."

Colin had nothing but questions in his eyes. He might have remembered her after the last Turning, but she could see now that he wasn't going to be able to tell her why.

"Never mind," she said. "We should get moving anyway. You have police here, yeah?"

He nodded. Her backpack hadn't soaked through, and the insides were still mostly dry. She shrugged it up onto her shoulder.

"Then we should be gone when they get here," she said. "Come on."

· · · • · • · · · ·

They shared a cab. Colin was heading back to his apartment, and Trina was heading wherever Colin was going, though she wasn't ready to tell him as much, at least not yet.

The driver picked them up at the end of an alley next to a boarded-up brick building. He frowned at the state of their dripping clothes as they ducked beneath the door, but stopped frowning when Colin raised the slider on the tip screen. He turned and disappeared as Colin pressed a button to close off the passenger compartment with a privacy barrier. The cab kept to the ground this time, trundling along the narrow roads.

"I wish there was more I could tell you," Trina said as she stared out the window, watching this new world as it passed by. "They almost caught up with me a couple times before. Well, more than a couple times. But I can't remember the last time they got that close."

That was a lie. She remembered all too well the night that The Burnout and The Cheerleader had herded her onto that barge. She could still hear herself scream as The Cheerleader's hand closed around her leg, the way it burned like icy fire. The marks of its fingers were still there, red lines in the meat of her calf that would not go away.

"It was a dog," Colin said. He had lost his glasses in the fall and his hands trembled as he rubbed at his eyes. "That's the only thing it could have been. It was a big dog. A very big dog, but still just a dog."

"Are you serious right now?" She took hold of his hands. They were cold, and they were shaking. She held onto them until he looked at her. "You saw what it was, how it came through the window? You know dogs don't move like that."

"I don't know what I saw!" He pulled away from her, and in that moment he seemed helpless and small. Trina had to remind herself that she had been through all this a hundred times, maybe more, but to him it was brand new. To him, it must be terrifying.

"It was chasing us," he said. "The mind does strange things when a person is under stress. Between that and the wild stories you've been putting in my head, it's a wonder I can trust my eyes at all."

Trina slumped back against the seat. Outside the window, the trees stretched up over the road and formed a canopy with their branches. Tall brick houses flashed by in their shade, their windows barred, their curtains drawn.

"And what about the coffee shop?" she asked. "You were right there with me. You saw everything change, same as I did, and you're going to say it was, what? Some trick of the light? A bad dream?"

"Young lady," he said, his voice heavy with patience, "you're the one with the stories about something changing. I said nothing of the sort."

"You don't remember the coffee shop, before it was the café? Ceramic mugs? Little tables? Truck stop across the street?"

"I've been going to that café before work nearly every day for the past four years. It's not a coffee shop, and as far as I know it never was a coffee shop, and I think I would have noticed a truck if it had stopped across the street."

She leaned in, searching his face, looking for any sign that he might just be messing with her. "So, the whole time we were talking, it was a café?"

He narrowed his eyes, confused by the question. "Well, yes. Of course."

"Did you see me sit down?"

He thought for a moment. "No, you were already there by the time I came in."

"But I was there, in the café. When you walked up. You saw me."

"Yes."

She cradled her chin in her hands, her elbows on her knees. "Tell me everything you remember."

He frowned, struggling to recall. His hands were no longer trembling and the look of fear was gone from his eyes. "I walked in. It was busy. I ordered my drink."

"What was it?"

"Red wine."

"Not coffee?"

"Not that late in the day. I'd be up all night."

"But I was there already? When you sat down?"

"Yes."

"And you're sure it was me. I looked the same? I sounded the same? You weren't talking to someone else?"

He puzzled at this a bit. "How would you be someone else?"

Trina shook her head. "I was me, right? What was I wearing? Was it this? Exactly the same? Not a different outfit? Not different colors?"

He studied her clothes, the worn jacket, the hoodie with frayed holes where the drawstring used to be, the faded t-shirt underneath. "Just the same. I'm sure of it."

"Same haircut? Same eye color? Everything?"

He sighed. "Look, will you please tell me what's the point of all this?"

She took a deep breath and pressed her hands down on her knees, steadying herself. "All right. What I told you before, about how reality is changing? It's not a lie, and it's not a joke. It's true. I go to sleep, and the world is one way, then I wake up and it's something completely different. The people are different. The places are different. Everything's just...different.

"Like earlier, in the café? When I sat down, that place was a coffee shop on the edge of a highway, and there was a truck stop across the road and there was a bus headed north that I was supposed to be on, but wasn't."

"I remember the bus," Colin said.

She stared deep into his eyes, only just noticing the little flecks of brown and green around his pupils. "You remember the bus! But I didn't get on that bus because

I was talking to *you*. And you didn't change the way everything else did. You were sitting there before, and you were still sitting there after. The whole world changed, but *you* didn't, and now we have to figure out why."

Colin sat back, watching her the way he had watched her in the little coffee shop. Only, his look was softer this time, tempered with empathy. It was a look of concern, but it held no hint of pity, and she found herself warming to it.

"Go ahead. You can say it. You think I'm nuts."

He smiled at her, and his smile was patient, almost paternal. "What I think," he said, "is that you're a very troubled young lady."

Trina rolled her eyes.

"And I can see that you're scared. Now whatever you're afraid of, whatever you're running from, we can find someone who will help. There are resources. Professionals—"

"I don't need some bullshit therapist or social worker. And you already saw what I'm running from. Stop pretending that you didn't."

He closed his eyes and rubbed at the light bristle of stubble on his cheek. "Try to see this from my point of view. Whatever changes you think are going on—" She opened her mouth to protest but he stopped her with a wave of his hand. "Whatever you saw in that *café*, to me it was just a normal day. Same as it was the day before, and the day before that, and the day before that."

"And it doesn't bother you that by this time tomorrow it's going to be something completely different? That you're probably going to forget everything about the world the way it is now? Because that's exactly what's happening to you, even if you can't tell."

"Miss Bell—"

"No, you're not getting this. When the world changes, everything changes. People. Governments. Mountains. Plants. Animals. Everything. Everything except me. Me, and now you."

He opened his mouth to speak, but stopped himself. His eyes narrowed, as if he were seeing something in her face that he couldn't quite put his finger on.

"How long has this been happening to you?"

She shook her head. "I don't know. As long as I can remember, and that's a long, long time. But in all that time, I have never met anyone who remembered me. Not ever."

"Which is exactly why I feel it is my responsibility to help you," Colin said. "Now, I don't know what it is that made you single me out, but it's been a long time since you've talked to someone, hasn't it?"

Trina said nothing, but only folded her arms and sank back against the seat. She thought of the driver of the pickup truck, of how he'd helped her when she'd most needed help, and seen her when she'd most needed to be seen. She hadn't even bothered to remember his name.

"My point is that I want to help you," Colin said. "If you'll let me help you, that is."

She frowned. Suddenly, she didn't want to look at him at all. Outside the window, a couple was holding hands at a sidewalk café, their legs intertwined beneath the table. On the corner, two girls huddled against a shop window, laughing at something on a shiny black tablet. A little white dog sat with its owner on a distant park bench, panting in the sun.

"Will you let me help you, Miss Bell?"

She watched his face, searching for the angle, searching for the lie. The worst part was that she understood too well why he didn't believe her. There had been a time when she hadn't believed it herself. There had been a time when she'd almost convinced herself that she was crazy, that all of this was just some fantasy she'd made up in her broken mind.

"Look," she said at last, "all I know is that that person right there, and that one, and that one...they're not going to be here tomorrow, but <u>you</u> might. And I can't risk letting you out of my sight, because if another Turning comes and you're not around, then I might never find you again, and I can't..."

She swallowed hard, but she wasn't about to let herself cry. Not for these people. Not for the truck driver. Not for this old man, no matter how sincere he might seem.

"So, if you want to help me, that's how you help me. Ok? You'll stick with me, and you'll wait. And after the next Turning, if you're gone, or I'm gone, then none of this will have mattered anyway."

They rode in silence, Trina gripping her elbows so hard that her knuckles went white, Colin with his hands steepled in front of his face. Trina listened to the sounds of the traffic and the people on the sidewalk as they rose and fell, like waves washing up on shore. Tomorrow, all of those sounds would be gone. Something altogether different would take their place, and no one out there had even the slightest idea.

At last Colin spoke, and when he did, the corners of his mouth curled up into a resigned little smile. "Well then," he said, "I hope you don't mind sleeping on the couch."

5

Colin's apartment was a small one-bedroom, down half a flight of stairs from the street in an old, three-story brownstone. He let them in with the same keycard he'd used at the library, and Trina made a beeline for the bathroom where she locked the door behind her. More than anything, she wanted a shower, but there was only a black panel where the faucets should be, and she didn't want to ask Colin how to work it.

The outside of her backpack had dried, and when she opened it, she was pleased to see that the insides were still mostly dry too. She pulled out a faded pair of jeans and a frayed sweater, and after she sniffed them a few times to make sure the smell of the canal hadn't gotten to them, she dressed herself quickly. She was used to dressing quickly, always afraid that she might lose her backpack in a Turning if she wasn't holding onto it. This time, she dressed quickly because she didn't want to look too long at herself, at the cuts and bruises on her skin, little scars that never seemed to fade.

When at last she emerged from the bathroom—her backpack over her shoulder, her wet clothes a little drier now and stuffed back inside—she felt lighter, as if the literal weight of the water in her jeans had been somehow holding her spirit down. Colin wasn't there to meet her, but she could hear the wood-on-wood creak of old drawers coming from behind the closed door that could only lead to the bedroom. She could feel his presence there, just on the other side of that door, and that feeling was the most comfort she'd had in a long time. Maybe as long as she could remember.

The rest of the apartment was small, but she set to exploring it anyway. The kitchen was clean. She guessed that it was probably never used. The white-painted cabinets were mostly bare, but for a few plates and mismatched glasses. Bachelors were the same no matter what the world was like. In the living room, a precarious stack of books leaned against an end table next to an overstuffed leather couch. The window curtains were drawn. When she pushed them aside, she could see the feet of the people walking by on the sidewalk, oblivious, like it was any other day.

Colin emerged from the bedroom with a pillow stacked on top of a knit blanket and a sheet covered with a flower pattern that looked like an impressionist painting. "Well, these are clean and the couch is fairly comfortable," he said. "At any rate, it should do until morning. Of course, you're welcome to the bedroom. I don't mind it out here a bit, if it sets you more at ease."

"The couch is just fine. Better than fine." She drifted back toward a set of shelves and watched as Colin shook out the sheet and let it settle over the couch. "I got stuck in a dust storm a few Turnings back and had to stay in a barn. The place hadn't been mucked out in ages and a horse kept trying to eat my hair. After that, a couch is a luxury."

"Turnings. That's when…"

"That's just what I call it when the world changes." She ran her fingers along the dusty collection of objects on top of a battered bookcase. A crystal plate. A model car with high fenders, looking old, like something lost to time. A chunk of quartz. An empty vase made of cut glass. "You know, everything just kind of turns around me."

He put the blanket down and watched her with a wary eye. "How many times has this happened to you?"

She picked up the vase and ran her fingers over its deep grooves, over its surface that rippled like melting ice. "Lost count," she said. "Dozens. Maybe a hundred."

"And before that?"

She put the vase back down and gave the model car a little push. It rocked back and forth, before it came to a stop. "I don't remember anything before that."

Colin sat down on the arm of the sofa and crossed his legs. "Nothing at all?"

"Not really," she said, but that was a lie. She remembered flowers. She remembered her grandfather's hands folded over her own, thick veins under paper-thin skin, like a roadmap of the whole world. She'd already caught herself staring at Colin's hands, hoping to see those same pathways, but they were nowhere to be found. "Nothing that makes any sense, anyway. I've got my name and I've got this backpack. That's about it."

He watched her face, studying it the way he had studied the puzzle in his newspaper. It made her uneasy. "You think I'm making this all up, don't you?"

"No," he said, quickly enough that it surprised her. "I can see that you believe what you're saying. For the time being, that's enough."

"But *you* don't believe it."

He sat and thought for a moment, measuring his words. "I believe in what can be seen. What can be measured, repeated. What you're claiming is...well, it's difficult. But if it means anything, I am trying."

She could see that he was. She could tell it by the way he looked at her, the first hints of a lopsided smile tugging at the corners of his mouth. She thought of the guy in the pickup truck, of the way he had measured her with his eyes, like he was taking inventory. He'd been kind, but there had been a need in that look, and she still chided herself for having been so eager to fill it. She saw nothing like that on Colin's face. He was just a man wanting to help her, asking for nothing in return. Somehow, that was worse.

"I don't see any pictures around," she said. "Not much of a family man, huh?"

He shook his head. "No, I'm afraid not."

"No parents?"

"Not since I was very young."

"Wife? Kids? Girlfriend? Boyfriend?"

He sighed, frowning. "You ask a great many questions for someone who still wants to crash on my couch."

She shrugged. "Just making sure you're not some kind of psycho-killer."

"Well, I can assure you that I'm not."

"Maybe," she said. "But you're still the first person like you that I've ever run into. You might be the only person like you in the whole world."

He went back to spreading the blanket over the couch, taking his time, paying more attention to the process than it seemed to deserve.

"You're really all alone here, aren't you?" she said.

"It seems to suit me."

She picked up the chunk of pink quartz and was surprised by the heft of it. "Now who's making up stories?"

When he turned back to her, there was a hint of sadness in his eyes that told her she had pushed him too far. "I suppose," he said, "that solitude is something that one gets used to over time. If that time is long enough, you come to expect it, and you stop looking for the alternatives. It becomes familiar, maybe even a little pleasant sometimes."

"It sounds nice," she said. "The familiar part, I mean."

He considered this. "Well, familiarity can be a kind of trap, I suppose. Even if it is a comforting one."

"Yeah, I get that." She set the chunk of quartz back on the shelf. "Don't worry, though. You're stuck with me, at least until morning."

"When everything changes?"

"When everything changes."

"And if it doesn't?"

She frowned. "Well, then, you're in luck. I'll leave and I'll never darken your door again."

"Or…"

She raised an eyebrow. "Or?"

"Or," he said, hesitating, "there's a halfway shelter about a mile away in Oldtown. It might be worth taking a look."

"And you just happened to have that one in your back pocket, did you?"

"I may have done a quick info trace while I was getting the blankets."

He smiled. It was a disarming, almost sheepish little smile, and she almost caught herself smiling back. It was nice to be cared for, even if just a little. She had forgotten how nice.

"I wouldn't worry about it," she said. "If there's one thing I've learned, it's that as soon as I start to get comfortable someplace, it goes away pretty fast."

"And are you?"

"Am I what?"

"Comfortable?"

She thought for a moment, surprised at the answer. "Yeah, I suppose I am. Or at least I will be, if that couch is as cushy as it looks. That blanket's something else, though. Is that sort of thing really in style here?"

He frowned as he looked down at the bright reds and blues, yellow sprays in the shapes of sunflowers. "No. Not for a long time now, anyway."

"If we're lucky, it'll be something better in the morning."

"And how would I know, exactly?" He folded his arms, and though he probably didn't mean it that way, it still felt like a dare. "According to you, I'll have no memory of the world the way it was before the change. The *Turning*. If that happens, then how do you plan to convince me that all of this ever existed in the first place?"

"Well, I've been thinking about that." She dropped down onto the couch. The cushions sank beneath her with a pleasant little woosh. "You don't remember the coffee shop at all?"

"I do not."

"But you remember talking to me, right? You remember everything we said to each other?"

"More or less, yes."

"Then it's simple. We just need to describe this place. In words. And we do it in a way that's repeatable, something we can memorize. Something there's no chance that we'd forget."

"A code?"

"A code." She smiled, and was pleased to see the old man smile back. "But it has to be simple, something there's no way you'd forget."

She stood up and paced the room, taking it all in. It was sparse, but it was enough. "Okay, how about this?" She spread her arms wide and spun on one heel. "Small room."

He nodded, following along. "Small room."

She picked up the piece of quartz. "Pink rock."

"Pink rock."

"Ugly lamp."

He looked over the tall brass lamp with its yellowed fabric shade. "Surely it's not that ugly."

"Stay with me here."

His eyes shimmered with amusement as he nodded. "Ugly lamp."

Trina flopped back down on the couch. "Flower blanket."

"Flower blanket."

"Okay, so say it back to me. Small room..."

"Pink rock. Ugly lamp—"

"Flower blanket!" Trina nearly leapt to her feet. At once feeling ecstatic with this newfound sense of control. "Small room. Pink rock. Ugly lamp. Flower blanket!"

Together, they said the words. They said them over and over again, turning them into a chant, a song to get stuck in their heads. Trina took the old man's hands in her own, and together they danced around and around, reciting the words like a mantra until they both fell back onto the couch. Colin struggled for breath and he waved off Trina's concerned glances until he caught it again.

"Small room. Pink rock. Ugly lamp. Flower blanket," he said at last. "I believe that it's in there to stay."

"Good, because first thing in the morning I'm going to make you say it back to me and you're going to get it right, yeah?"

"I will do my best."

"You'd better." Fatigue hit her all at once then, luring her deeper into the soft cushions of the couch. She squeezed her eyes shut to fight off a yawn.

Colin stood, and checked his watch. "Well, that I believe is my cue. You've already found the bathroom. And if you need anything in the night, I'll be right on the other side of that door."

Trina was already inching beneath the blanket, wrapping herself up in its gaudy flowers. She caught Colin's smile as he turned toward the bedroom. There was a faraway quality in his eyes that she didn't understand, but she was too tired to puzzle it out. She pulled her backpack beneath the blanket and wished that she could take back what she'd said about him being alone. She wished that she had just told him *thank you*, but by the time she figured that out, the door had already closed behind him.

6

Trina was slow to remember. She was not used to *having* to remember. Everything around her was dark, but she could sense the presence of the sun somewhere out beyond the heavy curtains. She remembered Colin. She had fallen asleep in his apartment, but it was morning now. Her backpack was still there, held close against her stomach. She had fallen asleep beneath the ugly blanket with the flowers. When she looked down, the blanket was still there.

She shot to her feet, her eyes adjusting to the dim light. The little shelf was still there against the far wall. The glass vase and the lump of quartz were exactly where she'd left them the night before. The dimensions of the room were all the same. The wood trim around the doors was still dark and worn with age.

"Colin!"

From behind the bedroom door, she heard a thump and the shuffle of feet. The door opened and Colin rushed in wearing a set of pale blue button-down pajamas, scratching at his matted hair.

"Good morning," he said through a yawn. His eyes were tired and confused, but as he saw Trina they quickly came into focus. "Oh, ah...small room. Pink rock—"

"No, forget that." She grabbed the edge of the blanket in her fist and held it out to him. "Don't you see? Everything's the same!"

He looked around, taking his time. "It does indeed seem to be exactly as I remember it." The tone in his voice wasn't smug, not exactly, but there was enough satisfaction in it to set Trina on edge. She dropped the blanket to the floor, stomped over to the window and threw the curtains wide. Beyond them was the same street-level view that had been there the night before. The shadows were different, and there were fewer feet walking by, but there was no mistaking that it was all exactly as it had been.

"Everything! Right down to the street lights. Damnit!"

Colin had found his glasses and was cleaning them with the hem of his shirt. "Honestly, I fail to see this as a bad thing."

She spun on him, fists clenched at her sides. "You fail to...how is this not a bad thing? I mean, I know for you it's all the same, but for me..."

That stung him a little. She could see it on his face, as sure as if she'd slapped him. When he spoke again, his words were slow and deliberate. "Well, perhaps whatever you thought was happening to you isn't happening anymore."

"*Was?*" She could hear her voice rising as she spoke. "Whatever <u>is</u> happening. I don't just *think* it's happening. It's happening."

He nodded. Trina knew how she must sound, and she swallowed hard to get herself under control. She could tell that Colin was trying to understand as much as she was, and all at once she felt bad for snapping at him.

"Either way," he said, "it's still a good thing. You're still here. I'm still here. Maybe the whole phenomenon has stopped."

She frowned, and tapped her foot on the floor. She wanted him to be right, but she refused to believe that it could be that easy. "No," she said, shaking her head. "Whoever's doing this to me is just messing with me now. They're just messing with me so that you'll think that I'm crazy and stop helping me."

Her hands were shaking and her lip was beginning to tremble. Colin watched her with widening eyes, overwhelmed, not knowing what to do. Trina thought of the two Shadows, pinned in place at the edge of the canal. Were they still there, or had the new day freed them? She looked at Colin, standing before her, helpless. What did she expect him to do when they came for her again? What did she expect would happen to him?

"This was stupid," she said, pushing past him toward the door. "I have to go."

She shouldered her backpack and got hold of the doorknob before she felt his hand close around her forearm. It was a gentle touch, so light that she could have broken away with barely any effort. Still, it stopped her cold. The wide-eyed helplessness was still on his face, but there was something else there, too. He was afraid for her, maybe afraid of what might happen to her if she went out there alone. For as much as she hadn't wanted to lose him, she hadn't thought until that moment that he might not want to lose her either.

She turned around and pulled him into an awkward hug. One of his buttons grazed her cheek as she buried her face against his chest, and she squeezed her eyes shut to hold back her tears. They spilled free anyway, and soaked into his shirt. Hesitating, he placed a gentle hand on the back of her head and smoothed her hair.

"Look," he told her, "I can't imagine what any of this must be like for you. And I won't pretend that I understand it. But I believe you. I do. And if you still want me to help you, then I *will* keep trying."

She breathed in the smell of him, crisp linen and dried sweat. He felt solid and real. He would not disappear from her life the way everyone else had disappeared. In that moment, she felt sure of it. In that moment, all of the uncertainty and the loneliness seemed to flow out of her. Now that it was gone, she didn't know if there was anything left in her to fill the space that it left behind.

The air shifted then. She felt the little rush, the way it made the little hairs at the back of her neck stand on end. She sensed it the way she might sense another person standing behind her. She squeezed her eyes shut and held onto Colin, knowing that he would come with her, that he had to come with her. The noises from the street were different now, the air drier and colder. But he was still there. The smell of him was the same, and she breathed it in.

"There," she said, without opening her eyes. It surprised her to hear that her voice didn't waver. "Just now. It just happened."

"Are you sure?" He broke away from her and took her by the arms. When she opened her eyes, she could still see the damp spot on his shirt that her tears had made.

"Yes," she said quietly. "Did you feel it?"

The trim around the doors was no longer the deep brown of stained wood, but bright white. A hasty paint job had slopped white streaks onto the yellowed walls. The dimensions of the place might have been the same, but it felt more cramped somehow. There was a desk, an old rolltop contraption full of little drawers and cubby holes stuffed with papers. The couch was still there, but its cushions were smaller and covered in deep green fabric. Though the sheets that hung half upon it seemed the same, the blanket was a loose-knit thing, with wide gaps between loops of faded yarn.

Colin looked around the place, taking in every detail from the iron radiator beneath the window to the tall bookcase with the blue and green spines of leather books tucked behind dusty glass doors. He grinned a curious grin, his eyes dancing as if he were seeing it all for the very first time.

"It's...exactly the way it always has been."

She frowned, and stared back at him through narrowed eyes.

"Ah, as far as I can tell," he added, taking a sudden interest in the floor.

"What about the code?"

"What about it?"

"Do you remember it!"

"Yes, of course." He squeezed his eyes shut, counting out the words before he said them. "Small room. Pink rock. Ugly lamp. Flower blanket."

Triumphant, she raised her index finger and pointed it at his nose. "Ha! There. You do remember."

"Well, yes, but..." He looked around the place, frowning. "Well, look here."

Trina's stomach did a little flip, like she was dropping from the top of a roller coaster. "What?" she asked, but deep down she already knew.

"Well, small room, obviously." He strode to the bookshelf, took a small object from on top of it, and held it out between his thumb and forefinger. "Pink rock."

It was no longer a large chunk of rough quartz, but a rounded pebble of soapstone, polished so that the wide, pink stripes stood out against the brown like ribbons of stretched taffy.

"Ugly lamp." The lamp was a heavy iron and stained-glass contraption, its fabric shade gone. "In fact, now that I'm looking at it again, I can see your point."

Trina felt a scream welling inside her, and clenched her jaw shut.

"And, flower blanket." He gestured toward the knitted thing that lay piled on the floor next to the couch. The pattern stood out, even among the wide loops and rough knots. Daisies, with dingy white petals and faded yellow centers.

Trina felt the rage wash over her and through her as it twisted into a dark and bottomless despair. She flopped down onto the couch, but instead of a woosh of cushions she was met with the sound of creaking springs.

He sat down beside her, his hands in his lap. "Perhaps we weren't specific enough."

She wished she had said "toy car." The little car was a statue of a horse now. She shook her head. "It wouldn't matter. We could describe a dog and when they changed the world, they'd just change everything around the dog and leave the dog the same. They're definitely messing with me."

"They? You mean those things that were chasing us."

"Yeah, them or whoever's been sending them after me. You still remember *them*, right?"

Colin nodded, but there was a kind of puzzlement on his face that made her wonder. Was he really remembering them as they had been. Or did he remember them as something else entirely?

She went to the window. The cars outside were gone. In their place were horses pulling carriages, some with two wheels, some with four. A kid ran by, brown coat and matching shorts, wearing a newsboy cap. He might have actually *been* a newsboy, for there were bundles of papers stacked by a little stand at the end of the road. All the men were wearing felt hats with wide brims, and the few women she could see were not walking alone.

Colin stepped in behind her. Together, they watched the people go by in silence until at last he said, softly, "Do you have any idea as to who *they* might be?"

There was a hush to his voice, a question beneath the question. He was really asking if *they* really existed at all, if this was all just happening in her head. "No. Just...it doesn't matter. Look." She pointed out the window, at the awnings above the windows of the tobacconist's shop across the street, at the worn cobbles set into the road. "What year is this?"

"What do you mean, what year?"

She shot him a look full of ice and daggers.

"Year of the Raven," he said. "Fourth transit since Succession. Why?"

She sighed and chided herself for thinking that the information might be helpful. "And yesterday? The year was the same?"

"Of course. Why wouldn't it be?"

She paused, crafting her words, working them into something that would make her sound reasonable. "Well, in the other realities, the ones I remember anyway, there was more technology than there is here. All the roads were paved and newspapers weren't so much of a thing anymore, and I don't even remember the last time I saw a horse-drawn carriage."

"How would you get anywhere without carriages?"

"Colin, we flew in a car yesterday."

"Flew?" The faraway look returned to his eyes. "I should think I would have remembered that."

Trina frowned. "Yeah, we never talked about it, did we? Anyway, it doesn't matter. My point is that is that, with every other Turning, the world changed but a lot stayed the same. Cars. Television. Airplanes. But this...this feels like a step back. A big step back."

He breathed deep, and his face became pained and confused. "I don't understand."

"No, you wouldn't, but it doesn't matter. The point is that this change is bigger than any of the ones I've been through before. Details always change. Places change. But at the end of the day it's still mostly familiar. But this..."

Outside, a greengrocer was pulling in crates of fruit from the sidewalk. Across the street, a man tipped his bowler hat to a woman who wore white gloves and a dress with a bustle that made her rear end look about three feet wide. She had an umbrella tucked beneath her arm, even though the sky showed not even the barest hint of rain.

"Yesterday was a bigger change, too. The flying cab. I've never seen anything like that before, in any of the

Turnings. I was just so busy trying to get to you that I never gave it a second thought."

Colin watched the people outside the window, clearly unsurprised by what he saw. Still, Trina could see that something was weighing on him and she knew, before he said anything, exactly what that something was.

"Is it at least possible," he said, "just possible, mind you...that everything that's been happening to you is just a product of your imagination?"

She frowned, and hesitated longer than she would have liked to. "No," she said, as much to convince herself as to convince him. "No, it's not."

At the end of the block, a man in a gray stovepipe hat ducked into a narrow booth that was painted a deep red. Written on its side in inviting block letters were the words PHONE CUBICLE. Trina spun around to face Colin. "I can prove it."

Grinning, she dropped to one knee to rummage through her backpack. "You have a phone in the apartment, right?"

"Yes," he said, a little bewildered. "In the bedroom. Why?"

"And it plugs into the wall? With wires?"

"How else would it—" He pinched the bridge of his nose, pained. "Yes, of course."

"And I bet talking is all you can do on it. No texting? No games? No memes?"

"I—"

"Never mind. Here." She stood and pressed the gleaming black rectangle into his hand. "Now, tell me what you make of that!"

It caught the light from the window as he turned it over between his fingers, a hatchwork of scratches set into its black-glass surface. "Well, it seems to be some kind of stone. Obsidian, perhaps? And the metal banding is quite uniform. Appears to be exceptional craftsmanship."

"Obsidian? No, give it here." She snatched it out of his hands and held down the button on the side. "This is a phone. This is what they're like in my reality. The *real* reality. And it connects to this thing called the Internet, which is just everything you ever wanted to know ever. And it doesn't need wires and it doesn't..." She pressed the button again, but it wasn't turning on.

"And of course it's still dead. Hang on a second." She rummaged in the backpack again unto she came away with a long white cord with a plug on the end. Colin watched her search the walls for a place to plug it in, but when she found one, it wouldn't fit. Her plug had two flat prongs jutting out from it. The outlet on the wall had only three narrow holes arranged in a triangle.

She groaned as she leaned back against the wall and slid down to the floor. She squeezed down on the little black rectangle until her hands shook. She wanted to throw the damn thing, wanted to watch it shatter to pieces against the wall. But then she'd have one less thing, one less *real* thing from that time before. As much as she hated it right now, she hated the thought of losing it even more.

Colin sat down on the floor beside her. He said nothing. He only sat, close enough to let her know that he was there, but far enough away to not intrude.

"You have to charge it," she said quietly. Her hair was in her face, which was fine because she didn't want to look at him. "I haven't been able to charge it, and it doesn't work if the battery's dead."

He nodded, but Trina could tell, even through the curtain of her hair, that he didn't understand. "Perhaps we can find some other way to—what did you say?—charge it?"

"Stop."

He tilted his head, questioning.

"Stop being so...damned reasonable." She smoothed her hair away from her face. "Just...I know how I look. I'm not an idiot. I know how ridiculous this all sounds. I know you think I'm crazy. So just...stop it."

He nodded, and in that nod was confirmation of everything that she had been trying not to admit to herself. He'd been going along with her, indulging her long enough to let her see the absurdity in everything she'd been saying. Of course he thought she was crazy. All he was doing now was letting her prove it.

"It was a stupid idea, anyway," she said. "There's no internet, no cell towers. I couldn't get anything out of it but lights and noise."

Colin seemed to consider this. "That's a shame. I'm rather fond of lights and noise."

She let herself smile at this. It worked to push away the hollow feeling that had settled in the pit of her stomach. "I'm not crazy, though," she said softly, and mostly to herself. "You can put that out of your head right now. If that's what you think of me, then I should just go, because I don't need that kind of help. And if you don't believe me then there's nothing you can do for me anyway."

They sat in silence for a moment. Colin stared at her until she finally met his eyes. "I believe you," he said. "But I will confess that I'm a bit out of my depth."

She didn't know what to say to that, because she was out of her depth too. The world outside was something completely new, and it frightened her. How was she supposed to navigate the place when she couldn't count on the basic rules that made it function?

She could wait. If it took a day, or two, or even a week, eventually this world would be gone and another would snap into its place. She could wait that long, assuming the Shadows didn't find her, but would Colin let her stay? She thought that he would, but would it be right for her to ask him to?

"You said yesterday that there was a halfway house or something that you thought could help?"

He blinked at this, surprised. "Yes!"

He raised a finger, telling her to wait, and trundled off to the bedroom. When he returned, he held a thick book in his hands, its edges frayed and dog-eared. Its cover was a deep green, and embossed across it in gold with swirling, baroque lettering was the word INFOSEARCH. He thumbed his way to a page he'd folded over and when he found it he turned the book around so she could see.

In the corner of the page was an ad in block lettering.

YOUNG LADIES!
Has hostile society cast you aside?
Adrift in Stormy Waters?
Have smoking, men or other mischief taken control
of your life?
We have the solution!

**Ms. Dixon's Home for the Dispossessed
200 South Royce, between Beaufort and Wain
No Appointment Necessary.**

Trina frowned at the wording. The casual sexism definitely fit with the Victorian feel of the place. What she'd seen outside the window had been familiar enough that she'd felt like she could at least navigate this world. She knew better than to trust that feeling, though. Just like she should know better than to trust anyone.

Next to the text was a line-drawing of a young woman, her hair swept back in a tidy bun, her dress pressed and pleated. Her chin was held high and the artist had given her the slightest hint of a self-satisfied smile. It was weird idealism, but all the same, Trina envied that smile. She wondered if she'd ever been able to pull off a smile like that, or if she ever would again.

"So, this is the place?"

Colin nodded somberly.

"And this is exactly the way it was last night? Same name, same ad? Same everything?"

"Well," his brows furrowed in thought. "Yes. I'm fairly certain."

Trina frowned at this. It was one thing to trust Colin to remember the words he had spoken to her, but it was another thing entirely to trust that he remembered events exactly the way they had happened. He hadn't remembered the coffee shop. He hadn't remembered the flying cabs. There was no way to be sure that he remembered this either.

"And you think they can help me."

Colin considered for a moment. "I think that it certainly could not hurt."

She studied his face, his guileless smile, the deep empathy in his eyes. He was being honest with her. He'd been honest with her from the start, and if he was wrong about this place being able to help her, then at least it was an honest wrong.

"Okay, then," she said.

"All right then," Colin said. "I'll get my coat."

He got to his feet and disappeared behind the bedroom door. When he returned, the book lay on the floor with the page torn out. The door hung open, and Trina was gone.

7

By the time she turned onto the high street, Trina was
hopelessly lost. She had gotten used to finding the
rhythm of a new place, learning her way quickly, doing
everything she could to blend in. Here, things felt familiar
and unfamiliar all at the same time, like seeing a picture
whose details she'd thought she'd remembered, but when
she looked again it was something else entirely.

The crowd carried her along, jostling her from one
intersection to the next, leaving her no time to get her
bearings. Her jeans and frayed sweatshirt drew looks
down the noses of women in long black dresses as she
ducked beneath the wide brims of their flower hats. The
men, perhaps sensing that she didn't belong, showed her
none of the deference they gave to those women. They
grimaced as they passed, like she was some kind of street
trash, and made it clear that they expected her to get out
of their way, not the other way around.

There was a flat cap lying on a crate next to a fruit
stand. Trina snatched it when the stockboy's back was
turned and tucked her hair up underneath it. She pulled
it low over her eyes as she fell in behind a group of men
in long wool coats, following in their wake as they swept
out a path with their canes and folded umbrellas. She cast
worried glances over her shoulder, knowing that, should

the Shadows find her here, there would be no room for her to run.

She checked the crumpled paper in her fist, looking for street names, and veered off across a wide intersection, halting and weaving to avoid the horse-drawn carts and carriages that showed no interest in slowing down for her. On the corner, a man in a threadbare coat and dark glasses played a steel guitar, his upturned hat at his feet. The whole place stank of rotted vegetables and horse sweat, punctuated by whiffs of who-knew-what drifting up from the sewer gratings, and it was enough to set her stomach churning.

Everywhere she looked, she found another thing that didn't fit. In those other worlds there had always been an underlying sense of sameness, a sense that everything was part of the same whole. Here, the place seemed to be daring her to make sense of it. Everywhere she looked was some new incongruity. A woman wearing a pair of wraparound sunglasses. A pizza in the window of a bakery. A beard dyed blue. She'd been out of place before, but here? Here, she was a complete stranger. Here, everything seemed wrong.

Yet, for all its differences, there were aspects of this new reality that still felt tantalizingly familiar. There were no cars in the street, no gasoline motors of any kind as far as she could tell, but there were still electric lines buzzing high above the sidewalks. She passed a shop window full of old-time gramophones with wide brass horns, and ornate wooden music boxes inlaid with silver and gold. They bore logos etched on plaques, logos that she felt certain she ought to recognize. An X in a circle. An apple with a bite taken out of it. Letters and acronyms that might have meant something to her once, but now just seemed like gibberish.

There was a cart standing next to the green-painted door of a bookshop. On it was a jumble of cheap-looking books, their bindings split, their edges worn. Trina tried to make herself small behind it as she searched the street, scanning the skies beyond the billowing chimneys for some clue as to which direction she should go. She showed the crumpled advertisement to the shopkeeper. He looked her up and down over the tops of his glasses before he gestured toward an intersection a block back in the direction she'd come from. She wanted to ask him more, but when she looked back he had already disappeared through the shop door.

A hard-topped cargo wagon trundled by, painted red and white and laden with brown-glass bottles. She followed it across the road, hopscotching her way around shallow puddles of dirty water. She almost collided with a round man in a stovepipe hat and mutton chops. He stared down at her with narrowed eyes but tipped his hat as she passed all the same. His hand was covered in tattoos that started at his knuckles and disappeared up into his coat sleeve.

It was all wrong, every last bit of it.

She reached a high bridge that crossed over a wide canal. A crowd was gathering there, its energy almost manic as the people massed against the rail. Something below had caught their collective attention. Trina shouldered them aside as she fought her way to the front of the press, ignoring shouts of indignation as she steadied herself against the rail.

One street over, on a lower bridge, a carriage had gone half over the side. Its great, black bulk listed sideways, wedged against a bent light post, propped up by the twisted iron railing. The horse that had drawn it hung out over the canal, suspended by its tangled harness. Bleeding and leg-broke, it scrambled for purchase against the brickwork arch, squealing and snorting as its harness began to slip.

Below, barge pilots plunged their long poles into the water to nudge their boats out of the way. The black water swirled in their wake, slick with surface oil that reflected the daylight in iridescent spirals. The carriage driver tugged at the horse's bonds, and was joined by others who hauled with all their might but could not budge the beast. One of the barge pilots stroked his white beard and shook his head as the horse's cries grew weaker. The leather strap around its neck slipped, and began to pull tight.

All around Trina, men lowered their eyes and women held handkerchiefs to their mouths, sneaking glances even as they turned away. Trina gripped the rail until her knuckles went white. Something about the colors swirling in the black water transfixed her, a note of dread plucked against the nerves of her spine, and she could not look away.

On that other bridge, a group of men had stripped out of their topcoats. Some had knives in their hands and they used them to saw frantically against the harness straps while others strained to loosen the buckles. The horse kicked once more, then grew still, but Trina barely noticed. Below her, the water churned, and every shimmering reflection seemed to beckon to her.

A hand at her back startled her out of her trance. It closed around the fabric of her sweatshirt and hauled her away from the rail. Only then did she realize how far she'd stretched out over the water. Another inch and she would have fallen.

Colin kept his grip on her, out of breath, his coat hanging open, his shoes barely tied. He turned her around and rubbed warmth into her arms that she hadn't realized she needed. "What's gotten into you? You almost went right over the side."

"This isn't right," she said.

"Yes," he said, looking concernedly over her shoulder at the crooked wagon, at the dangling horse, now dead. "I should think we'll want to move on before we're forced to witness any worse."

"No, I mean, everything's mixed up. Like they put a bunch of stuff that doesn't go together in a blender and just dumped it all over the place."

Colin winced and pinched the bridge of his nose, as if a sudden pain had gripped him there. "Of course," he said, with an edge in his voice that Trina hadn't heard before. "This all must be very tiring for you, keeping track of one change after another, but I assure you that everything is in its proper place."

There it was, that doubt in his voice again. It seemed to hang between them like an unspoken insult even as he hurried her away from the bridge. "No need to thank me, by the way," he said. "But consider yourself lucky that I knew which way you were headed. I don't imagine anyone else would have stopped you from falling. Come on, then."

She sulked behind him, trudging along in his footsteps, waiting for him to say something that would tell her that he still believed her, that she wasn't just imagining all this, but he didn't.

A teenage kid wound his way through the crowd carrying a wooden box of tools. He wore a bowler hat and the back of his vest was blazoned with a rounded logo, like an elongated checkmark. Up the street, an organ grinder cranked out a tune on the ornate cabinet strapped to his chest. A ferret on a string danced along his shoulders, and bared its teeth whenever someone passed too close.

"I'm sorry," she said.

"What was that?" He was pretending he hadn't heard her, and that made her smile a little.

"Don't make me say it again. It's just... I'm not used to needing help, okay? Or at least, I'm not used to thinking that having help might make any difference."

His strides became a little less stiff, and his pace slowed. "Unfortunately, the only way you'll know for sure is to actually let someone help you."

"Yeah," she said, not wanting to look at him. "I guess you're right. I just got spooked, I guess."

"By me?"

"No. By this. Just...all of it."

"Why?" he asked, making a pained face. "By your reckoning, this is the, what? third change since I've met you? If the whole world changes every time, I'd expect it to be quite different from what it was when you started, yes? Isn't it always wrong? From your point of view, I mean."

"No. I mean, yeah, but not like this." She frowned and tugged at Colin's arm to get him to stop. She pointed down the street at a set of yellow arches painted on a red sign hanging from a post outside a stone building with high windows. "You see that? That doesn't belong here. It's from my time, not this...whatever the hell this place is."

Colin considered for a second, then nodded. "Oh yes. They're everywhere, I'm afraid. But what do you mean 'your time?' We're all from the same time, aren't we? Or is that some new wrinkle you haven't told me about?"

She didn't like the condescension in his voice, but she let it go. She shook her head. "That's just it. Every other Turning, it's still been a modern world. There'd be changes here and there, like all the cars are electric or they hadn't figured out cordless phones yet. A few years ahead, twenty years back at most. But this..."

Her words trailed away as she came to a halt. They'd turned the corner once more, onto a grassy plaza lined with squat stone buildings, a mountainscape of turrets and pointed domes. Floating high above them was the great, curving hull of an airship. Its brassy skin blazed golden in the morning light, and rows of antennas along its spine gave it the look of some grand, giant ocean fish that had made a new home for itself in the sky.

Colin stopped and regarded her, fascinated once more. "I suppose that you've never seen a dirigible before."

"Not like that one, no." Glinting, it made a lazy turn along the diagonal path of the distant street, dragging its shadow across the faces of the buildings below. Trina stared at it as she followed Colin across the grassy plaza, unable to tear her eyes away from the clusters of propellers that seemed far too small to move something so enormous. She watched as boxy, whirling contraptions spilled from its sides and drifted to the porches of the buildings like maple seeds. It had almost floated out of sight when Colin came to a stop so abruptly that Trina nearly ran into him.

Colin put his hands on his hips and stared up at the squat rectangle of limestone and red brick that filled the block from one end to the other. Rows of narrow windows stretched up three stories toward the wide cornice that bordered its flat roof. Beneath a wrought-iron balcony stood two heavy oak doors set inside a tall, stone archway. Next to the arch was an unassuming copper plaque cut deep with stately, narrow lettering.

Ms. Dixon's Home for the Dispossessed
Est. 14 Harvest
Year of the Tortoise

Once more, Trina felt the doubt begin to creep over her, a nagging sense of unease that weighed heavy on her limbs. She'd become used to the feeling of separation that the constantly shifting world had given her, the sense that, no matter how strange or unbearable a given thing was, it would still be gone by morning. Now, standing before this place, she could almost believe that it had been there last night and would still be there tomorrow. The thought was like a little candle in her soul, and it warmed her. And yet, with it came another thought that she dreaded to even consider: that the world she found herself in might be solidifying, one place at a time, one person at a time, and soon there would be no returning to the world she once came from.

Colin laid a reassuring hand on her shoulder. "We don't have to go in if you don't want to."

She licked her lips, because her mouth was suddenly dry. "No. We didn't come all this way just to look in the windows. Besides, I want to see what it looks like when someone's dispossessed. Does a ghost come out of them or something? Do they turn into zombies?" She smiled at Colin, and Colin smiled back. All the same, it took her a few moments to steady herself enough to mount the steps and open the door.

8

Beyond the heavy doors was a wide lobby with a
high, coffered ceiling. The floor was marble, a grid
of white squares trimmed in black that made loud echoes
of their footsteps. At the far end was a long counter made
of dark wood, polished so highly that it shined like glass.
It was topped with a little brass bell that reminded Trina
of the motel with its buzzing neon sign. How long ago
had that been? A week? A month? It already seemed like
a lifetime.

The woman behind the desk rose to meet them. She
was young, Trina thought, not much older than herself,
standing pencil-straight in a plain green dress that seemed
made to show off all the bones in her shoulders. Her
coppery-red hair was pulled back and twisted into a plait
that seemed so much more simple and modern than the
complex buns and updos that she had seen on so many of
the women outside. She smiled as they approached her,
warm, but with a hint of caution.

"So good of you to come," the woman said, as if she had
been expecting them. "How can I help you?"

Trina realized at once that Colin was standing a full step
behind her, letting her take the lead. The problem was
that she had nothing to say, and hadn't given any thought
at all to what might happen after she opened that door.

She steadied her hands against the wooden counter. It was cool to the touch, and so reassuring that it made her want to tell this woman everything, to let it spill out of her like a great flood until the weight of it was gone. But all she did was stand there, unable to make a sound.

The woman behind the counter only smiled wider, bright red lips and perfect white teeth. She laid a hand on top of Trina's and leaned in close. "You're overwhelmed, I can tell. I was just the same way when I first arrived. It's all so...damned big."

Trina could tell by the twinkle in the woman's eyes that she was savoring her brief foray into profanity the same way she might savor a piece of chocolate. "How about we start with a little tour?" she asked, as if the thought had only just occurred to her. "I'm sure your companion won't mind if I steal you away for a bit. Would you, mister..."

"Oh. Um, Williams. Colin Williams." He extended his hand but she was already on her way around the counter to take it. She kept hold of Trina's hand as she moved, and gave it a reassuring little squeeze.

"Pleased to meet you both. I'm Ms. McCafferty. But please, call me Edie." They exchanged pleasantries for a few moments before Edie guided Colin into an overstuffed armchair flanked by two tall potted plants, explaining that they wouldn't be long, and that she could ring to have some tea brought to him if it would make the wait more comfortable. He shook his head and tried to catch Trina's eye. Trina warmed at the concern she saw on his face, and tried to smile back in a way that would let him know she would be okay.

And she really did feel like it might be okay. Okay the way it hadn't been in months. There was something so trustworthy in Edie's smile, in the gentle way she held out her hand toward the wide, curving staircase at the end of the lobby, that Trina might have been happy to follow her anywhere.

"This whole building used to be a hotel," Edie said, climbing the steps without hurry, reciting the words as if she had said them a hundred times before. "They built it back in the Year of the Dove. In fact, it was one of only three buildings that survived the Great Fire. I like to think that that makes us a stable little island, no matter what storms the outside world might throw at us."

She threw a conspiratorial wink back over her shoulder at Trina as they reached the landing, long legs in black heels taking the steps with measured grace. Trina looked down at her own frayed sweatshirt and dusty jeans, and hiked her backpack higher up on her shoulder.

"Of course, having been a hotel, that means the rooms are *quite* spacious. Most of our girls have a room all to themselves, though we do double up on occasion. But only when we know the girls will get along, and only when—"

"So, you live here too?"

Edie tilted her head as if she was amused by the interruption. "I do. My room is on the first floor. We have a few permanent staff, and some of the longer-term residents volunteer as house mothers, so there's always someone on-call twenty-eight hours a day. We keep at least two on every floor, so you're never more than a few steps—"

"You didn't have to do that, you know."

Edie pressed her lips together and straightened her spine, waiting for more.

"Colin," Trina said. "Downstairs. You didn't need to separate us. It was my idea to come here anyway. Well, it was his, but it was still my choice. He's helping me. He's a good guy."

Edie nodded, just once, but that nod seemed to drain the edges off her smile and turn the light in her eyes into something distant and a little sad. "You'll have to forgive me. I didn't mean to assume."

The stairs opened out onto a wide balcony that encircled a large atrium below. Trina drifted to the railing and looked down at the girls scattered on couches and threadbare chairs. Here four girls, scarcely older than teenagers, hunched over a table with playing cards in their hands. There a dark-haired woman sat sideways in an armchair, a book held close to her face. Still another curled up in a corner beneath a blanket, her eyes open, staring into the distance at nothing.

"Almost every girl who comes to us," Edie said, matter-of-factly, "is brought here by someone. And that someone doesn't always have their best interests in mind."

Edie balanced her forearms on the rail, standing close. "Men, sometimes families, treat these girls like refuse, to be dumped and forgotten. A girl becomes addicted to drugs, they bring her here. A daughter gets pregnant by her stepfather, they bring her here. Some people are just born to drink other people up, and when they're done, they barely care what happens to the empties. I see it all the time."

Trina turned to look at Edie, and saw that her eyes were dancing. "And most of these girls don't know it, but it's the best thing they could have done for them, because when they're ready to leave here, they're full again. They are *strong*, and whatever reason they have for being here doesn't matter anymore. And those people? Those people, more often than not, aren't a part of their lives anymore, because those people no longer matter."

Edie was close enough that their arms were almost touching, and Trina fought the urge to pull away. Edie seemed to sense this and started walking again. She kept her steps slow and measured, giving Trina time to follow.

"So, how about we start small," Edie said, her voice still low, like they were the only two people in the world. "How about we start with your name."

"Trina Bell." Trina smiled as she said it, the words tumbling out before she could think to hold them back. She'd been so used to leaving her name out of things because she knew no one would remember her anyway. She hadn't even told it to the man in the pickup truck. Now she'd given it twice in as many days. It felt good. It felt like she was taking something back.

"Trina." Edie lingered on the name, trying it out, looking at it from every angle. "That's lovely. I'm pleased to be able to welcome you to Ms. Dixon's home, Trina Bell. Now that we're acquainted, perhaps you'd like to tell me what brought you here today."

They passed beneath a high arch into the hallway beyond. Up ahead, a pair of girls rounded the corner, their voices high and playful. They slowed down when they caught sight of Edie, straightening their backs and smoothing at their skirts. Still, they were smiling as they passed, and Trina saw that Edie was smiling back at them.

"What about Ms. Dixon?" Trina asked. "Does she live here too?"

"Sadly, Ms. Dixon is no longer with us. She passed away about eight years ago."

They walked by a potted plant, the kind with wide, rubbery leaves. Trina ran one of the leaves between her fingers. It felt solid and smooth, and every bit of it was green, as if all the brown and withered bits had been trimmed away.

"But she was real? Like, you met her and talked to her and everything?"

If Edie was surprised by the question, there was no showing it on her face. "Of course," she said. "In fact, she was the one who welcomed me when I first came to this place."

"Did she have a first name?"

Edie nodded. "Alethea."

"And she was a good person? I mean, you could trust her and stuff? You could tell her things and she wouldn't think you were making it up or that you were crazy or anything?"

"She was," Edie said. "In fact, I'd venture to say that she was one of the most generous people I've ever known."

"Tell me something you remember about her. Something specific, I mean."

Edie began walking again, lips pressed thin as she searched her memories. Trina walked alongside her, watching her face, ready to find the lie, hoping fervently that there wouldn't be one.

"All right," Edie said, slowing her words to match her steps, as if they were walking back in time. "There was a day when we had a late spring snowfall. This was maybe twenty years ago. I was barely a teenager then, and only a resident. My old room is just at the end of this hall, in fact. But that morning, we were all out in the courtyard, residents and house mothers all together, throwing snowballs. Hardly anyone bothered with a coat, so we were all freezing." She was grinning now, a wide, open smile, and she turned her head aside to hide it. Trina caught herself smiling, too.

"And I had made this...*enormous* snowball." Edie made a circle with her hands the size of her head. "And Alethea—Ms. Dixon—had bent down to make one of her own. So, she was bending over, and she was facing away from me and the bustle of her dress was just so...big. In my defense, who could resist a target like that?"

She gave a little laugh that she immediately stifled. She straightened her back and squared her shoulders as she paused in front of one of the identical wooden doors. In her hand was a cartoonishly large ring of keys, each one at least two inches long and made of black iron.

"So, I pull my arm back, and I'm ready to throw. But Ms. Dixon must have had some kind of sixth sense about it because she stops what she's doing, turns around and puts her hands on her hips and says, 'Young lady, if you even think of throwing that snowball, you'll be doing laundry for a week!'"

The key turned and the lock clicked open. Trina smiled. "You totally threw that snowball, didn't you?"

Edie gave a little wink as the door swung wide. "Oh, I did."

They stepped inside onto green plush carpet. There was a wardrobe in one corner and a high-backed chair in the other. On the wall hung a little carving of a man in a loincloth tied to what looked like a wagon wheel. Trina wanted to ask about it, but stopped herself. Of everything in the room, it was the bed that really caught her eye. Four solid posts, with crisp sheets and pillows that looked big enough to swallow her whole. Her neck was still sore from sleeping on Colin's couch, and though she'd convinced herself that she wasn't tired, not really, she suddenly wanted nothing more than to take a nap.

"I spent the next week up to my elbows in wet towels and dirty underclothes." Edie motioned Trina over to the chair as she sat down on the edge of the bed, feet crossed, hands folded in her lap. "But in an odd way, that helped me to see the value of this place, and how every one of us was counting on each other to keep it running."

Trina sat down in the chair and tested its polished armrests. Her fingers traced little scratches in the wood, ridges where the varnish had been worn away. They were the marks of dozens of fingers, all the ones that had come before her own, year upon year upon year.

"The best part was that Ms. Dixon would come to visit me while I was working. She taught me how to get butter stains out of table linens and the quickest way to fold a bedsheet. But mostly, she just listened. Even when I wasn't talking about anything important, she still listened. And before long, I did start to tell her about the important things, and she listened to me then, too. You see, back then I was a bit unruly. Incorrigible, was what my parents called me. I was convinced that they had abandoned me here because they just didn't want to deal with me anymore, and about that I was not wrong."

Her face darkened a little, and Trina watched her, fascinated. She couldn't remember the last time she had looked at a person this long before, or hung this closely on the words they had to say. She couldn't remember the last time she'd been in a place that didn't feel as if it was about to be ripped away from her at any moment.

"But I talked, and she listened. And the more I talked, the more I began to find myself. That was when I saw the value in this place, the value in <u>her</u>. I've been here ever since. So, I suppose what I'm saying, Trina Bell, is that if you'd like to talk, about anything at all, it would be my privilege to listen."

Trina tapped her fingers on the arms of the chair, suddenly torn between saying nothing and saying everything. It was like meeting Colin all over again, and she felt that same need to be seen, that same fear of being forgotten. Her backpack was in her lap, and she fiddled with the little leather pull that hung from the zipper. Did they even have zippers in this reality? Could something as small as that, all by itself, be enough to prove to this woman—to herself—that she wasn't insane?

"I came here," Trina said, "thinking there was something here that I'm supposed to find. Something to help me make sense of some things I've been going through, you know? Only now, I'm not so sure that there really is anything to find. And maybe I was only thinking that there was so I could put off thinking about the rest of it, and how stupid and impossible it all is."

Edie nodded, considering. "And what did you plan to do once you found it?"

"No idea. There hasn't been much sense in making plans when nothing lasts. You just take one minute to the next, yeah? I've been doing that so long that I don't know if I even remember how to do anything else."

"Have you considered that, whatever it is you're looking for, maybe you've already found it?"

Edie was looking into Trina's eyes, so deeply that Trina wanted nothing more than to look away. She could feel the weight of Edie's sincerity as if it might crush her, as if it might grind her defenses down to dust. It was all she could do to remind herself that this woman was no more a part of her life than any of the others she had passed on the street that day, that she might disappear in the next Turning, or forget that Trina or this place had ever even been here at all.

And yet Trina couldn't look away. Just a day ago, she'd trusted no one, and in that time she had found a way to trust Colin, at least a little. Now she was starting to think that she could trust this woman, who she had only met a few minutes before. The idea terrified her, but she found herself holding onto it, nurturing it in her heart the way she might use her breath to kindle a flame.

There was a faint tapping against the doorframe accompanied by the soft clearing of a throat. "Ms. McCafferty?"

The girl in the doorway was dressed plainly but neatly, in the same conservative style she had seen on the other girls they'd passed in the halls.

"I'm sorry to interrupt, Ms. McCafferty, but Phoebe and I were taking the delivery just now and, well, we counted twice but we're short a case of canned peaches and two bags of cornmeal. They're on the list though, and Mister Turner's boy says he won't leave until we give him the full payment. So..."

"It's all right, Polly." She leaned toward Trina, making her a part of it. "Mister Turner likes to overcharge us now and then to keep us on our toes. Tell the boy I'll be down presently. And do not, under any circumstances, let Phoebe pay him anything before I get there, understood?"

The girl nodded, and her eyes flicked toward Trina as she disappeared from the doorway.

"Our Phoebe is more than a little sweet on that boy," Edie said. "She thinks no one's noticed, but by now it's a bit of an open secret. I do hope you'll keep it to yourself when I introduce her to you."

Edie was trying to connect with her the way they'd connected before, but the spell had been broken. Trina retreated again and wrung her hands together, ready to look anywhere but into Edie's eyes.

"The bathrooms seem nice," Trina said, tilting her head toward the open doorway and the clean white tiles beyond. "Hot and cold running water in every room, I suppose."

"One more perk of our former hotel status. You're welcome to wash up if you need to, or if you need a change of clothes..."

"Nah, I'm good."

Edie was grinning now. She saw how Trina was changing the subject, and wouldn't be deterred. The strange part was that Trina didn't mind.

"What do you say we continue the tour?" Edie reached out to take Trina by the hand. "There's someone I very much would like you to meet."

9

Edie led Trina to a room at the end of a quiet hallway. It sat behind heavy double doors with panes of frosted glass set in leaden frames, a wide room with wood-paneled walls and an ornate brass chandelier that hung like a spider from its high ceiling. Trina guessed that the place might have been a drawing room back in the building's hotel days, the kind of room where old men in bushy mustaches went to smoke and swirl brandy around in wide glass snifters. When she breathed deep, she thought she could still catch the faint whiff of cigar smoke on the air.

It was far too big to be an office, but had been given over to one anyway. An ornate bookcase lined one of the windowless walls, but it was only half filled and gathering dust. An empty desk sat in the corner next to an overstuffed couch and a high-backed chair of worn leather. The too-big room made everything in it seem small, even the man who was rising from behind the desk to greet her.

"Doctor?" Edie stood over Trina's shoulder, gently urging her through the doorway. "I'd like you to meet Trina Bell. Trina is taking a tour of our home today, and I thought that the two of you would want to get acquainted."

"Ah yes." He crossed the room with long, quick strides to offer her his hand. His hair was slicked back and shining, and he wore a slim brown suit with a little gold watch chain that dangled from his vest pocket. "I had heard we had a visitor. The girls are all buzzing about it. I'm afraid there's no keeping a secret in this place."

"Trina, this is Doctor Philip Sweet."

"Oh, we don't go in for titles much here. I'd be pleased if you called me Philip."

His hand was warm as she took it, his grip a little too strong. He stared down at her, friendly, but still almost demanding that she meet his eyes. When he shook her hand, it shook all the way up to her shoulder, and he didn't let go until she pulled away.

"Doctor Sweet is the physician here at Ms. Dixon's," Edie said, beaming, "and a very dear friend. Doctor, I was hoping that you wouldn't mind entertaining Miss Bell for a few moments while I assist Phoebe in the larder downstairs."

"The Turner boy again?" He didn't wait for Edie to confirm it before he leaned in and spoke to Trina in a stage whisper. "I do believe that that boy is more than a little smitten with her."

The cigar-smoke smell was in his clothes, sharp but faint, not so much a smell as a memory of a smell, and it seemed to spark in her a memory that was just out of reach. It made her want to lean in closer just so she could catch it again.

"But yes, it would be my pleasure." Trina could tell by the smile on his face that he meant it sincerely. And yet, there was something of the wolf in his heavy-lidded eyes, in the way he stared at her, almost daring her to look away.

This, too, seemed to tug at her memories, but in a way that set her nerves on edge. She decided that she did not like this man.

"Assuming, of course," Sweet said, "that it's all right with…Trina, was it?"

Trina nodded and smiled back at him as much as she could manage. She was on the train now and moving fast. She supposed there was no harm in riding it all the way to the next stop.

"Excellent," he said. "I've just asked Wendy to bring up some tea, so your timing is perfect."

Edie looked back at Trina, giving her room to object. When Trina didn't, she turned on her heel, but still made a point of leaving the large double doors open as she left. Doctor Sweet was standing too close, with no signs of moving until she did, so Trina drifted toward the half-empty bookshelves. An attempt had been made at filling the spaces with harmless-looking knickknacks that seemed all the more out of place for having been brought together in one place. There was a set of brass scales, and a pair of toy soldiers, their paint chipped and showing the lead beneath. A tarnished flute lay neglected in a felt-lined case next to a little statue of a cat carved out of jade. This she picked up and turned over in her hands, tracing its contours beneath her fingertips.

"Trina." Her name seemed strange coming from Sweet's mouth, and she wished that she had never given it away. "That's certainly not a common name. Is it short for something?"

"Yes." She set the little cat down and turned to a row of thick medical texts bound up in oiled leather. Brain Trauma and the Causes of Moral Disability. A Practical

Primer on Psychology. Phrenology and Predictors of Deviance. She pulled one out and flipped through its pages. They were brittle and musty with age. "So you're, what? You give everyone checkups? Turn your head and cough? That sort of thing?"

"Something like that." He fiddled with the little jade cat until it was back in its original place. "I come here three days a week to tend to the girls' medical needs. Though my interests and practice are more in the realm of psychotherapy. It's still something of an emerging science, but very promising in terms of treating various melancholies and deep-seated traumas."

"Yeah, I'm familiar." There was a box on a low shelf, red wood, with a polished brass hasp and a little brass crank sticking out from its side.

"Are you? I expect that puts you in the minority." The wolfish look was back in his eyes, evaluating her every move. "At any rate, I suppose you've already gathered that our friend Ms. McCafferty maneuvered us together in hopes that you might confide in me. So, I won't waste time in the attempt."

"Oh, no. By all means, attempt away." She opened the lid of the box and turned the crank. Music came, high and tinny, from a little clockwork mechanism inside. "Just don't expect too much. My brain's pretty small these days. I don't expect you'll be able to shrink it much more."

"Now that sounds like someone who's trying to convince herself that her thoughts aren't worth sharing." There was a patch of silver mirror inside the lid of the box. She watched the doctor's reflection inside it, blurry and distorted. "Of course, if you do decide there's something you'd like to tell me, anything you say will be held in the strictest confidence."

She thought about telling him. She could tell him everything and it wouldn't matter. She had told it over and over again in those early days, to anyone who would listen. It hadn't made a difference then, and it wouldn't make a difference now. Except, it had made a difference when she'd told it to Colin, because Colin had led her to this place. And this place felt right, even if this room did not. She wanted to tell this doctor, too, despite the fact that she didn't trust him. She wanted to see where he might lead her.

There came a gentle rap of knuckles on wood, and Trina turned to see a brown-haired girl pushing a polished-brass trolley cart through the open double doors. On it was a matching brass teapot and two porcelain cups. "Ah, thank you, Wendy." Doctor Sweet took hold of the cart and trundled it toward the desk. "Oh, and do shut the doors on your way out. There's a dear."

The girl gave a prim little nod and pulled the doors closed behind her. As the latches clicked shut, Sweet motioned toward the overstuffed chair for Trina to sit. "How do you take your tea? I like mine with lots of sugar. Comes with the name, I'm afraid." He smiled. It was a practiced smile, and it did not reach his eyes.

"And if I said I didn't want any?"

He paused with his back to her before he began to pour, as if considering. "Well, that would definitely be your loss. Keep this between us, but when I first came here, no one could make a decent cup of tea to save their lives. They'd make the water too hot, leave the leaves in too long. It was awful."

He lingered over the cups, taking his time with the sugar, letting each one fall in with a satisfying plop. "But, with a little time and attention—and sometimes a little pressure—all ills can be remedied." He turned around with a cup and saucer in each hand. He offered one to Trina. He held the cup out and looked her in the eye until she took it.

"You've been here a while, then?" Trina asked.

"More than a year. Please." He gestured toward the overstuffed chair, polite, but still seeming as if he was prepared to stand there forever unless she sat down. When she did, her jeans squeaked against the chair leather.

"And you?" He circled around behind Trina and placed his cup down on the desk. "I don't mean to be blunt, but you have the look about you of someone who could benefit from a stable situation."

The chair reminded her of the deep cushions of Colin's couch before they changed. She wondered if Colin was still out there waiting for her in the lobby. Did he have a teacup in his hand, too? Was he wondering where she was? She doubted it. He was probably already gone. She had no reason to expect him not to be. It was a minor miracle that he'd stayed with her as long as he had.

"Yeah, that's me," she said, looking down at her cup, at the dark liquid that rippled inside. "Just passing through. All the time."

Sweet sat down behind the desk. His chair gave a creak as he leaned back and steepled his fingers in front of his face. He stared at her, and she could feel him measuring her, like she was a specimen under glass. "Is that something you'd like to change?"

"And how am I supposed to do that?"

"Well, girls tend to come here when they've run out of options. They come here when there's nowhere else to go." He took a long sip of his tea, all the time looking pointedly into Trina's eyes. "They come here in all kinds of terrible states, but with time and a little trust, they start to open up. They start to talk about the things that brought them here, and before long, things start to get better."

The chair creaked again as he leaned in. "You do want things to get better, don't you?"

She stared down at the cup in her hands. He'd given it to her black, with a little spoon and three cubes of sugar arranged on the edge of the saucer. Her choice. She plucked up one of the cubes and stirred it in. It swirled the way the black water of the canal had swirled beneath the horse on the bridge. Looking into it she could almost see the poor thing's eye, panicked, rimmed in white.

"Maybe talking won't make a difference because it can't get better," she said. "Maybe you're not going to believe me anyway."

"And what is it about your situation that's so hard to believe?"

Trina raised the cup to her lips. Sweet watched her over his steepled fingers. "Just start at the beginning," he said.

She drank, inhaling the smell of the tea, all citrus and flowers. "My grandfather used to have roses in his backyard," she said, keeping the cup close to her face, breathing in its warmth. "Funny that I didn't remember that until just now. He had them all along the back of his house by the porch. I fell into them once when I was really little and cut my leg on the thorns. I think I still have the scar."

She had forgotten about the scar until that moment. She had looked at it a hundred times and never remembered where it had come from until now. Sweet watched her as she took another sip of the tea. This time, when she swallowed, it left a bitter taste in her mouth.

"I remember in the summers when I'd go to visit, we'd look at the flowers and he'd tell me to name a color. I'd say 'blue,' and he'd tell me to close my eyes and when I opened them again the roses would be blue. So then I'd say 'yellow' and we'd do it again and the flowers would be yellow."

She looked up at Sweet, at the light from the chandelier dancing in his eyes. Her words were barely more than a whisper because suddenly her mouth had gone dry.

"I'd name every color I could think of, over and over. And every time, I'd open my eyes and I'd see it right there in front of me. I could never figure out how he did it. But now..."

The chair creaked again. Sweet leaned in closer.

"What if... What if the thing that changed the flowers is the same thing that's changing the world now? And if my grandfather was doing it then, maybe that means that it's me that's doing it now."

Her hands were trembling, and the cup rattled on its saucer as she maneuvered it onto the desk. "I'm sorry," she said. "I know I'm not making any sense right now."

"No," Sweet said. "I think you're making perfect sense. The world *has* been changing all around us. And you're right. It is you. It's been you the whole time."

Trina tried to speak but no words would come out. Her throat felt as if it was being squeezed from the inside and it was getting hard to breathe.

"That's why I had to drug your tea. I must apologize for that. It's not the way I would have preferred to do this, but I'm afraid I'm not the only one with a stake in your future. I hope you'll forgive me."

Her vision blurred, but at the edges of it she could see something moving, dark shapes coalescing into darker shadows. She turned her head to face them, but the movement sent a spattering of stars across her eyes.

The Shadows drifted closer. She thought of Colin again, and tried to call out for him, but the world faded away before she could make a sound.

10

It was the cold that woke her, jolting through her limbs like icy needles. She tried to breathe, but her mouth was full of cloth that tasted of alcohol. What air she could get felt like knives inside her chest. She tried to raise her arms, but they wouldn't move. She was tied down to something hard in a green-tiled room. Her clothes were soaked to the skin and dripped fat drops of water onto the floor.

"Ah, you're awake," Doctor Sweet said with a hopeful note in his voice. "I'm very sorry about that. I had thought this would be quick, but given the circumstances I believe that it's more important to be thorough. I hope you'll understand."

He held a fire hose in his hands, and as he tugged back the handle a fresh torrent of freezing water struck her like an icy punch to the stomach. She twisted, but the straps at her chest and her hips held her firm. When she finally gathered enough breath to scream, the sound that came out was muffled and hopeless.

"Do you remember now?" Sweet asked, the handle still in his fist. "*Can* you remember now? I know it's unpleasant, but believe me when I tell you we wouldn't be doing this if it wasn't completely necessary."

Again, the water hit her, but she was ready this time and managed to keep from crying out. Still, she had to squeeze her eyes against the pain as the cold worked its needles into her. She tried to use her tongue to push the rag from her mouth, but it was in too deep.

"You know," Sweet said, "I have dedicated my entire adult life to the study of the human mind, and I never once imagined that I would ever encounter one with abilities like yours." He pulled back the stream of water enough to be heard, but not enough to stop it from stinging. His voice was casual, no different than when he had poured her tea. "The implications are staggering. To be able to exert your will so perfectly, so completely. It changes everything we thought we knew about biology, spirituality, metaphysics. I should think that if I had the time for a complete study, you'd make me quite a wealthy man indeed."

There was a drain in the center of the floor where the water ran down. Sweet stood astride it, flanked by two wide, porcelain tubs that crouched on stubby, clawed feet. Their canvas coverings lay at angles, stretched taut over metal frames, each with a single hole, big enough for a person's head to poke through. Moon-shaped electric lamps blared out from the corners on articulated metal stands. The whole place was done over from floor to ceiling in mildewy green tile. Trina could see a wide metal door in the darkness behind Sweet, just a few steps away and yet impossibly far.

Sweet snapped the water off then, as if a thought had just occurred to him. He set the hose aside and stepped toward her, leaning in close. "You mustn't think that's what motivates me, though." He smoothed her dripping hair away from her eyes with a tender hand. Trina bucked against the straps. "I care very deeply about all my charges. Even you. In fact, you especially. And I want you to know that, if there were any other way to make us all safe from you, I would take it. I swear."

The strap at her forehead had soaked through enough to let her head slip sideways a bit. There were no windows in this place. Was she in a basement? It didn't make sense that an old hotel would have a basement like this. This place felt more like a hospital, not modern, but obsolete long before she had ever been born. And yet, there hadn't been a Turning. There couldn't have. Sweet was still here, and he remembered who she was.

Sweet stepped back behind the lights to a small, porcelain counter where the contents of her backpack were laid out like museum pieces in a display. Her useless phone. Her spare clothes, still crumpled and damp from the canal. A little toy car she'd forgotten she'd had. This last he took up in his hand, delicately spinning the wheels against his fingers, smiling at the whirring sound they made.

"I have no end of questions, but there's just no time. The risk...allowing someone like you to just roam free, to keep doing what you do... Well, the dangers are too obvious."

He grabbed hold of one of the lamps, and its wheels screeched as he dragged it toward her. In his other hand he brought along a stainless-steel cart. On it was plastic bottle of rubbing alcohol and a tray of sharp-looking metal implements that gleamed in the electric light.

"I'd really hoped that the shock of the hydrotherapy would be enough to bring us back to where we started.

But if we can't go back, we need to take steps to make sure *you* don't go forward. Fortunately, it's a very simple procedure. Quite quick, actually. Two taps then done. And afterward, you'll still be with us, and if what they've told me is true, everything will be set back to rights."

He paused then, as if struck by a thought, and laid his glasses upon the cart. He leaned in close, his voice barely a whisper. "I want to ask you something, but you'll have to promise me that you won't cry out. The procedure is for your benefit, but if you cry out, I'll have to rush and my hands might slip. If that happens, I can't be responsible for your safety. Do you understand?"

She tried to nod, but her head wouldn't move. Still, he must have seen the desperate agreement in her eyes because he unraveled the cloth from her mouth and used it to wipe some of the damp from around her lips. She swallowed. Her mouth was dry, her throat swollen, and though she wanted to plead with him to let her go, she could not make the words come.

"Tell me," he said, his breath low in her ear, "this new place you've made for us, where did it come from? Has it always existed? Has it just been here, waiting for us? Or did you conjure it somehow? It all seems so impossible that, if I hadn't seen it with my own eyes, hadn't *felt* the change as it came over me, I'd scarcely believe it."

There *had* been a Turning, then. There'd been a Turning and he still remembered her. More than that, he knew this place had changed. That was more than Colin had done, more than anyone had ever done. It should be impossible, but still, he *knew*.

She swallowed again and felt some of the moisture return to her mouth. When she spoke, the words came out in a croaking whisper. "Look, I don't know what you think I did, or who you think I am, but I came here with my friend, and he's out there waiting. He's probably looking for me right now. And the Turnings? It's not me. I don't know how they're happening. I swear—"

He frowned and pulled the rag up again. She tried to scream but her cries were cut off by the cloth, by Sweet's fingers pushing it back into her mouth, deep enough to make her gag.

"That's a shame," he said. "I was hoping that you might be honest with me. I already know all about you, you see. I knew all about you before you even stepped foot in my office. They told me you would come here. They knew it was inevitable that you would find this place eventually, and we were ready for you."

Something stirred at the corners of her vision, dark forms drifting closer. Seven figures, shimmering, bending the world around them.

"They told me everything," Sweet said. "They showed me what you've been doing to this world. The chaos. The destruction. Supplanting one reality with another, over and over and over again."

There was a tremble in Sweet's voice as the Shadows approached. The instruments on the cart rattled as he stumbled back into the safety of the electric lights. The Shadows fanned out around them. As their passage curled the tiles and bent the tubs aside, Trina could feel their vibrations on the air, like the low rumble of a passing train.

"They set me in your path to stop you," Sweet said. "And though it pains me—it really does—that's exactly what I intend to do."

The Tall Man drifted closer, looming over her until all she could see was the empty void where its face ought to be. She could feel the pull of the thing, an electromagnetic hum, a gravity that threatened to draw her in despite the straps that held her down. She tried to scream, to pull free, but all she could do was to squeeze her eyes shut and wish the thing away. Over and over, she repeated the words in her mind, pleading with the thing, begging it to leave her alone, until at last she felt it retreat. Its pull went slack, and the hum subsided until she could barely feel it there at all.

When she opened her eyes again, Sweet was there in the Shadow's place, leaning over her. His face was full of concern, and in that moment, his eyes seemed almost kind.

"I don't suppose it will do any harm now to tell you that my first thought was that we should kill you outright." He smoothed a strand of wet hair away from her forehead. "But I don't want to hurt you. That's not the kind of person I am. And that should tell you how seriously I'm taking this. I am not, at heart, a violent man."

Trina was breathing hard now, her nostrils flaring. She tried to turn her head again, but all she could move were her eyes. They found the metal door in the far wall, and saw the long handle begin to turn. Inch by inch it opened, spilling light from the hallway in a narrow beam upon the floor.

"In any event, there's too much risk. There's no telling what might happen to the world if you were to suddenly just...end. This way is so much better. For everyone. I promise you."

An unruly head of blonde hair peeked through the crack in the door, trying hard not to be seen. The girl's face was in darkness, but still Trina could see her eyes, two points of reflected light, shining wide and full of fear.

"And when I'm done, you'll be right as rain." Sweet laid a hand on her cheek, watching her with a patient smile. "Just two taps. You'll see. It's entirely safe, and when it's done you won't remember a thing. It's the memory that's causing the problem, you see. It's still there, hidden away like a cancer, hidden so deep that you don't even know that it's there."

Trina's eyes darted back to the door. The girl was there, her hair hanging in great draggles past her shoulders, frozen, watching. Trina jerked against the straps at her wrists, trying to make some gesture that would signal the girl to run, to get help. All she could manage was to flap her hands uselessly. The girl didn't move.

"Remove the memory, and we remove the danger entirely. This world and everyone in it will be safe. That's what we both want, isn't it? For everyone to be safe?" Trina looked back at Doctor Sweet and tried to nod, to show him that she understood, that she would give him what he wanted. He looked down at her, patient, almost compassionate. She tried to hold his gaze, to keep his attention long enough for the girl in the doorway to see what was going on. Long enough for her to slip away and find help.

Sweet must have seen the agreement in her eyes, because he pressed a gentle hand to her cheek. "That's good," he said. "This will all go so much more quickly if you cooperate."

The air buzzed with anticipation as he pulled the cart closer. The alcohol sloshed in its plastic bottle. Every implement in the tray was sharp and shining. Trina stole a glance back at the door, but it was closed now. The girl was gone.

Sweet swung the lamp back over her head and took up one of the instruments between his fingers. It gleamed as he turned it over in the light, a pick made of stainless steel, eight inches long and sharpened to a wicked point.

Trina strained at her bonds. She tried to speak past the rag in her mouth, to say anything that would keep him talking long enough for the girl to find Edie, to find Colin, to find anyone. But the girl wasn't coming back. In her heart she knew it was true, and there was nothing she could do to change it.

"It's just a matter of separating the frontal lobes of the brain from the prefrontal cortex." Sweet's voice was clipped and clinical, the voice of a teacher. He twirled the tip of the long pick in demonstration. "Just a few quick turns and it's all done."

Trina pulled again. The belts at her wrists dug deep furrows into her skin. She tried to raise her hips but her knees would not bend. The Shadows retreated, leaving the doctor room to do his work. Trina could still feel them hovering at the edges of the room, their electric hum crackling the air, waiting, watching.

"We'll go in through the top of the eye socket. That's where the bone is thinnest. Like an eggshell, really." He picked up another instrument from the tray, a steel hammer so small that it might have been a toy. "Strange that I never knew about this treatment until today, and yet at the same time I remember it as if I've been practicing it my whole life. Of course, I would have preferred that you had remained unconscious until the procedure was finished. But as long as you cooperate, the pain should be absolutely minimal. Just a little pinch and then done."

He brought the lamp down close to Trina's face and she had to squint against the brightness of it. She could feel its heat on her skin, warming the damp that soaked through her clothes. Her breath was coming faster now, flaring her nostrils and stinging her throat. She squeezed her eyes shut and felt the strap across her forehead slip. A millimeter, then another, then nothing. She was stuck fast, like a bug pinned to a board. She tried to scream, to force the rag from her mouth with her tongue, but the effort only made her gag.

Sweet leaned his elbow into her chest to steady himself and drove away what little wind Trina had left. Her eyes popped open and she could see the silvery point of the pick, just inches away.

"Steady now, and eyes open if you please. The last thing I want is to hurt you, but if you keep on like this, I can't be responsible for what might happen."

She wanted to close her eyes but she couldn't, not with the glinting point of the silver pick looming so close. She thought of the flowers, how she would put her hands over her face and call out the colors and the colors would be there, the flowers alive, their petals soft beneath her fingers. Sweet tightened his grip on the little hammer, and she remembered the feel of her grandfather's hand on her shoulder. Steady. Strong.

The world went dark. The air around her stirred, as if it had been sucked away, only to rush back in again. The electric hum of the Shadows was gone, as if some great switch had been thrown. When the light returned, the green-tiled walls were replaced with red brick, and the musty smell in the air had been traded for the faint scent of earth and horse manure.

Sweet was still there, but his white lab coat had turned back into the vest and rolled-up sleeves he had worn when she'd first met him. The hammer was in his hands. So was the pick, but their handles were wooden now, not steel. Sweet seemed to forget them as he and straightened to take in his new surroundings with widening eyes.

"Absolutely extraordinary."

Trina strained once more. The thick belts that had held her wrists were ropes now, thin and frayed. The left one gave as she pulled, an inch, maybe two. The table she'd been strapped to had become a wooden pallet tilted against the wall. She twisted her body and was surprised to find that she could move. The belt at her waist was gone.

The tubs were gone, too. In their place were shelves stacked with heavy burlap bags, wooden bins filled with potatoes, glass jars laid out in rows, lit by a single lantern perched on a stool. Trina knew at once that this must be the larder that Edie had mentioned before, that they were back in Ms. Dixon's home, in its basement. Her eyes darted, searching for the Shadows, but the Shadows had disappeared.

"This is amazing!" Sweet cried. "I didn't think it possible, but you've brought us right back to where we started."

While Sweet's back was turned, Trina jerked her arm again. She pulled with every last bit of strength she had left, straining against the ropes until they burned furrows into her wrists. Her left arm moved an inch, then another, and then finally, with a snap of rope and a cracking of wood, it came free.

Trina stared at her hand, at the red marks in her wrist, almost not believing. Sweet hadn't seen her, but he might turn around again at any moment. Trina's head was still stuck, but she reached for her other hand, working by feel to find the knot and work it loose.

"And yet," Sweet said in awe, "I still remember that other world. I remember it all. Don't you see?"

He turned on her then, and when he saw her pulling at the knot his face twisted into a dark frown. He took hold of her arm and used his knee to pin it down against her side.

"The Others were ready for you. Even as you tried to run from them, they were always one step ahead of you."

He took up the pick again. Trina tried to cry out, but the cloth gag was now a heavy rubber bit between her teeth, pressing down on her tongue and strangling the sound before it ever had a chance to rise.

"They made it so that you could not change me. All my knowledge, all my memories. They kept me the same so that I could fulfill their purpose. So I could finish what they'd started."

Her left arm was pinned beneath Sweet's weight, but she'd loosened the rope on her other wrist enough to wiggle it free. She tried to push him away, but her muscles were burning and all her strength was gone. She punched at his ribs, but she was so weak that he didn't even notice.

Sweet brought the hammer up, the silver pick rusted now, and just inches from her eye. "And so help me, I *will* finish it."

Trina stretched out with her free hand, feeling frantically for something, anything. The cart with Sweet's tools was changed but still in reach. She felt again, and this time her hand closed around something heavy. She swung hard and smashed it against the doctor's head.

Sweet howled, and dropped the pick onto Trina's chest as he staggered back. She flung it away, and sent it rattling across the wooden floor. She could smell the alcohol from the glass bottle she'd smashed against Sweet's head. It misted the air and stung her eyes.

She had almost worked her way free when Sweet turned on her, sputtering with pain and rage. The side of his face gleamed in the lantern light, wet and shining, with shards of glass stuck deep in his skin. He fell upon her and wrapped his hands around her throat.

"I won't let you!" he cried. "I won't let you take this world from me!"

His thumbs pressed down on her windpipe, and though she twisted and pulled she could not shake him loose. The gag was still in her mouth, but she had no wind left to speak. Her vision was narrowing and full of stars. She reached out and found the brass handle of the lantern. Gripping it with both hands, she mustered the last of her strength, and swung.

The lantern exploded against the side of Sweet's head in a shower of glass, igniting the alcohol and engulfing him in bright blue flame. He staggered back, screaming as Trina pulled the rubber bit from her mouth. Gasping for air, she set to work undoing the rest of the ropes. Sweet fell to the floor, batting at the flames. They had reached his shoulders, blue fire turning to orange as it spread across his chest. Trina tugged the knots at her feet loose and scrambled toward the door, leaving the doctor writhing on the ground behind her.

11

Trina's legs were alive with pins and needles as she crashed through the door and stumbled into the shadowy hallway. She could hear Sweet's screams, thick with pain and rage, trailing away behind her. There were lights overhead, glass bulbs strung on bare wire, dim and flickering. They marked a path to a distant set of double doors, and she lurched unsteadily to follow it.

She had to find Edie. Edie wasn't a part of this. She couldn't be. She'd been kind and she'd wanted to help. She couldn't have known that Sweet would turn on her, couldn't have known about the fire hose in that basement that wasn't even a part of her world. She couldn't have known about that wicked, gleaming ice pick that still seemed to hover before Trina's eyes every time she closed them.

Unless Edie had been in on it from the beginning. Unless this place had been one big trap to bring her to Sweet. To bring her to the Shadows.

The lights flickered and plunged the hallway into darkness. An instant later they returned, so bright they were almost blinding. The walls had transformed again, this time from rough wood to painted cinder-block, the lights to harsh fluorescents. Their electric hum raised the hairs on the back of Trina's neck as she skidded to a stop.

The dimensions of the hallway hadn't changed, only its trappings, as if a new skin had been overlaid atop the old one, a skin of scuffed tile flooring and metal doors in metal frames. A neatly laid row of lights along the ceiling marked the way to a new set of double doors with square windows and long metal handles. The lights wavered again a moment later, and when they came back, the hallway had changed again, back to that dim-lit world of horse-smells and dirty floorboards.

Colin was still out there, somewhere. She'd been gone so long that he had to be looking for her by now. If not, then surely he was still sitting in that overstuffed chair, waiting for her in whatever had become of that old hotel lobby. Whatever Sweet had done, whatever Edie *might* have done, she was still sure about Colin. He wouldn't just abandon her. He wouldn't leave her down here, alone in the dark.

Her shoes were wet, her jeans soaked through. The muscles in her legs were frozen and they made every step feel like she was trudging through wet concrete. She'd left her backpack behind, along with her phone and her clothes and everything she'd brought with her from the real world. She couldn't risk going back for it, not with Sweet still there, burning on the floor.

His screams had stopped, or was it just that she couldn't hear them? She didn't want to believe she had killed him, no matter that she'd had no choice. She thought to turn back, to try to help him, but she didn't know what would be worse, finding him dead or finding him still alive.

The world flickered again and returned to that brightly-lit hallway. Trina stumbled, her head ringing, toward the distant double doors, hoping against hope that they might lead her back upstairs. She tried the handles of the metal doors as she passed. Each one was labeled with neat lettering on Bakelite signs. Isolation Ward. Electro-Convulsive Therapy. Every one of them was locked. She listened for voices, but heard nothing but the echoes of her footsteps, of her frantic and gasping breaths.

A thought occurred to her then, as insistent as the fluorescent lights above her head. What if Colin wasn't looking for her at all? What if the Shadows had already found him, the same way they'd found her?

The next door was wider than the others, windowless, with a great black sign that spelled out RESTRICTED in red block letters. She shouldered into it and shoved down on the handle. It was locked. There was a fire extinguisher in the glass case on the wall, and she thought about using it to smash her way through. How long had she been away? An hour? Maybe more? Why hadn't anyone come looking? There had been a girl in the doorway. Their eyes had met. She'd gone to find help. Or had she just gone?

Water rained down on her head in a sudden, misting spray. The fire sprinklers had turned on, reviving the chill in her already-wet skin. Trina tried the door again, hoping that some automatic lock would pop it open, but it wouldn't budge. Someone had to be on their way now, if only to shut the water off. They had to be.

The lights dimmed again, and the metal door became a heavy slab of wood. The RESTRICTED sign was gone, and in its place were hand-painted letters in white that read KEEP OUT. A rusted padlock on a hasp held it shut, but when she tried to reach for the lock it disappeared, and the metal door returned.

Pain bloomed behind Trina's eyes. The water had begun to pool around her feet, and it came up in great splashes with every step. From somewhere behind her came the hollow crash of a door banging open. She looked back and Sweet was standing in the doorway of the hydrotherapy room, his chest heaving. Half of his hair was gone, burned down to his raw and reddened scalp, his left eye a blackened ruin.

Trina threw herself against the double doors. She tugged at them furiously, but they were locked tight. She tried again and nearly fell back into the water. It was ankle-deep now, deeper than the sprinklers alone could account for.

Sweet closed the gap between them in long, splashing strides. He caught her hair in his fist and yanked her off her feet. At once he was on top of her, his hands around her throat. The water foamed around them. It closed over her face and left her sputtering.

"Put it back," Sweet spat, pulling her close. "This place is in my head now. It's not real. It doesn't belong here! Put it back!"

She tried to speak, to tell him that she didn't know how, that she wasn't doing this, but he forced her back down beneath the surface before she could say a word. Through the churning water she watched the lights gutter like a candle flame, taking the world with them. Sweet's face stayed the same, one mad eye dancing in the flickering blue light, his scalp burned raw.

Once more the lights flared. Trina tried to hold her breath, but her heart was racing too fast. Her chest heaved, and her lungs filled with water. It tasted stagnant and muddy, like the bottom of a river. All strength left her arms, and her vision began to darken. She thought of her grandfather. She thought of the flowers, but in that moment they had no color at all.

At once the hands let go of her throat and she was able to breathe again. She broke the surface, gasping and hacking the water from her lungs as she fought to right herself. Sweet lay floating next to her, his body limp.

"Go!"

Edie McCafferty loomed over them. Her hair was pulled back in a tight ponytail and she had traded her plain, green dress for a sodden white lab coat that dragged in the swirling water. She wore glasses with heavy, black frames and held a fire extinguisher in both hands, cocked back, as if at any moment she might bring it back down on Sweet's head.

"Go on," she said. "Get upstairs. Go!"

Trina struggled her way up to her feet. The water was at her knees as she sloshed toward the big double doors that stood open now to the stairway beyond. She paused between them and turned back to Edie, who stood over Sweet, watching him, as if the two of them were the only things left in the world.

"Where's Colin?"

Edie turned her head, but didn't take her eyes off of Sweet. "Who?"

Trina's heart sank. The lights changed again, and Edie changed with them. Now she was just as she had been when Trina had first met her. Wide strands of hair had come loose from the plait at her back. Her green dress swirled in the rising water.

"Colin," Trina said. "Old man. Tall. He was waiting for me."

Edie gave a quick nod, as if she didn't need reminding. "Of course," she said, looking down at her hands. They were empty but bent, as if something heavy had been there just a moment before. Doctor Sweet stirred, floating listlessly in the swirling water. The lights snapped back to full brightness, and Edie was the Edie in the lab coat again, the fire extinguisher back in her hands.

"Where is he?"

The Edie in the lab coat shook her head. "Whoever he is, if he's smart, he's already gone." She nudged Sweet's body with her foot. He rolled onto his back and coughed up a spray of water. "You need to leave. Now. I'll be fine. Just go!"

Trina turned and stomped up the stairwell. Water was pouring down the steps in a torrent, and she had to hug her body to the handrail to keep from being swept back down. The metal rail turned to rough wood in her hands, and dug deep splinters into her palms. Her feet slipped. Every step was like walking up a waterfall. The sound of it filled her ears and echoed through the small space as she struggled to the top.

She barely recognized the atrium at the top of the stairs. The dark wood paneling was gone, lost to institutional cinderblock painted a dull, creamy yellow. Where there had been couches before, there now sat row after row of narrow beds framed with metal tubing. Side tables and tray stands lay on their sides, half submerged in the ankle-deep muddy water that stretched from wall to wall.

"Colin!"

The only answer was her own voice echoed back to her, and she knew at once that she was wasting her breath. That didn't stop her from calling out again as she splashed toward the hospital lobby. She looked back at the stairwell, no longer a waterfall but a rising lagoon. She thought of Edie standing over Sweet with the fire extinguisher in her hands, and knew that there was no way either of them had made it out in time.

Water poured in through the gap beneath the lobby door. Trina pulled it open and the rush came in so fast that it nearly swept her off her feet. She waded into it, picking her way past vinyl couches, wading among floating potted plants until at last she reached the entryway.

Outside, the sky was dark and full of low, roiling clouds. The rain poured down in heavy sheets so thick that she couldn't see to the other side of the street. There were lights in the distant windows, skyscrapers of metal and glass. If any of the carriages and horses she'd seen still existed here, they'd been swept away in the torrent that had transformed the street into a muddy, rushing river.

Trina retreated behind the doors and found herself back in the lobby of the old hotel. She slogged toward the wide, curving staircase, hoping to find a way up. The first few stairs were underwater, but the rest were dry, and she let the current draw her toward them. As she drifted closer, she could see that there was something moving in the water at the base of the stairs, a dark spot bulging just below the surface. It swirled lazily as it rose, coalescing into a head, then shoulders, rising up out of the churning muck, a Shadow in the shape of a child.

Trina turned back for the entrance, but the water was at her waist now, thwarting her. She chanced a glimpse over her shoulder at The Child. The water around its feet had churned into a raging whirlpool. She could feel its current pulling her back toward the staircase as it drained the flood waters away into nothingness. Floating in the air above the maelstrom, The Child reached out for her, its fingers splayed, its outlines writhing.

Trina struggled to pull away, fighting with every step. She could see that other current through the doorway, the raging river where the road used to be, foaming beneath the sheeting rain. With her last bit of strength and a single deep breath, she hurled herself into it.

The flow of the water took her, and she surrendered to it, bobbing like a cork in a storm-tossed ocean. It swept her down the road and scraped her body along the rough cobblestones. A light post drifted past and she tried to grab hold, but the current was too strong. The effort sent her spinning. Something heavy struck the back of her head with a hollow-sounding thud. Her mouth filled with muddy water, and the world began to dim. In the moment before it went dark, Trina had the fleeting sense that someone else was in the water, holding out their hands to her. She stretched out to meet them, but they were too far out of reach.

12

The sun was high, and it bore down on Trina's head without a single cloud for shade. The cracked blacktop beneath her feet had become an angry thing, intent on burning away every last bit of the will she had to keep walking. She could see the small town at the distant end of the road, hunched and shimmering through the heat, a collection of dark outlines so far away that it barely seemed worth chasing.

She'd awoken in the water, wrapped around an exposed cluster of roots that she had no memory of grabbing onto. The climb up the riverbank had left her shoes caked and muddy, and her clothes had taken the better part of the morning to dry. Now that they had, they felt coarse and gritty against her skin. Dried mud flaked away from her feet with every step, falling behind her like a trail of breadcrumbs.

There was a little girl with curly black hair up ahead, kicking in the dirt at the side of the road. Her faded floral dress was worn down to tatters and her head was down as she searched for something on the ground. She looked up at Trina with wary eyes set in a dirty face. She smiled. Trina wanted to smile back, but found that she wasn't able to.

There were crops planted in neat rows on either side of the road, patchy with soybeans and stunted corn. If the summery heat was anything to judge by, they should have been taller. Trina scanned the horizon for some sign of a house or a farm that the child might belong to, but there were no houses to be seen and the town still seemed impossibly far away.

The little girl dropped quick to the ground and came up with something clasped between her hands. She opened them, and a grasshopper sprang out to flutter on stubby wings into the weeds. Trina wondered where the grasshopper had come from. Had it always been there, before the Turning, before she ever came to this place? None of the usual questions made sense anymore, and any answers she found were as changeable as the current in the river that had brought her here. She watched the girl, grimy and alone, and wanted to tell her that she was sorry.

Something up the road caught the little girl's eye, and her face darkened as she squinted in its direction. It trundled toward them, large and kicking up dust. By the time Trina turned back, the girl was already off running, curls bouncing as she skipped between the stunted rows of dried crops, and in a moment, she was gone. Trina set herself back to walking. It was all she had left, and there was nothing in that distant point of movement that could possibly be worth stopping for.

She heard the sounds of the thing as it drew closer, the high, uneven whine of the engine, the heavy rumble of tires on asphalt. She heard it slow as it pulled up behind her, big and rattling, engine belts slipping. The horn sounded, two quick toots, high and friendly, like something from a circus clown. It made her start, but it did not break her stride.

The engine gunned and the truck pulled up alongside her to match her pace. It was a flatbed truck with six wheels and slatted sides, riding high, belching thick clouds of black smoke that stung at her nostrils. It was painted an olive green that had covered over tan with road dust. Through the grime she could see the emblem painted on its side, a black squid, its head pointed like the tip of a bullet. One set of tentacles was wrapped around a bundle of arrows, the other around a lightning bolt.

"Hey, little girl. You need a ride?"

A skinny guy in rolled-up sleeves hauled himself up until he was half hanging out of the passenger window. Though Trina didn't turn to look at him, she could still see his smile, wide and sly, his eyes dancing.

"No need to be shy, my dear. I've had all my shots and I don't bite, not 'less I'm asked to, at least."

A tittering of laughter rose from the back of the truck. Twenty soldiers, maybe more, huddled restless against the slats.

"If you're going in to town, I'm the best guide for miles. I know the place like the freckles on the back of my hand. Show you the sights? Take a nice, moonlit walk through the park? No need to worry, sweetheart. Plenty of chaperones up there keepin' their *eyes* on us."

More laughter rose at this, and somehow the guy's smile grew even wider.

"All right, lock it down, Janowski." This was a new voice, a familiar voice, and it made Trina stop in her tracks. The truck squealed to a halt and a woman jumped down from the tailgate. She was tall and thin in faded camouflage fatigues, with her hair tucked up beneath a helmet that sat crooked on her head.

When she spoke to Trina, her voice was low and warm, like a fire on a cold night. "What's the matter, sweetheart? Are you lost?"

Trina tried to speak, but she was too caught up in the woman's eyes, in the little strands of bright-red hair that hung loose at the sides of her face. The last time Trina had seen her, she had been up to her knees in water, standing over a madman with a fire extinguisher in her hands. The last time Trina had thought about this woman, she'd been certain that she was dead.

"I think you scared her, Sarge," said Janowski, still hanging out the window, all teeth and close-cropped hair. "Maybe she'll feel safer riding up front with me."

"Button it! Or you and your gear can double-time it behind us all the way back to base. Clear?"

Janowski's face fell, and he slunk back inside the window. The chatter from the back of the truck stopped as sharply as if a switch had been turned off.

"Don't mind these goons," the sergeant said. "They like to mouth off tough, but they're mostly harmless."

The truck shuddered, let out a great bang and a thick puff of smoke, then grew still. A wave of anxious grumbling rippled through the back of the flatbed.

"Okay, Janowski," the sergeant called over her shoulder, her eyes never leaving Trina's. "You know the drill. Biggest mouth starts 'er back up, so get on it."

Janowski seemed to deflate as he opened the door of the cab. "Aw, come on, Sarge. That's the fourth time today. Let Davison do it for once. My arms are ready to fall off."

"That's an order, Janowski."

Janowski clambered down without another word. From beneath the truck's grille, he unfolded a heavy metal crank and threw all his weight against it. As it turned, he stared at the back of the sergeant's head with eyes angry enough to set it on fire.

The sergeant smiled at Trina, a private smile, just for the two of them. There were two chevrons stitched to her shoulder, and beneath them was a patch with the black squid clutching its lightning and its arrows. On her right breast was an embroidered name tag that read DEVERAUX.

"Are you heading into town? Do you have people there?"

Trina stared at the name tag, but the name tag was wrong. Her name was Edie McCafferty. It had been Edie McCafferty in that other world, and in that other world Edie McCafferty had saved her life.

Janowski strained at the crank. With one last turn, it swung loose, and the engine shuddered to life. The grin came back to his face as he rubbed at his shoulder and hopped back into the cab.

"We can give you a ride," the sergeant said. "You'll be safe in the back. With me. If that's okay with you."

Trina nodded, and together they climbed into the back of the truck. The soldiers made room, shifting their packs and their rifles as the sergeant made her way up to the front. She slapped her hand twice against the back of the cab, and the truck lurched forward, spewing a gust of black smoke into the air.

"You got a name, kid?"

Of course I have a name, Trina thought. *I told it to you yesterday. I told you my name and I trusted you and now I've lost Colin. I've lost everything.*

"Trina."

The sergeant nodded and held her hand out until Trina took it. "I'm Sergeant Deveraux. Evangeline Deveraux. People who know me just call me Edie."

· · · ● ● ● ● · ·

They sat in silence, bouncing as the truck heaved and pitched down the empty road. Soldiers leaned against each other and tilted their helmets over their weary eyes. It surprised Trina that there were more women than men packed into those identical uniforms, some barely older than children. Narrow-framed and bootworn, they swayed, not seeming to notice the jolts of the road, the groaning of rusted wheel-springs. Those who were still awake had a distance in their eyes, a hardness in the set of their jaws. Wherever Trina had found herself, it was clear that it was no easy place to be.

Trina watched Edie. Or Evangeline, or whatever she was called in this place. She had the soldier's faraway look in her eyes, but when she caught Trina staring at her, the distance would melt away and the corners of her mouth would curl up in a little smile. In those moments, there was no doubt in Trina's mind that this was the same woman she had met at Ms. Dixon's home, the same woman who had promised to help her, and hadn't called her crazy. In those moments, it was impossible for Trina to not smile back.

But the smile didn't last. Even Edie's good will couldn't shield her from the soldiers' doubtful glances. Trina could feel them whenever her head was turned, and she could scarcely blame them. She didn't trust this place any more than they trusted her. They all looked away from her when she tried to meet their eyes. All, that was, but two of them. They sat apart from the rest, a man and a woman, their backs straight, their eyes watchful. They wore long brown coats with high collars over their fatigues, and they each wore a looped string of beads on one arm, adorned with a single silver medallion. Their eyes followed her every move, watching her the way a cat watches injured prey.

The farm fields and drainage ditches gave way to clapboard houses and close-cropped lawns. Sprays of green plants overflowed from neat little boxes beneath the windows as water sprayed skyward in lazy arcs from rotating sprinklers. The cars in the driveways were all freshly-washed, with chrome bumpers and high tail fins that caught the noonday sun. Each one had a crank set into its grille, like the one Janowski had used to start the truck. Far above the sidewalk, electrical wires sagged and dry leaves choked the rusted transformers that clung to leaning wooden poles. A stray dog chased their truck, barking, for a quarter mile before it finally gave up and drifted away.

It wasn't until they bounced across the river bridge and turned onto the main street that Trina finally began to see other people. She watched them through the slats in the side of the truck as they walked past glass shopfronts in the shade of green canvas awnings. They kept their eyes on the ground as the truck passed, as if they were wary of attracting too much attention.

The truck pulled into a side lot alongside a row of identical flatbeds and a few open-top Jeeps. The soldiers piled out in pairs and Trina followed, taking pains to keep her distance from the two with the beaded armbands.

They had parked next to a tall, red-brick building trimmed in limestone. She knew it immediately from its wide, corniced roof and wrought-iron balcony. It was so familiar, so perfect in its dimensions that it might have been plucked whole from that other world and dropped here amid the loops of barbed concertina wire that topped the chain-link fence and surrounded the forest of green tents that grew like mushrooms on the wide back lawn.

Trina watched the soldiers go, their packs and long rifles slung over their shoulders. They moved with purpose, each of them with a place where they were supposed to be, a place where they belonged. All of them except for her. As they walked double-time they took extra steps to make a wide path around a rough wooden platform in the center of the lawn. On it were two sets of stocks, each with three holes, just high enough for a kneeling person to put their head and arms through.

"Hey, kid. Are you coming?"

Edie stood apart from the hustle of bodies, looking impatiently over her shoulder. She carried herself differently, this new Edie, jaw jutting and head cocked to one side. The quiet elegance was gone, given way to a rough and worldly swagger, but Trina felt safe with her all the same. She fell in behind Edie and they veered off through a gap in the fence past the entrance to the big brick building. Next to the double doors where there should have been a plaque was a hand-lettered white sign that read NO UNACCOMPANIED CIVILIANS BEYOND THIS POINT.

"What is this place?"

"This is F.O.B. India Lima." Edie spread her arms wide as if to encompass the place. It was the same gesture that

Trina had seen her make when they toured the old hotel. "Forward Operations Base. First line of defense against the Viper."

Above their heads, a flag flapped in the breeze. It bore the same squid that was on the sides of all the vehicles, blazoned on a field of blue.

"The Viper?"

"Damn right. But don't worry. There's no way they're gonna get a reach this far in, not with the Blinkers out there squatting on the interstate." She nodded in the direction of a distant water tower. A bulging cylinder clung to the side of it like a malignant growth, big and dark with rounded edges, held on with thick, black cables.

"I know the place doesn't look like much, but you should have seen it when we moved in. Used to be a convent or some other thing. Abandoned for years. Took forever to get the toilets working. If you need a hot meal, I can hook you up with a ration chit as long as you promise not to ask where it came from."

She stopped walking and turned back to Trina, blocking her path, giving her full attention.

"How about you, kid? What's your story? You're not V.P.R. You're not local. You carrying any transit papers?"

"Papers? Uh, no." Trina patted down her pockets, but they were empty.

"I'll pretend I didn't hear that. You got people around? Someone who can vouch for you?"

Trina searched her face, looking for some sign of recognition, but found none. "You really don't remember me, do you?"

"If I should, don't take it personal. I see a lot of faces out there in the DMZ. Things move fast. Too much of it just kind of runs together."

"Forget it," Trina said, her eyes on her shoes. "It's not important."

"You've got people though, right? Family? Someone who'd claim you? If not, we've got to get you on the next civilian transport down to Springfield. They'll take good care of you, but it's a long-ass ride in this heat. You're way better off staying where you're at."

"My, uh, my uncle."

"Your uncle have a name?"

"Colin," Trina said. "Colin Williams. He works at the library. I think."

Edie nodded. "Okay, then. Let's get you cleaned up. I'll take you to Corporal Beaumont. She'll set you up with a shower and a change of clothes. If you need medical attention, there's a hospital tent out back. Tell the doc I sent you and he'll get you whatever you need."

Trina felt her stomach clench. "The doc?"

"Yeah, but don't worry. He's a pussycat. Just don't mention the bandages, all right? His face got burned up pretty bad. Says it was a fuse box, exploded on him a few months back. He's still a whiz with a scalpel, but I don't think he's ever going to look right again."

13

Corporal Beaumont turned out to be a woman with buzz-cut blonde hair who carried a clipboard in the crook of her arm the way a mother might carry a child. She frowned as she took in the state of Trina's muddy clothes, but true to Edie's word, she pointed Trina to the corner of the camp where the showers were located. They were little more than canvas stalls fed from barrels perched on high poles with water that had warmed in the sun. There was no privacy, but there was no one there to see her anyway and the towels were clean, even if they were a little coarse. As the dirt swirled down the drain, she could smell the river in it, and the lingering ghost of rubbing alcohol.

When she was done, there was a stack of fresh things on the crate where she'd left her dirty clothes. Shoes. Underwear. A pair of faded jeans that was only a little too big on her and a gray t-shirt with UAF stenciled on the front in big block letters. A little wooden token poked out from between the layers, a circle the size of a poker chip. It was painted white and stamped with the image of the squid, only this squid was holding a knife and a fork. Trina looked for Edie so she could thank her, but Edie was nowhere to be found.

The new clothes smelled strongly of cheap detergent. Trina breathed them in and tried to remember the last time she'd been clean. Had it been in the motel with the flickering sign? She'd been so afraid of losing her backpack then, and hadn't let it out of her sight. Now the backpack was gone, along with everything she had brought with her from the real world, her world. With her old clothes gone, there was nothing left of that world for her to lose.

The mess tent stood at the opposite end of camp, a three-peaked mountain of canvas full of rows of long white tables on uneven ground that had been rubbed bare by the passage of boots and time. Weary soldiers and grubby civilians queued up in the shade, but each group kept to itself and did not mingle with the others. Beyond the tent was a high fence strung with razor wire. It circled the yard and the brick and limestone building, and she could see no civilians on the other side.

Trina fell in line behind a group of soldiers and watched as they gave their tokens to a burly man in an apron. When she handed him the little wooden circle, he looked down at her, squinting, and for a moment she was sure he was going to tell her to leave. But he only waved her on, and in a moment she was holding a tin tray, its compartments filled with runny piles in various shades of brown and green, and a half-circle of fried bread that looked too dry to ever get moldy. Still, she couldn't help but notice that he'd given her less than the others.

The long tables under the tent were half-empty, with people seated in clusters of twos and threes. The civilians kept to one side of the tent, eating with their heads down. Trina set out to join them, looking for a hiding spot, some place where she could blend in. She stiffened when she saw a hand shoot up from the soldiers' section and wave her over.

"Well hello," Janowski said, standing up to guide her into an empty seat. He was chewing with his mouth open, trying to catch her eye. "I knew there was only so long that you'd be able to resist my charms."

He flinched as an elbow caught him in the hip, thrown by the girl with the choppy black hair sitting next to him. "Let her be, Janowski. Besides, you have about as much charm as a box elder bug."

"Hey, do not speak ill of the box elder bug." His smile was wide, and there were bits of food in it. "Box elder bugs have charms to spare."

"Then next time I see one, I'll apologize for comparing it to you." He moved to get his arm around her and put her in a head lock, but she ducked it, grinning, and pushed him away. It was an affectionate, almost brotherly gesture, and it made Trina smile. She slid into a seat across from them and prodded experimentally at the chunks that glistened in the pool of brown gravy on her tray. They looked like meat, but she couldn't be sure. She wasn't all that hungry, anyway.

"It tastes better than it looks." The blond soldier sitting next to her didn't look up from his plate, and he spoke so softly that she could barely be sure that he was talking to her at all. "You'll probably want to eat the stew first, though. Helps you appreciate the rest."

"Blasphemy! Chef Crawford over there is a true artiste." Janowski lifted his spoon and let the contents plop back down onto his tray to punctuate the point. "Half the reason I joined up was they promised me I could eat like this every day."

"Really?" the girl asked frowning. "What's the other half?"

"Oh, the fresh air. The scintillating conversation. That, and the occasional snake hunt." He held out his fist to the blond, who bumped it with his own, but there was no joy in it, no energy. Trina realized then why these two seemed so familiar. They were the same teenagers who'd pushed her out of the car after they'd tried to rob her. They seemed harmless now. The blond one was new, though. Him, she would have remembered right away. There was a heaviness to the set of his shoulders, a weariness that seemed to mirror her own. It made her feel like she could trust him. It made her feel like she could trust all of them.

"How about you, kid?" The girl with the black hair eyed her up cautiously. "You looking to join the people's militia, do your time and write your own ticket?"

They all called her kid, but most of the soldiers she'd seen looked much younger than she was. Some, like Janowski, looked young enough to have been her kid brother. She hugged her shoulder, touched the scars beneath her t-shirt, and suddenly felt old. "No," she said. "I'm just looking for someone."

"This someone wouldn't happen to be a boyfriend, would he?" Janowski took another elbow to the ribs, but this time he didn't seem to notice.

"No. Just a friend." Trina remembered pushing aside the door at the top of the stairs to find that Colin wasn't there and felt the same clenching absence in her chest. "I think."

"On base or in town?" the blond soldier asked, still looking down, still speaking softly.

"I don't know."

"Well," the dark-haired girl said, "if he's on base, Sarge'll help you track him down. She knows this place cold. Every rule, every reg. Everyone who goes in or out."

"And it's clear she's already taken a liking to you," Janowski said, using his fork to indicate her new clean clothes. "When we picked you up, you looked like the horse bucked you off and dragged you both ways through the manure pile." He took another elbow to the ribs, hard enough this time to make him yelp.

The girl leaned in, speaking confidentially. "Usually, scroungers don't get white tickets. Meat's strictly for personnel."

There was a group of civilians at the edge of a far table, three women and a little boy who couldn't have been older than six. Trina had felt their eyes on her when she'd walked in, but now they wouldn't look her way. They huddled over bowls of something like oatmeal, their clothes dirty, their eyes haunted.

Trina looked down at her food again and felt guilty. "If it's a problem, I can go."

'No, no. I won't stand for that. No way." Janowski trailed a piece of bread through the gravy on his plate and stuffed it into his mouth. "You're with us now. Blood brothers and sworn protectors until death or the end of time!"

The girl rolled her eyes. "He just means we'll help you out if we can. I'm Briggs, by the way." She held out her hand and Trina took it. "This sparkling conversationalist here is Woods."

The blonde soldier gave a nod in acknowledgement and tilted his head toward Janowski. "I gather you and this idiot are already acquainted."

"She knows the name, but not the legend," Janowski said, grinning as he chewed. "An oversight that I would be more than happy to correct."

Trina felt her face getting hot and looked away. She'd seen that look in his face before, or at least something like it, on that desert highway all those turnings ago. There'd been a touch of malice in it then, but there wasn't so much as a hint of that now. He was still the same, and yet he was someone completely different. It made her wonder how different this world's Edie was from the one she'd left behind. It made her wonder if this new Edie would believe her at all.

She stabbed at her stew with her fork, and to her surprise, it really did taste better than it looked. Her hunger kicked in then, and before she could stop herself she was wolfing the stuff down.

"How about you?" The blond soldier—Woods—was looking at her in a way that was interested and disinterested all at once. "You got a name, rookie?"

She wiped her mouth with the back of her hand. Only then did she realize that there were tears on her cheeks. "Trina," she said. "Trina Bell."

Woods nodded. He wasn't just looking at her. He was watching her eyes, like he expected her to get up and leave at any second, like he was used to people not sticking around. "All right, Bell. Welcome to the I.L."

She tried to smile at him, but he was already turning away. Janowski stared at them with his mouth open in mock surprise. Briggs raised an eyebrow. "I do believe that's the most we've heard out of Woods all week."

"Clearly, the lady has magical powers." Janowski threw himself down on the table in supplication. "Please, O powerful one, tell us the secrets of your sorcery!"

Even Woods smiled at this, if only a little. Around a mouthful of food, he asked, "So where you headed? Once you find your friend, that is."

Trina took up the half-circle of bread from her tray and began to worry a piece off of the end of it. She'd had a plan, back when she thought she knew where the Turnings were coming from. Now that plan seemed like nothing more than wishful thinking.

They showed me what you've been doing to this world. The chaos. The destruction.

Doctor Sweet's words still rang in her mind. He was out there somewhere, probably somewhere in this very camp. Had he been right about her? Had he been right about the Turnings being her fault?

She dropped the bread back onto the tray. It was torn now, and when she saw how her hands had mangled the thing, she no longer wanted to eat it. "I don't know where I'm going anymore," she said. "North, I guess."

"North." Janowski sat up straight and eyed Trina with exaggerated attention. "Ah, the promised land!"

Briggs shook her head. "Not much chance of that. They shut down travel visas months ago. Even if you manage to find a bison to carry you over, it's still a tough crossing."

"V.P.R.'s got the roads locked down." Janowski said. "Must have something good up there, if you're willing to make that hike."

"No." Trina stared down at her tray, at the torn bread with the marks of her fingers still on it. "I thought I did, a while ago. Everything's kind of flipped upside-down since then."

"Must have flipped pretty hard," Woods said, "judging by the way we found you."

Trina remembered then that she'd seen him before, in the truck. He'd had his helmet down over his eyes, his arms folded, pretending to sleep. But he hadn't been sleeping. She'd been able to tell by the way his body had moved, his muscles tightening, his body bracing itself against every jostle and bump in the road.

"All the more reason to put them rightside-up again as quickly as possible." Janowski leaned forward and cupped his chin in his hands. "So, tell us more about this mysterious friend of yours."

She might have taken his posture for more clowning, except Briggs was leaning forward too. Woods watched attentively, even if it was only from the corners of his eyes.

"His name is Colin Williams. Maybe you've seen him? Older guy. Whitish hair. Glasses."

"An older man," Janowski breathed, making it sound scandalous. Briggs kicked him under the table.

"He'd be working at the library," Trina said. "If there even is a library around here."

Briggs nodded. "I haven't heard the name, but yeah, there's a library. Just off Main Street, by the old church."

Trina didn't want to smile. If she smiled that meant that she thought there was a real hope of finding him, and the only thing worse than having hope was having it taken away. Still, she couldn't stop herself. "Can you give me directions?"

"I can take you."

They all turned in unison to Woods, who was caught off-guard by the sudden attention. He recovered himself quickly and turned back to his plate.

"I can get there on my own," Trina said quickly.

Woods shrugged. "I'm off rotation until 22:00, and it's all the way on the other side of town. Besides, you'll probably need some help getting through the checkpoint."

"Oh yeah. That's a tough walk alone for a girl without any transit papers." Janowski pitched forward as Briggs slapped him hard on the back of his head. "Ow! What? It's not like I don't hear things."

"Wait, that's for real?" Briggs leaned in and kept her voice low. "Girl, are you in the wind right now?"

"I... I must have lost them in the river." She thought of her backpack, of her spare clothes, of the phone that was all she'd had left of the world she'd left behind. All of it was lost now. Papers seemed like the least of her problems.

"The X.O. can get her a temporary resident status," Briggs said, "especially if we find her friend and get him to take her in. Elsewise, she'll end up at a work camp with the rest of the refugees."

"Either way, she'll need an escort to get off base," Woods said.

"You make it sound so romantic." Janowski folded his hands against his cheek and rolled his eyes dreamily skyward. "Just a girl and a man—more or less—out on the town in the middle of an occupation."

Briggs rolled her eyes. "Don't you have duty in the motor pool, like, ten minutes ago?"

Janowski checked his watch and his eyes went wide. "Correct you are. I must away." He took hold of Trina's hand and held it as if he might kiss the back of it. "It has been a rare pleasure meeting you, my dear lady. I do hope we will see each other again, someday when this war is done and the hearts of men are not so hard and cruel."

He gave a quick bow as he backed away from the table. Briggs rolled her eyes as he left, then rose to follow him. "Same goes for me," she said. "But, you know, without the assholery. Be careful, ok."

Woods stood up, pulled a cap from his pocket and wrestled it down onto his head. "All right, Bell," he said with an attempt at a smile. "What do you say we find your friend?"

·········

Trina and Woods scraped out their trays while Briggs and Janowski set off for the motor pool beyond the old red-brick hotel that Trina could still only think of as Ms. Dixon's Home. She watched them go, easy in each other's company, trading shoulder punches, stumbling against each other on purpose. Seeing them like that carved out a hollow place in her chest. She thought of the guy with the pickup truck, of the rise and fall of his chest as he slept next to her, and felt a strange twinge of guilt that she hadn't bothered to ask him his name.

The tents of the camp were arranged in two neat rows, with the three longest ones on one side and a collection of smaller ones on the other. Between them was a wide strip of patchy lawn crisscrossed with dirt paths where soldiers rushed back and forth. Near the fence, a group of children in oversized UAF shirts chased a ball of rags tied together with string. If there were parents they belonged to, Trina couldn't see them.

Woods led her straight down the center of the camp, toward a narrow break in the fence flanked by a wooden gatehouse. They were out in the open, and it felt like everyone in the place was watching her. Woods must have sensed her hesitation. "Don't worry" he said. "Most of these guys are kittens. But if anyone gives you a hard time at the gate, just show them your badge and let me do the talking, okay?"

She nodded, but she didn't care about the soldiers, not even the ones with the beads around their arms that lurked at the fringes like vultures waiting for an animal to die. She was fixated on the longest of the tents, the one with the red and white cross on its roof. If Doctor Sweet was here—and Trina was certain now that he was—that was exactly where he'd be. She struggled to keep up with Woods' long strides and tried in vain to steer them toward the far side of the lawn.

"Let me borrow your hat."

He looked back at her, squinting. "My hat?"

She trotted up alongside him, maneuvering so that his body between her and the med tent. "Just give it. Please?"

He shrugged and handed her the hat. She pulled it down onto her head and kept her eyes down, not wanting to look any of the passing soldiers in the eye in case they might see her face and be able to describe it later. They were almost to the gatehouse, and she could feel herself starting to relax. She could see the main street beyond the fence, the high church steeple rising in the distance. If Colin was in this world, he was somewhere just beyond that steeple. She was beginning to believe, for the first time since she'd pulled herself out of the river, that she might actually be able to find him.

"Corporal. A word."

Woods turned in mid-stride and stiffened to attention. Trina stiffened too. She knew that voice, affable but with a low note of silky menace. She kept her head low as she turned around, but she could still see his bandages and the thick pad of gauze wrapped tight to the side of the man's head, covering the spot where she'd burned him.

"At ease," Doctor Sweet said. "I'm looking for Major Turner. Is he back from The Palace yet?"

Woods unclenched and moved his hands behind his back. "Turner, sir?"

Sweet sighed and pinched the bridge of his nose. "Carlson, I mean." His voice was heavy with exasperation. "Major Carlson. Is he back?"

"Couldn't say, sir. I've been out on the line. Just got back. But I thought I saw his car on the lot on the way in. If he's here, you'll probably catch him up in his office."

Sweet frowned. He wore the same loose fatigues as Woods beneath a crisp white lab coat. A single silver lieutenant's bar glinted from his collar, and from the arm of his coat dangled a silver medallion at the end of a beaded chain. He slapped at the stack of papers in his hand. "Did you know that it takes five requisition forms and three brass autographs just to get penicillin in this place? Penicillin! All these advancements and I might as well go back to using bromine and mercury for as long as it takes the stuff to get here!"

He was speaking to Woods, but he was staring right at Trina. She could feel the heat of his gaze as she tried to stay hidden beneath the brim of the cap.

"For infection, you see?" His one good eye widened as he stared down at her. "Can't leave it untreated, or there's no telling how far it will spread."

"I'm afraid I wouldn't know, sir." Woods must have seen the way Sweet was looking at her, because he shifted his weight forward to pull Sweet's attention back to him. Trina hoped that neither of them would notice that she was shaking.

"I wouldn't expect you to, Corporal," Sweet said, "and count yourself lucky. It's almost as if this whole place has been purpose-built just to make my life difficult."

He stared down at Trina until the heat of his gaze gave her no choice but to look up at him. She could see the angry red skin peeking out from the edges of the bandages, raw and glistening with ointment. One eye was covered with that thick pad of gauze, but the other was wide and eager.

"Is this civilian in your charge?" Sweet asked.

"Yes, sir. I was just escorting her off base."

"Escorting her where, Corporal?"

Trina's legs began to tingle with a mad urge to run. The gatehouse was right there, just a few steps away. The guard might try to stop her, but a guard wasn't a Shadow. It wouldn't take much to get past him. Once she was on the other side, she could just keep running and be gone before Sweet or anyone else could catch her.

"She's got family out over the bridge," Woods said, offhandedly. "She needed an assist and I got the detail." It wasn't a lie, not exactly, and Woods put just enough boredom into the words to make it sound routine.

"Stuck babysitting. Well, I can't say I envy you." Sweet turned to Trina. "Though you certainly appear to be in good hands...miss?"

Trina balled her fists. He knew damn well who she was and she was too tired for games. She forced a smile. "Wendy," she said, trying to keep the ice out of her voice. "Pleased to meet you."

He held out his hand until she took it. "Philip Sweet. *Lieutenant* Philip Sweet." He squeezed down on her fingers until she couldn't help but pull away. She swallowed hard, remembering how that hand had felt squeezing down on her throat.

"Don't mind the bandages," Sweet said. "It was just a bit of an accident. I got careless, but I've learned my lesson. It won't happen again."

He turned his eye on Woods, looking him up and down, evaluating. Woods' face was so impassive that it might have been carved out of stone.

"Corporal, what do you say you take these forms up to Major Carlson, get his signature for me? I can get your scrounger here where she needs to go."

Woods flicked his gaze toward Trina. Her eyes were wide, pleading with him without saying a word. She knew that Sweet could see it too, but her heart was beating too fast for her to care.

Woods seemed to consider for a moment and said, "Sorry, sir. Sergeant put me on this one special. Wants me to double-time it too, be back by eighteen hundred."

Trina risked a quick glance at Sweet, only to find that he was staring right at her. He caught the look, and the corners of his mouth turned up in a predatory smile.

"I could make it an order, Corporal."

Woods straightened back to attention. "Yes, sir."

There was a pause as Sweet considered, a pause so long and so silent that Trina's own heartbeat seemed to rise up just to fill the void. He looked over the papers in his hands, taking his time, letting the threat hang between them, watching Trina from the corner of his eye.

"No," he said at last. "I wouldn't want to get on Edie's bad side. Last time I did that I found myself locked in the juvenile ward for three hours without my keys, and every nurse on the floor off doing who knows what."

Woods kept his stoic face, but Trina could still see his brows knitting in confusion. "Sir?"

"At Ms. Dixon's," Sweet said, impatient. "In the old library. The one with the brass fireplace."

Woods squinted. "You mean the admin building, sir?"

"I know what the building is, Corporal!" What was left of his face turned red as he spat the words. Woods snapped back to attention and kept his eyes forward. Sweet pressed the papers to his forehead, breathing deep. When he took them away, the smile was back, but it was strained.

"As you were, Corporal," Sweet said, bringing his voice back under control. A spot of reddish brown had bloomed in the gauze at the side of his head, and it was spreading.

"You're lucky to have this one looking out for you, *Wendy*." Sweet made a point of staring at Trina when he spoke, his good eye narrowed and wary. "It's a dangerous world out there. I'd hate to think what might happen to you without him. Oh, and Corporal?"

Woods eyed him warily. Sweet reached up and tapped the unburnt side of his head with one finger.

"Get yourself a lid. You're out of uniform."

There was a slight limp in the doctor's step as he left them. Trina barely noticed. She was already out beyond the sandbag barricades, walking on stiff legs so fast that Woods had to jog to keep up.

14

They had gone a full two blocks before Trina's muscles relaxed enough to let her slow down. She paused on the main street beneath the wide shadow of a movie theater marquee, her hands on her knees. Her throat had gone dry and as she struggled to breathe she remembered the way Sweet's hands had tightened around her throat. When she swallowed, she could still feel his thumbs pressing down on her windpipe.

Woods was there, a few steps behind her. When she turned around, he was squinting up at the marquee, shading his eyes with his hand. It was the kind of theater that might have gone out of style thirty years ago in her own world, with a little box office out front and only enough room for one screen inside. The bulbs around the marquee were dark and its crooked letters read WELCOME EASTERN CONF LIBERATORS. Someone had thrown something through one of the dirty windows that made a tidy hole at the center of a spiderweb of cracks. No one had bothered to fix it.

"I used to like movies." Woods stepped in close, frowning at the hole in the glass. "You ever been to one?"

"Movies?" She remembered a time when she'd stopped following the maps, when she'd passed a day between

Turnings hunched in the back of a theater, watching the same show over and over. "Yeah. All the time."

Woods watched her face, and his brow furrowed slightly as if something about what she'd just said hadn't made sense. The look was gone in an instant, and he started walking again, slow enough for her to catch up.

"I always liked the idea of sitting in the dark with a bunch of people you've never met, everyone all focused on the same thing. But no one has to talk about it or draw any attention to it. You're all just...there."

A kid with red hair and a sunburned face rode past them on a dented blue bicycle. He might have been seven, maybe eight. There was something about seeing a kid that age that tugged at Trina's insides, like the memory of some old wound. As he rode by, his eyes drifted to the pistol at Woods' side with equal parts fascination and fear. Woods didn't seem to notice him, didn't seem to react at all.

He hadn't asked her about their encounter with Sweet. He'd seen the way the doctor had looked at her, and he had to know that something was going on. Still, he hadn't said a word. To look at him, it was as if nothing had happened at all. If he was waiting for her to explain herself, he had to know that she wasn't going to. He seemed all right with that, and knowing that he didn't expect anything of her helped Trina relax, if only a little.

"Is that why you joined the militia?" she asked. "Everyone all focused on the same thing?"

Woods shook his head. "No, I joined up to get out of Ohio. You know, like the posters say. 'See the world, spread the word.' But now I'm stuck in the I.L., which isn't exactly a step up. Anyway, I only mentioned it because it popped into my mind just now. It's funny. I've passed by this theater maybe a dozen times in the last three months and never gave it a second look. I'd almost forgotten that movies ever used to be a thing. Last time I saw one I couldn't have been much older than that kid back there." He cocked a thumb over his shoulder, but the kid on the bike was long gone.

"I think it had a spaceship in it," he said, struggling with the memory. "Maybe a cat?"

She looked back up the street. The base was out of sight, but there was water up ahead, a little bridge hunched over the narrow river. Everywhere were little shopfronts that crowded close to the sidewalk. Their windows were dark, but that didn't stop the few people on the street from hurrying their way between them. Like the marquee, all the electric lights were either off or broken. In the distance loomed a blue water tower with a pointed roof. A weird black structure bulged from its side. Its thick black cables wound around the supports like creeping vines.

Trina made a point of getting in front of Woods, of forcing him to look at her. "What's the earliest thing you remember?"

"My dad," he said, without having to think. "He left around the time the Blinkers came. Before that...well, I don't like to talk about it all that much."

A bell on a shop door across the street made a high and friendly ringing, a sound at odds with the dark mood of the people on the street. The sun was high and there wasn't a single cloud in the sky, and yet the whole place seemed as if it were covered in some shadow that everyone but Trina could see. No one paused to talk to each other or even make eye contact as they passed by. They kept their heads down and their steps quick, as if they wanted nothing so much as to be indoors and out of sight.

"But you remember," she said. "Not *that*, necessarily, but everything that's happened to you, the choices you made. It's all, like, vivid. It all still feels real?"

"I suppose so," he said. "I mean, it's not like I have perfect recall or anything, but I remember the high points. Why do you ask?"

Trina shrugged. "It's just something I've been thinking about. Like, places and things are only real to us because we remember them. So, is it remembering them that makes them real? Or would they still be real even if we forgot all about them? And if we forget—like, really forget—then maybe when the past is past it's just...gone."

Woods clasped his hands behind his back, walking at-ease as he considered. "You know, I read somewhere that memory isn't a permanent thing, like you're taking it out of a box and looking at it and putting it back just like you found it. Every time we remember something, it's like we're putting it back together again. Sometimes we add things. Sometimes we take them away. But every time we remember it, it's just a little bit different than the last. So maybe memories don't matter as much as we think they do. Maybe memories are just what we decide we want them to be."

She stopped walking and after a moment he stopped, too.

"What?"

"Nothing," she said. "I'm impressed, that's all. You've got some depth to you, soldier."

He smiled. She'd embarrassed him, and she liked that she could embarrass him. "Not what you'd expect from a grunt from the O.H.?"

"Not what I'd expect from anyone, anymore. But lately the whole world's full of surprises."

Escalations, she thought.

He nodded. There was deep understanding in that nod, and it frightened her a little. "What about you, then?"

"What about me, what?"

"Your memories," he said. "What's the first thing you remember?"

She drew in a deep breath and took her time deciding whether to answer.

"I remember my grandfather," she said at last. "I think he died when I was pretty young. I don't remember much these days, but I remember that. It's just images, really. He'd do these...well, I guess you'd call them magic tricks. I mean, really amazing. He tried to teach me how to do them too, but I never could figure out how."

They walked in silence for a while, Woods setting the pace, taking his time. Trina walked beside him. With the sun at her back and a breeze brushing her skin, she could almost let herself believe that they were just two people out for a stroll, with no other purpose but to enjoy the day. He knew where they were going, and she was content to follow, to let someone else make the decisions for a change. It was nice to have a plan, even if that plan was somebody else's.

"I didn't thank you," she said. "For helping me. Back at the base."

"It seemed like you and the doc had some history."

She swallowed. Her throat still hurt and when she breathed deep she could still smell muddy river water. "Yeah, I guess that's one way you could put it."

He nodded, as if he understood, and left it there.

They passed by a store that had vacuum cleaners in the window, steel monsters all fat and curvy like giant electric shavers. The sign on the door said CLOSED, and it looked like the place had been that way for years. A poster hung next to it, a painting of a sleek green convertible with a crank in the grille, the driver smiling wide beneath his fedora hat. In the passenger seat next to him was a coiled and leering snake, its tongue darting between its pointed teeth. Beneath the picture were the words, WHEN YOU RIDE ALONE, YOU RIDE WITH THE VIPER!

"But, you know..." He chose each word carefully, as if he were walking across a minefield. "If you're in some kind of trouble or something..."

"It's nothing I can't handle."

"But if you needed help. Not that you *need* help, but if you did. I could..."

She shook her head. "I wouldn't want to get you in trouble."

He shrugged. "It wouldn't be the first time. Definitely won't be the last." He smiled then. It was the first smile she'd seen him make, and it didn't seem at all out of place.

"Thanks," she said. "I like you, Woods. You're sweet." The words came out easily, before she'd had a chance to stop them, and she was surprised to realize that she meant them.

"Nah," he said, the smile gone now. "I'm just trying to make sure I get my hat back."

She plucked the hat from her head and made a show of looking it over before she slapped it against Woods' chest. "You can wear it for now," she said, "but I'm keeping it."

He smiled again, and the darkness that he seemed to carry with him lifted a bit. "Nate," he said.

"What?"

"My name. You can call me Nate. If you want to."

Nate. She turned the name over and over again in her mind, testing the feel of it. It suited him, this soldier. It seemed to suit every bit of his tall and lanky frame, as if Nate was the only name he ever could have possibly had. Knowing it made her uneasy. Corporal Woods, she could deal with. Corporal Woods could be held at arms' length and kept there for as long as she needed to. But Nate? Nate was something different entirely.

A woman in a pale green dress hurried past them. Her dark hair was done up in a curly poodle cut, her dress fastened high at the neck. She stepped off the sidewalk and into the street to keep from getting too close. Trina could feel the way the woman's eyes lingered on them long after she passed.

"Tell me something you remember," Trina said. "Any memory. Anything at all, as long as it's a good one."

"Okay." The skin around his eyes scrunched a little, then his cheeks flushed hot as he held back a little chuckle. "All right. Well, there was this guy I used to run with in secondary school. Name was Mikey Sloane. Little guy. Funny as hell. Anyhow, somewhere along the way, he got it into his head that he wouldn't have to do his turn in the service if he was ruled mentally unfit. Couldn't stop talking about it all year long. I kept telling him that it didn't matter, but he just would not listen."

He was laughing now, his eyes distant but dancing. "So, graduation day comes along. And we're all there—gowns and badges and everything—getting ready to go up on stage and get our promotion and enlistment papers. But Mikey, he's nowhere to be seen. So they start calling names and we all start lining up, and from the back of the auditorium someone starts screaming. So I look back, and Mikey comes running down the aisle, buck-ass naked. And he's..."

The laughter came quicker now, his face lighting up so brightly that Trina couldn't help but light up a little, too.

"...and he's yelling at the top of his lungs, 'I'm going to the dance but I can't find my cumberbund! Has anybody seen my cumberbund?'"

Trina watched him lose himself to laughter, laughter that just got worse the more he tried to keep it at bay. The story wasn't all that funny to her, but it was better than funny. It was *real*. He remembered it because he had lived it, and it still lived in him. It meant that there was no way she could have created this place, not if Woods, if *Nate*, had a memory like that. It meant that Sweet had to be wrong about her. He had to be.

Trina waited until he caught his breath before she asked, "Did it work?"

"No, it didn't," Woods said as he wiped his eyes. "He took ten lashes and spent two days in confinement. They shipped him out the next week. He died in the Battle of Gallows Crossing. I probably shouldn't even be telling you this. You're going to get the wrong idea about me and start thinking I run with subversive types."

"Would that be such a bad thing?"

His laughter stopped abruptly, as if her question had swallowed it whole. It was all the answer that she needed.

"Why are you asking me all this stuff about memories anyway?"

"No reason," she said, but then she saw his face darken with doubt. "No, that's not really true, exactly. It's just that...well, I've been going through some stuff lately."

She might have been content to leave it there but for the way he walked with his head cocked in her direction, the ease with which he listened without prompting, without any demands that she make sense or that she even keep speaking. It was enough to make the words flow out of her before she could even think to hold them back.

"Everything's been so surreal lately, and I've been trying to figure out what it all means. It used to be I thought that I was just kind of adrift, you know? That the things that were happening to me were because someone else was doing them *to* me."

She searched his face, looking for some sign that she should stop, some hint of what might be going on inside his head. All she saw was that same guileless look, so open that it might have meant anything, or nothing at all.

"And it got to where nothing around me seemed real, and as long as nothing around me was real, then nothing that happened around me or even *to* me mattered at all. But now...I dunno. I'm starting to wonder if maybe it's just been me the whole time. Maybe I've been doing it to myself all along."

Woods nodded, ever so slightly, but if he was agreeing with her or just thinking it over, she couldn't tell.

"It's okay," she said. "I sound like an idiot. I won't get mad if you tell me so."

"No," he said. "I don't think you sound like an idiot at all. I actually think it's kind of good when things don't make sense. If things don't make sense to me, it means they're not a part of who I am, and I'm not really a part of them. Not any more than I have to be, anyway."

They came to the corner, and as they rounded it, it occurred to Trina that there hadn't been any cars on the road, or vehicles of any kind save for a few bicycles. People hurried past the darkened shop windows on foot and let out long breaths as they reached that corner, like kids rushing past a graveyard.

"Sometimes I wish it was different, too," Woods said. "But then I have to remind myself that different isn't always better."

A wide, grassy plaza lay ahead of them. At its center stood a towering building with a wide, domed roof and white columns. Between the columns hung a long, black banner blazoned with the image of the squid with lightning in its tentacles. At the base of the building's wide steps, a wooden platform had been raised, a narrow stage beneath a long wooden beam. Four bodies hung by their necks from that beam, from ropes cinched tight around the burlap sacks that covered their heads.

"Is that what you're trying to remember?" Woods asked her. "The world the way it was before?"

She barely heard him. She was transfixed by the bodies on the gallows. Two were men, hanging side by side in identical brown suits. Next to them was a woman, the red of her dress so bright that it seemed almost as if she'd worn it in a final act of defiance.

But it was the body on the far end, nearest the sidewalk, that Trina couldn't look away from. Shorter than the rest, his rope had been made long, so that his feet hung even with the others. He wore short pants, as if he'd planned on spending the day at the park with a baseball glove in his hand. He couldn't have been much older than ten.

Woods walked on ahead of her, and it was only then that she realized she had stopped in her tracks. He hadn't seemed to notice the bodies. His eyes had been on some faraway point beyond the hardware store and the bookshop at the end of the plaza. It was as if he were seeing past all of it, to some other world than this one.

"Oh, crap," he said. "I'm sorry. I come this way so many times I didn't even think—"

"No," she said, still not taking her eyes off the boy. "It's all right. I need to see."

The hoods over their heads were a mercy. Trina didn't think that she could bear to see their faces. The way their heads tilted sideways made them look like they were asking her a question. She could see no trapdoor in the floor of the stage, no sharp drop, no quick end. These people had been hauled up and left to strangle.

"What did they do?"

Woods was silent for a while, and Trina couldn't tell if he was trying to find the right answer or if he was just afraid to say. He was walking quickly now, as if he wanted to hurry them past the gallows so it could be forgotten.

"Spies, most likely," he said at last. "There are a lot of subversives around town, especially with being so close to the front. There's a network, lets them feed information back to the Vipers. They steal supplies sometimes too. Right off the trucks if they can."

Now that they were closer, she could see that the kid's shoes were missing. One of his socks was loose. It dangled from his foot, grimy and wet. His knees were dirty, covered in scrapes that would never heal. For a fleeting, terrible moment, she had the mad idea that she knew this child, that she would recognize him if only she could lift the hood and see his face.

"You make it sound like you think they deserve it."

Woods considered, and drew in a deep breath. "They do. In a way. I guess. Not that they can really help it, I suppose. I imagine people do all kinds of desperate things when there's a war on."

"But you're still okay with just...killing people in the street?"

"No. I just..." He looked over his shoulder to make sure that they were alone, and stepped in close. He spoke in a whisper, but there was an edge in it that hissed. "Keep your voice down, willya? Of course I'm not okay with it. I don't want anyone to die, especially not like that. I hate it, all right?"

He stood tall again and let out a long breath. Trina could see that his lip was trembling. "Everyone just wants things to go back the way they were, but they can't. The Blinkers made sure of that when they killed all the electrics. They left us in the dark and we had no choice but to start over any way we could."

Trina had been so focused on the bodies and the gallows that she hadn't even noticed the dark shape on the side of the courthouse dome. It was larger than the one on the water tower, a sleek, black lozenge the size of a bus. It clung to the roof with long coiled tentacles that wound across the dome like ivy, twining their way between the columns of the high bell tower. They pulsed lazily in the sun, bulging as they stretched, like a snake digesting a mouse.

"You may not remember the world the way it was," Woods said, "but I do, okay? Nothing's ever going to be that way again, but we're trying to build something new. Something better. And I have a duty to help see that through."

Trina said nothing. She was too afraid that if she said anything more, she'd risk being counted as one of those subversives, risk getting a bag over her head and a rope around her neck. Her eyes drifted to the pistol strapped to Woods' hip, and wondered how little it would take for him to use it.

"Look," Woods said, "it's just another block or so, but we can take the long way. You don't have to look at any of this."

She had already pushed past him, walking stiff-legged, so fast she was almost running. The Blinker on the courthouse roof expanded and contracted as if in some dreamless slumber. She tried to tell herself that none of this was real. She tried to tell herself that it wasn't her who had made it real.

Woods caught up to her and pulled at her elbow. "Come on. It's okay. How about you tell me about your friend."

Trina jerked her arm away. "He's not my friend. I don't even know if he's still alive." She wiped her sleeve across her eyes. She'd expected tears, but there were none. "The library. You said it's close?"

"Well, yeah. Just past the church over there."

I can find my own way," she said, leaving him standing bewildered on the sidewalk. "I don't want to keep you from your duty."

15

By the time she reached the library, Trina could barely breathe. It felt as if iron bands had been pulled tight against her chest and a nest of rats was gnawing at her insides. She pressed her forehead to the rough stone wall, let its edges bite into her skin. She pressed until it hurt, until this new pain pushed aside all the other pain. She squeezed her eyes shut, but all she could see was a little boy hanging from the end of a rope.

This was a world full of monsters, and no one but a monster would have any part in making it. Not on purpose. It was a cruel joke, another prison in an endless series of prisons to punish her for who knew what. She couldn't let herself believe that she was responsible for anything in this world. She couldn't let herself believe that Sweet had been right about her, about any of it. She pressed her palms to her eyes and tried to drive his words from her mind, but they only grew roots, echoing louder and louder.

They showed me what you've been doing to this world. Over and over and over again.

The stone wall was cool in the shade, and she let it hold her up. She looked back down the road to see if Woods had followed her, but Woods wasn't there. She could still see the top of the courthouse dome peeking up over the low buildings, the black coils of the Blinker swelling around it like some enormous octopus. Her fists were balled tight. As she breathed, she felt them unclench by degrees. Her nails left little red crescents in the meat of her palms.

The planters along the steps that led up to the library door were full of flowers, wide sprays of daisies and zinnias in bright clusters of yellow and white. She stared at the nearest one until she'd memorized its contours. She held it in her mind as she closed her eyes.

Red, she thought, over and over. *Red. Red.*

She mouthed the words as she pictured the color of the flower changing, the whole world changing. *Red. Red. Red.*

She opened her eyes. The flowers were still the same, white and yellow. The great, black Blinker still coiled around the courthouse dome. And somewhere beyond the merciful curtain of the shop buildings, the same child still dangled from the same rope.

A woman hurried by with a young girl, a mother holding her daughter's hand. The little girl ran to keep up. Both of them threw furtive glances at Trina over their shoulders. Trina wondered if they would report her, this suspicious woman talking to herself outside the library. Would they think she was one of the subversive types that Woods had warned her about? Was Woods on his way back to the base even now, on his way to report her? On his way to tell Doctor Sweet? Or Lieutenant Sweet? Or whatever it was he called himself in this place?

She didn't think so, but she had no reason to *not* think so. Did she really believe that this man she'd just met would spare her just because they'd shared a walk together? This man who she'd known for all of five minutes? This man she had trusted because she had been desperate for any kind of meaningful human contact? Because he had been nice to her, the way the guy in the pickup truck had been nice to her?

She forced herself to breathe, forced her limbs to stop shaking. The Shadows were still out there. Sweet was still out there. If either of them managed to find her before she found Colin, she might never find him again. Everything else was secondary, and she had to put it out of her mind long enough to do what she came here to do. If the soldiers came for her, then so be it. This place would be gone in a day or two anyway. Whatever was going to happen to this world when the Turning came, it couldn't come fast enough.

The library door creaked open at a push. It was hot inside, and Trina's clothes began to cling to her almost as soon as she stepped across the threshold. Dust swam in the light that filtered in through the narrow windows. Cobwebby oil lanterns sat darkened on the rows of long tables next to forgotten stacks of unshelved books. The air was thick with the smell of wood polish and the musty scent of old paper, and there was not a single person to be seen. It seemed a place fit only for ghosts.

It wasn't the same library as the one where she had first found Colin, but it was close enough that she could see its echo at every turn. The desk out front was made of faded cherrywood this time, but there was no one behind it to greet her. There was no grand castle turret, but the rotunda still rose high above her head, lined with books all the way to the vaulted ceiling. Its shelves were crisscrossed with winding iron balconies and sliding wooden ladders.

She let her hand linger on the wide wooden banister as she climbed the spiral staircase that rose along the rotunda shelves. The floating platforms from that other world seemed little more than a child's fantasy. Below her, the mosaic tile floor still had the same spiral pattern, but in this world the colors were all wrong.

Step by step, she rose along the bookshelves, retracing the fall she and Colin had taken in that other world. She wondered if some version of them had run from the Shadows in this world too, some other Colin, some other Trina, different, but almost the same. If that other Colin was here, would he remember her at all?

When she found him, he was back in his tiny office, behind a desk so wide that it seemed impossible that it had ever fit through the door. Every inch of it was strewn with papers and books, each stacked on top of another, abandoned in the middle of reading. More books were stacked in precarious towers on the floor. Colin sat at the center of it all in a high-backed chair, like a little boat in the eye of a hurricane. His head was cradled in his hands.

"Colin?"

He started at the sound of her voice. She saw his eyes then, sunken and rimmed with red, his face slack with exhaustion. He stared at her, befuddled, as if he was looking at a stranger. Trina's heart sank, for in that moment her worst fear was realized. This wasn't her Colin. It was some other Colin entirely, and this Colin did not know her.

"Miss Bell?"

Trina tried to hold back the cry of joy that rose in her throat. It came out as a bark of laughter as Colin got up from his chair. In an instant, he was around the desk, pulling her into his arms. He still felt exactly like the Colin she knew. He felt safe, the way her grandfather had felt safe. He still smelled of soap and crisp linen, only now it came with the faint scent of wood smoke and burning lamp oil.

"My dear girl, where did you disappear to?" He held her out at arm's length, and his eyes went wide as he noticed her clothes. "Oh, no. Don't tell me that you've enlisted."

She looked down at the shirt Edie had given her, the gray cloth with the military lettering. "What? God, no. My clothes got wrecked in the flood, so they gave me new ones is all."

His brows furrowed at this. "Flood? What flood?"

"How do you not remember the flood? The whole street was underwater. I almost drowned."

His eyes grew distant, searching for a memory. For an instant it seemed as if he might have found it, but it was gone as soon as it came. "Trina, there hasn't been a cloud in the sky. Not a drop of rain for weeks."

She stared at him, and wondered if this really was some other Colin after all. The last time she'd seen him, he'd been in the lobby of the old hotel. What if all those back-and-forth Turnings had left him behind? She still had the bump on the back her head from when the flood had swept her away. She'd thought that she remembered him reaching out to her, trying to save her from the rushing water. Had he ever even been there at all?

"I thought that I'd lost you." she whispered.

"You never lost me," he said. "But when you didn't come back, well, I suppose I assumed that you'd forgotten about me. So, I left the base and went home."

"You *assumed*?" She pushed him away, harder than she'd meant to. Papers fell as he stumbled back against the desk. "So you just left me there? You didn't think to…I don't know, check on me? You never wondered what those people might be up to? A bunch of strangers?"

"You seemed to be in safe hands at the time."

"Safe hands! He tortured me. He tried to drown me! I almost died."

He stared at her with his mouth open, not understanding. "He who?"

"Sweet. The doctor." Only, Colin hadn't known about Sweet. He'd only met Edie. He couldn't have known about the fire hose, about the ice pick. "Never mind. It doesn't matter."

Colin didn't seem to hear her. His look was far away, as if he was trying to fill in the blanks in a puzzle whose boundaries he didn't understand. "I should remember leaving," he said at last. "But I don't. I remember waiting for you. I remember being alone for quite a while, which is strange because I can't imagine why anyone would be left alone for that long on a military base. In fact, now that I think of it, it seems odd that they even let us in the building at all."

There was a dreamy quality to his voice, like a man on the edge of sleep. His words were clear, but they seemed to surprise him as they came out of his mouth, as if they were being spoken by someone else entirely.

"The next thing I recall, I was sitting at home, in my apartment. Isn't that strange? I'd almost forgotten the whole thing entirely, except that I noticed the geode that I keep on top of the old radio cabinet. You remember it. The one with the pink crystals?"

He smiled then, and in that moment he seemed to come back to himself. "That's when I remembered our mantra. Small room. Pink rock. Ugly lamp. Flower blanket. Then it all came flooding back to me. Isn't that extraordinary?"

Trina barely heard him. He'd waited, but he'd left. He went back home as if none of it had ever happened. All this time, he hadn't been looking for her at all.

"I can't believe you left me," she said quietly.

Colin seemed chastened. "The duty sergeant seemed to have your best interests at heart, and she certainly seemed to know the lay of the place. How strange that I didn't consider that you might be in danger."

For the first time she noticed the deep shadows under his eyes and wondered when was the last time he'd gotten any sleep.

"But, you're absolutely right," he whispered. "It's a military base in the middle of a war. It should have occurred to me that they might have taken you into custody. Or worse."

His face was stricken, and when he looked up at her she could see the weight of the memory in his sunken cheeks, his trembling chin.

"I'm sorry, Trina. I'm so sorry."

She turned away, suddenly unable to look him in the eye. "How long have I been gone?"

He thought for a moment. "Three days, nearly. Counting today and the day we visited the base. Fifty, perhaps fifty-five hours."

She'd lost a day, then. But did that mean that she'd been unconscious that long? Or were the Turnings starting to change the way time moved as well?

"Once I realized my mistake," he said, "I waited for you at my apartment, but I was afraid that you might have forgotten where I lived. So, when you hadn't turned up by the next morning I went back to the base and inquired at the gate. But no one had seen you or even remembered us being there. That's when I decided to wait for you here."

"How did you know I'd come back here?"

He seemed taken aback at this, another question that didn't make sense. "You'd already found me here once. It didn't seem unlikely that you'd find me again."

"And you've been waiting here this whole time?"

"Yes."

"For two days?"

He shrugged, considering. "Yes."

She huffed a bit at this. All her anger was draining away, and her cheeks had begun to grow hot.

"And it turns out that it's a very good thing that I did." He waved her closer as he dug into a pile of papers on his desk. "I was thinking about the building at the military base. It suddenly struck me as strange that we'd find ourselves there of all places. Then I remembered how you'd insisted on calling it by its former name, the one that I found in that old phone directory. Ms. Dixon's Home for the Dispossessed."

He spun an open book around to her and tapped the picture on the page. "Which, in turn, started me wondering what it might have been before that."

The picture was of Ms. Dixon's Home, the same brick and limestone building, the same wrought-iron balconies. But this was before the high chain fences and the coils of barbed wire. Long before, if the book's brittle and yellowed paper was any indication. Beneath the caption in plain block type were the words Millbrook College c.3917.

"That's the old notation, pre-occupation," he said. "That puts it at about 85 years ago."

"A college? Not a hotel? Not a hospital?"

He frowned. She shook her head to tell him that it didn't matter. "So, it was a school. So what?"

"Ah, but not just any school. Millbrook College was the leading center for theoretical physics in all the three provinces. It was closed down not long after the Blinkers came. Without working instruments, there just wasn't much point, but before that, if you were studying advanced physics or relativity or any number of things, you did it here."

He shuffled through a stack of papers, huffed in annoyance, and then set it aside. Beneath it was an oversized book filled with bound newspapers that eclipsed the mess on the desk when he opened it.

"Then I remembered that you'd told me you were looking for a particle accelerator. So, I did some digging. Most of the records were electronic and therefore unreadable, but I did manage to unearth this."

He flattened out the brittle newsprint with his palms. There, on page five of an edition dated February 30th, 3821, was a short article, less than half a column of text and no pictures. The headline read, MILLBROOK RESEARCHERS SET TO PROBE ATOMIC MYSTERIES.

"Apparently," Colin said, "three scientists from Millbrook College's Applied Physics department were studying the nature of subatomic particles using a device called an induction accelerator to create high-energy beams of electrons."

"A particle accelerator," she said. "It's been here the whole time?"

"In the basement of that very building." He leaned back in his chair, smiling triumphantly. "Now, look at the date."

She watched his face, waiting.

"It's three days before the first Blinkers appeared."

"And when the Blinkers came, the electricity stopped working."

"Precisely." He was practically beaming. "It's far too perfect to be a coincidence."

Trina touched her hand to the paper, felt the subtle indentations of the words, and saw that her fingers were trembling. If what the article said was true, then she'd been right about the particle accelerator all along. But if Sweet was telling the truth about her, then there was no such thing as a coincidence. Her subconscious had made those articles and planted them here, just as it had everything else.

They showed me what you've been doing to this world. Over and over and over again.

She shook her head. "It doesn't mean anything. There aren't any Blinkers where I come from. This is the only world where I've seen anything like them."

His brows wrinkled again. "Really? I was certain that we passed at least three of them on our way to the base together."

She didn't want to tell him anything more about what the world had been like for them that day, with the horse-drawn carriages and the giant airship in the sky. She could already see the puzzlement in his eyes, the searching for memories that he couldn't quite catch. If she told him any more, she was afraid it might break him.

"In any case, it's not the point." All at once his eyes were clear, all hint of that inward turning gone. "What matters is that the place you've been trying to reach may have been right under your nose all along."

She looked at the faded picture of the building again, at the wide-open lawn at the base of the stone steps. Between the barbed wire and the armed guards, that building seemed farther away than ever, now. She wanted to believe that this place was the key she'd been looking for, but there were so many barriers in the way. But were the barriers something the Shadows had set in her way, or something she had put there herself?

"So, how do these Blinkers work, anyway? How do they shut down the power?"

"No one knows." Again, Colin fumbled with the papers, and when he looked up his eyes were alive with the thrill of the chase. "As near as anyone can tell, they emit some kind of field that makes the use of conventional electrical devices impossible. Of course, the human nervous system is electrical, so it's not as if they suppress electrical activity entirely, but a common theory is that they're somehow able to shut down any current that extends above a certain amperage. But that's impossible to test, let alone verify. No one's been able to create an instrument that can measure the effect."

It was one more obstacle in a series of obstacles, as if the world had sensed her getting close to a solution and raised more roadblocks in her way.

"And they just showed up one day?" she asked. "The way people are acting, you'd think they'd always been here."

"For many people, they have." He pushed his glasses higher up on his nose. "It's been almost a generation. Many people alive now barely have any concept of what electricity even was."

He paused here, a question forming on his lips that he seemed almost afraid to ask. "But that polished stone you showed me. That device in your bag. You say you've never seen the Blinkers before. Do I take that to mean that you've been to a place that still uses electricity?"

"I have," Trina said, and crouched down so that she could look Colin in the eye. "And you have too. There was electricity in your apartment on the day we got separated. The ugly lamp. That was an electric lamp. Don't you remember?"

She regretted her words immediately, because Colin squeezed his eyes shut as if the thought were causing him physical pain. "I remember... That is to say, I thought... It was just a passing notion, really. Maybe even a dream. But that lamp is an oil lamp. It always has been."

Trina chewed at her tongue to offset the sinking feeling in her stomach. "Forget it," she said. "The phone's gone anyway. I'm probably just confused."

"I'm sorry," he said, back in control now. "I know it's a lot to digest. But it's not the Blinkers that are of interest so much as what became of the *building*."

He pushed another piece of paper into her hands. "That's a clipping from the Herald's public notices section. The building stood abandoned for more than five years after the college ceased operation. Left derelict and in complete disrepair. It was the kind of place that kids threw stones at just to break the windows."

She handed the paper back to him without reading it. She'd felt safe behind these windows, once. She didn't want to think about them being broken.

"At any rate," Colin said, "it became a hotbed for minor crimes. Drifters, drug addicts and the like. There was something in the police blotter about it every week. At least until September of 3829."

He unearthed another of the giant books of newspapers and spread it out before her. This time, it was a front-page headline. FEDS BUST LOCAL RUM RUNNERS.

"They'd been using it as a warehouse. Shipments in the dead of night, round-the-clock guards. The mayor and the police chief in their pockets. It's all there if you care to read it. It's fascinating, but what's of real interest in regards to your situation is something that was said at the trial."

Here he patted the cover of a thick tome bound in black leather, embossed in gold with the words, PROCEEDINGS OF THE CRIMINAL COURTS, 3830 VOL IX.

"The ringleader, a man by the name of Frank Dorsey, testified that they had broken through a basement wall that led to an old cistern, well below ground. According to his story, he had found an old transistor radio the night before in a box full of items left there from the old Millbrook college days, and forgotten that he'd put it in his coat pocket. But when he approached that concrete cistern, the radio began to work again."

He said this last in a breathless whisper. Trina had to remind herself that, to her, an old radio was just an old radio. But to Colin and everyone else in this world without electricity, it must have seemed like a miracle.

"It was just static, mind you, but even that much should have been impossible. And, of course, the story was laughed at and disregarded as just another urban legend. There was no end to Millbrook College stories at the time, everything from axe murderers to restless spirits to little gray men who glowed in the dark. Dorsey died suddenly of cancer before the trial ended, so no one paid any attention to the claim or ever bothered to investigate it. Six months later, the building sold for a very reasonable price to Ms. Althea Dixon, who fixed the place up and made it into a home for girls."

The papers on Colin's desk were like drifts of snow. Thick books threatened to slide off the edges, the way that icebergs slid off into the ocean. It seemed as if the entire history of this world had been laid out before her, every last detail, every hidden thing. For the first time, she felt like she could figure everything out, all of it, if only she could look deep enough.

"Did you come across any mention of a doctor?" She knew the answer before the words even left her lips. "At the base? His name's Philip Sweet."

"You mentioned him earlier," Colin said. "Did you say that he tortured you? I hope you don't mean literally."

"Just... Did you find anything about him?"

"Not that I can recall. I think I would have remembered the name. Why?"

"It's nothing. Forget it." She didn't want to tell him the rest, that Sweet knew about the Turnings, too. That he'd told her that they were her fault and tried to drown her for it. She didn't want to tell him that Sweet was still out there, and that he remembered her.

"So, what's in the cistern?" she asked.

"I hesitate to stray too far from the information at hand," Colin said. "You see, in the records of the building permits related to the renovations, I came across an inspection report. Some extensive brickwork was done in order to rehabilitate the building's basement. In those records, there's no mention of a cistern or even anything like a cistern. If it exists, which I'm convinced that it does, it would have been sealed up when the renovations were made."

"But why would they seal it up?"

He shrugged. "Any number of reasons. It could have been a safety issue. Or perhaps they didn't know it was there and they only thought they were repairing a wall. In any event, I don't believe that they had any idea about Mister Dorsey's claim, or that there was any reason to suspect that there was anything out of the ordinary related to the building. In fact, I couldn't find any reference to any strange phenomena or happenings on the site at all after Ms. Dixon took possession."

The light was still dancing in Colin's eyes, undeterred by this seeming dead end. The longer it lingered, the more Trina found that it was catching. "All right then," she said. "Tell me the rest."

"You already know the rest," he said, beaming. "The militia came in three years ago and commandeered the building, and that was the end of Ms. Dixon's Home."

He snapped the book shut, and it sent up a puff of dust that twinkled and spun in the beam of light from the window. Trina chewed her lip as she thought about all those girls being put out on the street. She wondered if this world's version of Edie had lived in that place, or if she had any inkling of what might be hidden beneath it.

"But consider this." Colin was on his feet now, and starting to pace the little stretch of floor behind the desk. "The militia could have chosen just about anywhere for their base. The secondary school is newer and closer to the front. The courthouse has far more space. I could go on. So, what is it about this place, a place that has no apparent strategic value, that would make them choose it above all others?"

"A hole in the ground that makes old radios buzz for five minutes?"

"Not just old radios," Colin said, "but a place where potentially any electronic equipment becomes functional again. A place where the Blinkers either do not or *cannot* reach."

There had been a door in the basement in that other world, one with RESTRICTED painted on it in red letters. It had stayed locked, even when the world changed around her. More obstacles. She shook her head. "It's a nice idea, but it's an awful lot of wishful thinking."

"Is it? You said yourself that you believed a particle accelerator was to blame for your situation. And where did we find ourselves but in the very building that used to house the only working particle accelerator in the province? A particle accelerator that was activated just before the Blinkers arrived to shut it down? It seems to me that's a little too much to be just a coincidence."

They showed me what you've been doing to this world. Sweet's voice echoed in her mind. *Over and over and over again.*

"Yeah, well, I've had a lot of time to reconsider that. And anyway, the world I came from, the Blinkers were never a part of it."

"How do you know?"

She opened her mouth, but realized that she didn't have an answer.

"You've said yourself that you have very little recollection of the time before your situation began. With all the realities you've been experiencing, how do you know that *this* isn't the correct one?"

She breathed deep and turned the idea over, let it settle upon her mind like new-fallen snow. She had become used to Colin not having as much information as she did, but now he seemed to have hit upon something new. Something strange enough to almost make sense.

"No," Trina said at last. "It's just too convenient. It can't be right."

"Can't it?" He was talking quickly now, all signs of his earlier confusion gone. "You said yourself that every time the world changes, you end up back where you started. What if the reason you haven't been able to leave isn't because you're being kept away from something? What if you keep coming back to this place because you're already exactly where you need to be?"

Another thought occurred to her then, more terrible than all the others: what if Sweet had lied? If she didn't make these worlds, and all this was being done to her by the Shadows or whoever was behind them, the whole story might be some elaborate ploy to lure her back to the base, to Sweet. What if, by going back, she'd be walking right into a trap?

"Of course, we've already been inside the place once, but getting down to the basement of the building might prove challenging. In fact, I'd expect we'd encounter a fair amount of resistance. But I've had some thoughts in that direction, and I—"

"No."

"Beg pardon?"

"If I go back," she said, "you can't come with me."

"Surely, you're not suggesting that you go back there alone?"

"You said yourself that this might be exactly where I need to be. If that's the case, I won't have any problems getting in. And besides..."

She stopped herself. If she wasn't supposed to be there, then it wouldn't matter to her, because there would be another Turning soon enough. But Colin? Colin could still get hurt, maybe even killed. And even if he didn't, if another Turning came and he was with her when it happened, what would it mean for him then? She could see the toll that his conflicting memories were taking on him. How long would it be before there was nothing of him left?

"Look," she said. "I mean...I don't know where I'd be right now if you hadn't helped me. And if there's a chance that I can get out of this, stop the Turnings from happening, it's because of you."

He smiled, and she suddenly found herself unable to look him in the eye. "But I can't let you take any more risks for me." Her throat felt full, her words choked. "I couldn't live with myself if..."

She steadied herself against the desk. Colin reached out and put his hand on top of hers. "Do you know what I was doing with my time before I met you?"

He looked at her until she met his gaze, patient and fatherly. "I was simply marking the days. Each one was exactly like the last, nothing changing, with nothing to fear or look forward to. If you'd asked me what I'd be doing two weeks from now, or a year, or ten years, I could have told you because it would have been exactly what I was doing that day. And I was perfectly content because I didn't believe that it could be any other way."

Again came the lump in her throat, the threat of losing her grip.

"You changed that for me," he said. "And there's no going back. So, if it means a little danger here and there, I consider it a very small price to pay. So, for good or ill, I'm afraid you're stuck with me."

They stood together in silence as she thought about all the reasons why he should stay behind. She'd already put this man in danger once without a giving it second thought. She had thought of him as being immune to the Turnings somehow, that the changes they brought couldn't touch him. She'd been careless and selfish, and now he was nearly as adrift as she was. She tried to find the words to tell him that she couldn't let him go with her, but just looking into his eyes was enough to tell her that he wouldn't take no for an answer.

"All right," she said at last. "We'll go. But you're going to have to follow my lead."

"You have a plan, then?"

"Not really," she said. "Not yet. But we need to find someone to let us into that basement, I think I might know a guy."

16

"Well, as I live and breathe. The prodigal has returned." Janowski wiped his hands on a rag as he strode toward the fence, leaving the jeep he was working on with its front jacked up in the air and a wheel laying on the ground. "Let me guess, our man Woods failed in his mission and you've come back looking for a real guide to show you a night on the town."

"Something like that," Trina said, regretting the words as soon as she saw the way they made his eyes light up. "Actually, I need your help with something."

"Well, you're in luck then, because I am most definitely in a helping mood." He gave her a playful wink, inviting her to be playful back. "Just tell me what needs doing and count on me to get it done."

Trina folded her arms. "I need to get into the base."

"Oh, well that's simple. You still have your civvy badge, yeah? Get you right back through the gate. Easy peasy lemon squeezy."

"Well, yeah, but…" She weighed the risks again, not sure if she could trust him, knowing that she didn't have a lot of options. "What if I needed to get into a place where civilians weren't strictly allowed to go, exactly?"

She let her gaze drift over his shoulder, toward the tall brick building with the wrought-iron balcony. The light in his eyes gave way to confusion. "The offices? Why'd you want to go in there? It's nothing but desks and file cabinets and grumpy officers in starchy uniforms. Way above my pay grade."

"But you can get me in? I mean, you *are* the guy who knows the place like the freckles on the back of his hand, right?"

Janowski rubbed at the stubble on his chin and let out a harsh snort of a laugh. When he looked at her again, the playful twinkle was gone from his eye. He shook his head. "Nah. I get caught with a civilian in a restricted area, it's a caning for sure. And the last thing my record, or my backside, needs is another one of those, thanks very much."

"You could always tell them you were just sneaking me in for a little, you know, private time. They'll buy that, right?"

"Ah, you wound me. That might take a few strokes off, just for amusing the Sarge. But it's not worth the risk. Not even if I thought you were going to make good on the offer."

A head poked out from behind the jeep that Janowski had been working on. It was Briggs. She kept her eyes on her work but Trina still caught her veiled glances in their direction. She was watching, but doing everything she could to not look like she was watching.

"Speaking of the Sarge," Janowski said, "you can just go up there and ask for her yourself. She already knows who you are, and if there's anyone likely to help you along, it'd be her."

Trina shook her head and stepped back from the fence, wanting to put a little distance between them. "No, I can't go to Edie." There was a question in the way he looked at her, but she didn't have an answer. Edie had helped her before, in that other world. She had helped her in this one, too. Trina wondered if it was only that she was afraid that one had nothing to do with the other, that Edie would forget her again after this world, too. Or was it that she couldn't face the possibility that Edie really had meant to lead her to Sweet, and that she might do it again.

"I just can't, okay?"

He held up his hands. "Fair enough, but there are limits to my charity. If you want me to risk my cheeks and my sterling reputation, you're going to have to tell me why."

She let out a long sigh. "I need to get into the basement."

"The basement? Waste of time. The only thing down there is storerooms and broken furniture."

"Then it shouldn't be a problem getting me in, right?"

He frowned, and looked down on her with more skepticism than she might have given him credit for. "This is an awful lot of sneaky-sneak for something you keep telling me shouldn't be a problem. Makes me wonder about the parts you're not telling me."

The wind blew cold across her shoulders. The sun would be setting soon. That's when Colin told her to be ready. He wouldn't say what he had in mind, but he seemed to think it would be enough to buy her the time that she needed. Already she could see the activity in the camp slowing down, tapering off for the night. Sweet was still out there, somewhere in that sea of tents, and he'd know that she was coming back.

"All right," she said. "It's just that I'd prefer that a certain someone didn't know I was there."

"Ah, so your date with Young Master Woods went even worse than I'd imagined. Shame. I really thought you two kids had what it took to go the distance."

She rubbed at her arms and tried to drive the chill away. She couldn't feel the next Turning coming on, but it *would* come. It always did. If she wanted to see what this world kept hidden behind that RESTRICTED door, she was running out of time. "No," she said. "It's not Woods. It's the doctor. Doctor Sweet."

"The L.T. with the mummy wrap all 'round his face?"

"That's him."

Janowski's eyes went wide as he sucked in a breath. "The plot thickens!"

From somewhere behind him came the sound of a tool being dropped, a ringing of metal loud enough to make Trina's muscles tense. She looked back to the jeep but Briggs wasn't there. At once Trina was aware of how out in the open they were, how anyone might be watching.

"Wait," Janowski said. "You wouldn't happen to be *responsible* for said mummy wrap, would you?"

Trina said nothing, but the longer she said nothing, the surer he seemed to know that it was true.

"Oh, you naughty girl. I mean, I liked you before, but now I might have to marry you." He rubbed at his chin again, considering. "All right. I'll get you inside without the doc seeing, though you *will* owe me, and when it comes to favors, I always collect. I'll be done with this business in half an hour. Meet me outside the main gate then and I'll get you into the place all quiet-like. Good?"

· · · · · · · · · ·

It was more than an hour before Janowski showed up at the gate, cupping his hand to his eyes to block out the setting sun, looking for her in the most obvious way possible. That was all right. She hadn't expected him to be subtle, and if anyone saw them they'd just assume that the two of them were sneaking off somewhere to be alone together. As a cover story, it wasn't bad, and she didn't have a better one.

She'd spent the time sitting on a park bench a block away, watching the gate while she pretended to read a beat-up paperback that she'd taken from the stacks in the library. She'd told herself that she was watching for Edie to pass by, but really she'd been watching for Sweet. Just the thought of seeing him again was enough to start her stomach churning, but the thought that she might not see him coming was even worse. The Shadows were somewhere out there, too. She could feel them, like a subtle trembling in the air, like a song just beyond hearing.

"What took you so long?" Janowski asked, taking her by the arm. "I've been waiting here forever."

He hustled her through the gatehouse so quickly that she didn't even have time to be annoyed. The soldier there wrote down the number on her badge. Her name wasn't on it, so she gave him a fake one. Trina wondered what would happen if Sweet got his hands on that list and somehow figured out that she was back on the base. She wondered if he was out there watching her even now.

"No need to worry about the doc, darlin'," Janowski said, as if he'd read her mind. "I passed by the med tent on the way over, and he was in the middle of stitching up some poor sap who laid his arm open trying to strip down a 50 cal. He'll be hours."

Trina realized then that she envied Sweet. It didn't seem fair that he should have a place in this world, that he should be surrounded by people who at least knew who he was when she was stuck starting over with every Turning. It didn't seem right that he should have a life when she didn't.

At least she still had Colin. The sun was almost down, and whatever he was planning would be happening soon. She didn't think she'd be able to forgive herself if he ended up getting hurt, but he'd ushered her out of the library with barely any chance for her to protest. After everything, he still wanted to help her. She hoped that she was still worthy of that help, assuming she ever had been.

Janowski pulled her along as they walked toward the high inner fence. "Wait," she said. "What about Edie?"

"The Sarge? She'll be in her office on the second floor. Right there in the corner, see?" He pointed to a window where the dim light of an oil lamp was flickering somewhere inside. "I'll talk you in past the desk clerk, but I'm afraid that's the best I'll be able to do. If Sarge sees me lurking around, she's liable to brush us both off. I got caught sneaking in a few bottles of contraband about a week ago, and I don't think she's forgotten about it yet. But if you do run into her and you could see clear to put in a good word or two, I'll be your friend 'til the end. Now, put your arm around me."

"What?"

"Just put your arm around me."

She did as he said, and he immediately fell against her. She staggered beneath his weight, but held him up as he veered drunkenly toward the gap in the fence. The guard there smirked as they passed. Janowski paused long enough to give a wobbly salute before they stumbled on.

"You gotta make it awkward," Janowski said when they had lurched out of earshot. "Make 'em look but never see you. That's the key."

He took the building's stone steps two at a time, and bowed low as he swept the doors open for her. She hurried inside and tried not to look at the sign that read NO UNACCOMPANIED CIVILIANS BEYOND THIS POINT. Suddenly, she was afraid that she wouldn't recognize the place, that it would be just another dead end. The lobby was dark, and it took her eyes a second to adjust. When they did, she could make out the narrow counter and the staircase curving up into the shadows, but without light, everything seemed sinister and strange.

A single soldier sat behind the counter, working by lantern light. He barely looked up as the doors slammed behind them. Janowski shot him a grin, not bothering to slow his stride, moving like he owned the place. He took a clipboard off the counter and pretended to sign his name before he put it back down, just out of the soldier's reach. The soldier let them go without saying a word.

It was brighter in the atrium beyond the double doors, where the early evening light still filtered in through the high skylight. Trina looked up at the walkways above, grateful to see that the railings hadn't changed, grateful to see the spot where she and Edie had first spoken in that other world. There were metal desks where the couches used to be, perfectly spaced in neat rows, and a huge topographic map suspended like a tapestry from the far wall. Apart from that, the place was the same, right down to the wide fireplace and the stone floor that rang beneath their footsteps.

The desks were empty, and all the lanterns had been doused. Everything around her had the air of winding down, of settling in for the lightless night. It made her wonder if this was how nights had been in her own reality, in the old days before electric lights were ever a thing. She remembered her phone, now lost in that other world, lost because of Doctor Sweet. She knew how it worked but she couldn't remember having ever actually used it. What if it had never been hers at all? It might just be an artifact of some other turning, a detail lost in the fog of a dozen remembered worlds. What if Colin was right? What if this world was the real one after all?

"Okay, we gotta double-time it if we're going to get you out of here before blackout." Janowski trotted past her and waved at her to follow. "Over this way. Hurry."

He led her down the row of desks, past squeaky-looking metal chairs and papers piled high in letter trays. They were working their way to a door at the far end of the atrium. The last time she'd seen that door, she'd been slogging through water, and everything on the floor below had been flooded. Now she was going back, and she had no idea what was waiting for her.

"Just follow my lead if there's anyone on duty down there," Janowski said. "If we're lucky, it'll be Corporal Diaz. She's a little sweet on me. Bit obvious about it, too. Can't blame the girl. So just—"

He paused with his hand on the door handle, his head tilted like a dog that's just heard something rustling in the brush. An instant later, Trina heard it too, the high drone of a hand-cranked siren, rising and falling like something out of an old cartoon.

"Shit."

"What? What is it?"

"Perimeter alarm," he said, looking back to the double doors that led to the outside. "Probably nothing, but I need to be on station or it's my ass. I gotta go."

Trina grabbed him by the arm as he turned. "Wait. You're just going to leave me here?"

"Just go on down. Hard part's done. If Diaz is there, just tell her I sent you. If it's not...I don't know. Baffle them with bullshit until I get back." She watched him go, listening to the sounds of his boots on the stones until the siren overtook them and she stood in the empty room, alone.

The siren meant that, whatever Colin had planned, it was happening out there right now. It was working, too. She could hear the voices of the soldiers beneath the din, growing fainter as they were drawn away. She fought the urge to follow them, to find out if Colin was all right. With the piercing wail of the siren rising over and over like an accusation, all she could think of was the gallows at the courthouse, of the child hanging from a rope.

The door wasn't locked, and when she pulled it open she could see the steps disappearing down into shadowy depths where it seemed they'd forgotten to light the lamps at all. She didn't give herself time to change her mind. She moved quickly, hoping that there was no one down there to hear her coming, hoping that Sweet wasn't already down there, waiting for her.

But there was no one there. Not Sweet, not even Corporal Diaz. The place was empty but for a desk and a few token lanterns, and it took Trina's eyes a moment to adjust to the dimmer light. And yet, even in the darkness, she could make out the borders of the long hallway that stretched out before her, the familiar doorways lining either side. The fluorescent lights were gone, and the painted cinderblock here was mortared stone. Still, there was no mistaking that this was the basement of the hotel, the basement of the hospital. This was the place where Sweet had almost killed her.

The sound of the siren didn't reach down here. It was as if the darkness had swallowed it whole. Trina kept close to the walls as she moved, listening for voices, for any sound that might warn her that she was not alone. All she could hear were her own quickening breaths and the faint shuffle of her feet upon the dusty stone floor.

She found the door she was looking for. A lantern had been hung on a hook beside it, as if to say to anyone who might be looking that this place was important, that this door, more than any of the others, was deserving of its own light. It was made of metal, painted green and set in a thick band of mortar that was newer than the rest. Next to it was a hand-lettered sign.

RESTRICTED AREA. AUTHORIZED
PERSONNEL ONLY BEYOND THIS POINT.

Trina placed her hand upon the door handle. She'd expected it to be cold, but it was warm to the touch. She'd expected there to be a guard, too. If this really was the place she thought it was, then surely there *should* be a guard. But then, if it was the place, maybe she was meant to be here. Maybe whoever or whatever was responsible for the turnings had cleared the way for her, and all she had to do was open the door.

She closed her fist around the handle. In those other worlds, it had been locked. It would have to be locked in this one, unless the way had been cleared for her, unless she had cleared the way herself. She closed her eyes. She breathed deep and imagined the handle turning beneath her hand. She imagined the flowers and her grandfather's voice in her ear. She imagined the lock clicking open. She imagined the flowers turning blue.

17

The handle turned. The door swung open, and Trina opened her eyes. In the shadows beyond the doorway, a metal staircase led down into the darkness. She took the lantern down from its hook with trembling hands and held it out in front of her like a shield. The steps were rusted steel, and she could hear the rain of dust flaking away beneath her feet. The air grew colder as she went. By the time she reached the iron catwalk some thirty steps down, she was rubbing at her arms for warmth. It felt as if she were descending into a tomb.

Above her head, a string of old, dead light bulbs hung from a ceiling beam. She followed it around one corner, then another. The walls curved, the poured concrete smooth and seamless. Another catwalk ran along the inside of the curve, circling back onto itself in a wide O. The circle was bisected by a metal bridge that stretched out over empty air. Trina gripped the guardrail and held the lantern out over the void, but she could not see the bottom.

She listened for the siren again, but could hear nothing but her own breathing. Any minute now the soldiers would come, and they would find her down here. Would they arrest her? Would they hang her body in front of the courthouse? Or would they just leave her down here, alone, until the next Turning, not knowing what happened to Colin, not knowing if he was even still alive?

On the far side of the pit was a landing with more steps leading up, but the steps were crumbled and broken, like a mouthful of rotten teeth. There was a metal door at the base of those stairs, an oblong hatch that opened onto a small room barely the size of a closet. It had a glass window that looked out over the pit, but it was so streaked with grime that she could barely see through it.

She rubbed at the goosebumps the cold had raised on her arms. Only, it wasn't just the cold. There was something in the air, an energy that tightened her scalp and tugged at the little hairs on her skin. She'd felt a sensation just like it every time the Turnings came, but here it was distant, like a nagging ache. Like background noise. It told her that she was in the right place even as it made her wonder how much time she had left before this world disappeared and she would have to start all over again.

Inside the little room, a bank of controls had been mounted beneath the window. On it was a series of dials and toggle switches with gauges set above them. Trina tried one of the switches. It made a hollow, metallic thunk, but the needles on the gauges above it didn't budge. She tried another, then another, flipping them on and off again like a monkey in a behavioral experiment. Nothing she did had any effect on the needles, and each throw of the switches felt more and more desperate. Finally, she gave up trying. There was no more electricity here than there was anywhere else, and coming down here had been a stupid idea.

She leaned back against the cold concrete and closed her eyes. When she did, she could almost picture her grandfather, the little lines around his eyes, the thin lips curling up at their edges. Hints of a picture, but never the whole. If she'd only been able to learn what he knew, maybe she could imagine this world back to the way it was, before the war, before the little boy and the gallows. Only, she couldn't remember the world the way it had been, the way it should be. She couldn't even remember her grandfather's face.

She chased after his image in her mind, but it retreated as quickly as she could follow. It led her on, like a firefly in a dark forest, flaring and shrinking, close enough to touch but too fleeting to hold. She thought of the flowers. She smelled the sweet scent of them, and at once she felt her grandfather's hand on her shoulder, heard his voice whisper in her ear.

Don't imagine that you can change them, he told her. *Know that they already are exactly as you wish to see them. Know that that is the way they always have been.*

Trina's eyes snapped open, and the memory receded like a speeding train. Still, she knew it had been real by the heat that rose in her cheeks, by the tingle of the little hairs at the back of her neck. She had remembered her grandfather's voice, really remembered it, for the first time since all of this had begun. It still echoed in her mind, deep and sonorous and ageless. She could feel the truth of it, the reality of it, like an anchor in a stormy sea.

Out beyond the hatch, she could just make out the faint outlines of the catwalk stretching out over the yawning concrete pit. It all seemed brighter somehow, brighter than just her eyes adjusting to the darkness could account for. The space beyond the doorway was bathed in a new glow, a muted blue light that threw long shadows up the walls and onto the domed ceiling.

Trembling, Trina stepped out of the control room and onto the rusted walkway. She held her breath as the hollow sound of her footsteps rang through the ancient metal. There was a light at the base of the pit, pale and blue, like moonlight on water. It suffused the air beneath her feet, illuminating long pipes and bundles of electrical cables on the walls. For the first time she could see the full depth of the pit forty feet below her, maybe more. Standing at the edge was like standing on the roof of a tall building, and looking down was enough to make her feel dizzy.

Was this what had brought the memory to her, this light in a place where all light had died? Was this what she had come here to see, what the Shadows had been trying to keep her from finding? The thought made her giddy. Had she at last found the very thing that was responsible for the Turnings, the cause of all her uncertainties, all her suffering? After all her running, all her searching, had the answers been this close the whole time?

She remembered again what Doctor Sweet had told her, and a new thought emerged, more terrible than the others. What if this place was just some product of her mind, some construct of her imagination? What if there were no answers? What if the light was only here because she had put it here herself?

She closed her eyes again, and wrung the railing in her fists. She held the light in her mind as she tried to coax it to grow brighter, but the light only seemed to fall away. Again, she tried to picture her grandfather's face, but all she could see was Colin's face, Sweet's face, Woods' face. This last one lingered, smiling at her the way that he had smiled at her on the street with the sun at his back and his eyes in shadow. She tried to hold onto it, but the more she chased it, the more it twisted, until it became a new face, lifeless and pale. It was the face she'd imagined hiding under the hood at the courthouse. It was the face of the little boy, hanging from a rope.

The railing gave way with a crack, and she felt herself start to fall. Her eyes snapped open, but the light was gone. Her stomach lurched as her arms pinwheeled, searching for something to hold onto, but finding nothing. Then, all at once, she stopped. She hung over the pit in the dark, suspended, defying gravity. A tug at the waistband of her jeans hauled her back from the edge. She stumbled, but an arm around her middle kept her on her feet.

"Jesus, kid. Watch out. It's not a diving board."

Trina turned and saw Woods there, his face bathed in orange light. They were leaning against the concrete wall, his lantern swinging at the end of his outstretched arm. He gave her an uneasy smile as he held onto her, steadying her as she caught her breath.

"What are you doing all the way down here, anyway?"

She untangled herself from him, smoothing down her clothes, reassuring herself that she was still there, still alive. She stared at him in disbelief until she could speak again. "How are you here?"

"I should be asking you that. This is a restricted area. You're not supposed to be here."

"No, I mean, how did you get here? I was all by myself just a second ago."

His brow furrowed. "The stairs. I followed you down."

"No, you didn't." She brought her foot down and the hollow ringing of metal echoed through the chamber. "See? I would have heard you."

He raised his hands up to mollify her. The lantern swung wild, throwing odd shadows. "Look, would you just..." He lowered his voice to a whisper. "Keep it down, okay? Someone's going to hear us."

"How did you know I was down here?" Her pulse was thudding in her ears, every muscle screaming at her to run. She'd closed the door at the top of the stairs, made a point of shutting it behind her. No one could have known that she was here. Not even Janowski knew that she was here.

"I..." He paused, just for an instant, but in that instant his eyes were searching, almost confused. "I saw you. You went through the door and I followed you down."

"The hallway was empty." The stairs leading back up were on the other side of him. If she was going to run, she'd have to take the long way around to reach them, and he was standing too close. "You weren't there. No one was there. And you couldn't have come down the stairs. I would have seen the light."

"Look, you're not as sneaky as you think you are. If I could see you come down here, then so could anybody else. And I just..." He straightened his back, tensing as if he were expecting to get hit. "I just didn't want you to get in trouble is all."

"Then why didn't I see you come down here? I should have seen your lantern. I would have heard you coming." Deep down, she already knew the answer. She hadn't seen him come down the stairs because he hadn't come down the stairs at all. He hadn't been there behind her until the exact moment when she needed him to be.

"Your eyes were closed," he said. "I called to you, but you didn't hear me. What were you doing all the way out on the edge like that, anyway? Were you trying to get yourself killed?"

She looked back to the spot where she had been standing. The railing had broken away, but she never heard it hit the bottom. Already the doubt was beginning to creep in. Had she just been that distracted? Had she really not noticed him? "I... I just thought I saw something down there."

Woods scratched the stubbly hair at the back of his head. In the harsh light of the lantern, he looked younger somehow, younger even than he had the last time she'd seen him. "Look, we should get out of here before I get put in the stocks, and you get thrown off base, or..."

He stopped himself there, but she knew what he meant. When she closed her eyes she could still see the face of the little boy, or at least the face her thoughts had made for him, with his skin pale and his thin lips turning blue. She could almost believe that she had seen that boy somewhere before.

She looked over the edge of the pit. Between Woods' lantern and her own, the whole place was brighter now, but she still could not see to the bottom. The blue glow that had been there a moment ago was completely gone.

"What were they doing in this place, anyway?" she asked.

Woods crept closer to the edge and peered tentatively down. "I don't know," he said. "They never told me and its none of my business, anyway. Can we go?"

The lantern gave enough light that she could see all the way to the far side of the pit, to a rusted ladder bolted onto the concrete. "Do you think I could get down there?"

"What? No." He took a step back, as if the mere thought might propel him over the edge. "Why?"

"I bet I can get down there." Trina was already halfway around the circle before Woods could collect himself enough to follow. There was a gap in the railing where the ladder led down, and by the time he caught up with her, she was already testing it with her foot.

"You're crazy," he said, holding his lantern out over the dark pit. "It's got to be at least fifty feet down. You'll break your neck."

"I'll be fine. Just give me your light." He handed it to her without taking time to think about it. She bounced on the first rung to test the ladder some more. It groaned, but it held.

"Look, Trina. If I get caught down here, it's my ass."

"Then don't get caught down here." She took her first steps gingerly, moving slow, keeping careful hold of the lantern. "Just take the other light and go. I'll be up in a minute."

"What do you think is down there?"

"Nothing. Maybe everything."

"What if you get hurt?"

"I won't. Just go."

He looked over his shoulder at the stairs, but that was the last that she saw of him. It took all her attention to negotiate her way down. The lantern rocked against the metal rungs, hard enough that she thought it might break. Rust rained down beneath her feet, and as the dust reached her lungs she held her breath for fear that coughing might make her lose her grip.

She kept her eyes on her feet as she climbed. The flame in the lantern was weak, its flickering light barely enough to reach farther than a few rungs below her. Beyond that light, there was only the dark, and no hint of the bottom below. Her heart quickened as she tested each rung, less sure with each step that they would take her weight, less sure that they would ever end.

When her feet finally touched the concrete floor, she looked back up at the place where she had started. There was no light at the top of the pit. She wondered if Woods had taken the other lantern, and felt a sudden twinge of regret at the way she'd told him to leave. She didn't want to think about being alone down here. She didn't want to think that the Turning might come before she could see him again.

There was sign posted beside the ladder. It was old and faded, but she could still make out the words.

CAUTION
RADIATION AREA
AUTHORIZED PERSONNEL ONLY

She lifted the lantern higher to get a better look at the place. A ring of dead light bulbs set in wire cages circled the pit like jewels in a rusted crown. Patches of bare concrete dotted the walls, with empty pipes and drooping cables hung between them. Whatever equipment had been down here had been gone for years, maybe decades. It was as if she had discovered some ancient tomb only to find that it had been plundered long ago. All the answers she had hoped to find were gone, if they had ever been here at all.

And yet, there was one spot in this place that did not feel empty, a spot in the center of the pit where her light did not reach. When she turned the lantern upon it, it seemed to push the light back, as if the darkness around it was a shroud, some physical thing that light could not penetrate. No matter where she moved, it stayed perpetually in shadow.

She took a step toward it, and as she did, the air around her seemed to grow colder. She was gripped by the sudden feeling that she was not alone. She raised the lantern higher, searching, and held her breath, afraid to make a sound.

She crouched low as she approached the dark patch, holding the light out as if she might banish it. She could see its borders now, fuzzy and indistinct, like a blurred photograph, a dark absence of space barely bigger than she was. The dusty concrete curved and shimmered around it. The very air it touched seemed alive with crackling energy. And yet, she could tell that this darkness was nothing like the Shadows that had been pursuing her. This was something else entirely. This was something new.

Trina bent close and regarded the patch of shadow in the flickering light of the lantern. With an unsteady hand, she reached out and touched its shimmering surface. It felt as if she were touching the side of a beehive. Alive, it hummed beneath her fingers, its raw energy surging up her arm and down her spine until her whole body buzzed with it.

She pushed down, felt it resist then give way. She watched her fingers warp and bend as though she was seeing them in a funhouse mirror. Her fingers disappeared, then her hand, all the way past her wrist. She was about to stop when her fingertips brushed against something wet and corpse-cold. There was no mistaking it for anything other than skin.

She felt farther, and found an arm clad in sodden cloth, a hand so small she could cup it in her own. She felt along the wet clothing and laid her hand across an icy cheek. She thought again of that boy, swinging dead from the gallows. She thought of the face that she had given him in her mind, and wondered if it was possible she was touching that same face now. When her fingers brushed against his lips, she could feel that his mouth was full of water.

Something changed in the air then, a shift in pressure like the opening of a window, and she pulled her hand back as if she'd been stung. She'd felt the gravity of the thing, a suction that tugged at her fingertips and threatened to pull her inside. The shadow seemed to swell and breathe. Its borders were alive, its surface boiling and rippling as if the gentle beehive had become a nest of angry hornets.

Trina scrambled back. Her foot caught the lantern and sent it skidding sideways across the floor. The glass cracked and the oil spilled along the dusty ground, igniting in a flash of blue fire. It burned quickly, and by the time she reached the ladder, the light was nearly gone. She could no longer see the shadowy mass on the floor, but she could still feel it growing, could still feel the way it pulsed with mad, insistent energy.

The ladder creaked beneath her weight as she climbed. The fire below her burned itself out, and the darkness that followed was so total that she couldn't be sure where it ended and she began. She moved by feel in the dark. The rungs of the ladder rang with every step, but she no longer cared if anyone heard her.

She could just make out the edge of the pit above her, limned in dim light. If Woods had gone, then at least he had left the other lantern behind. She was glad for that much, and didn't like the idea of trying to find her way out without it. She looked back, certain that the thing on the floor had followed her, that even now it was reaching out with an inky black hand to pull her back down.

But there was nothing there. She could see all the way to the bottom of the pit, far below her now. The fire was gone, but a faint glow had taken its place, and it took her brain a few frantic moments to understand why. It was the circle of ancient electric bulbs strung around the base of the pit. She could feel their steady hum reverberating through the steel as she climbed. They were coming to life, and growing brighter by the moment.

She took the rungs faster now. She was almost at the top, and she could see shadows moving there in the lamplight. Woods was up there, waiting for her. He had to be. Trina's arms were tired, but they found new strength at the thought. She pulled herself up, ignoring the way the corroded metal dug into her palms, ignoring the creak of old bolts and the rain of rust that fell beneath her shoes.

Her foot slipped and missed the rung. All at once she was hanging from her hands over the empty space, her legs pinwheeling, scraping against the sides of the ladder. The metal gave a sickening screech as it started to give. A hand thrust down from the edge of the pit. She took hold of it and didn't let go. With help, she scrambled the rest of the way up and collapsed, panting, onto the steel walkway.

It wasn't Woods who'd pulled her up. Woods was on his knees near the stairs with his hands behind his back. Two soldiers stood on either side of him, each of them with the beaded armbands dangling from their biceps. A dark silhouette crouched next to her, one with gauze wrapped around his head.

"Hello, Trina." Doctor Sweet leaned in close, close enough that she could see the delight in his unbandaged eye. "Or is it Wendy now? Such a shame that we were interrupted in our last meeting. I'm looking forward to picking up where we left off."

18

Sweet kept his hand on the back of Trina's neck and squeezed down hard enough to send her to her knees. No one was near enough to the stocks to see them. The grassy plaza was nearly empty, save for a handful of civilians and distracted soldiers staring out beyond the barbed wire to the distant church steeple. It was set off from the darkening sky by a flickering orange haze that rose up from the ground like a sinister fog. Something beyond the church was burning, and the sinking feeling in Trina's stomach told her that it could only be one thing. Colin had set the library on fire.

Woods was already on the ground by her side. He tried to stand, but one of the soldiers with the beaded armbands sent a kick into the back of his knee and drove him down again. He raised his head, defiant, and stared Sweet right in his one good eye. "I invoke my right to tribunal under the Uniform Code of Service, Section twelve, Paragraph three. I demand to see my commanding officer, who will then—"

Sweet's other hand still had the pistol in it, and he swung it against the side of Woods' head. Woods saw the blow coming and rolled with it, but it still connected with a heavy thunk, like a baseball hitting a catcher's mitt.

Woods spat on the ground, and Trina saw that there was blood in it.

"...who will then appoint an advocate to oversee my defense."

Woods had repeated that demand all the way up from the basement, so many times that the soldiers with the armbands had begun to share barely-concealed glances of concern at Sweet's silence. They said nothing, because, in this world, Philip Sweet outranked them both.

"One of the first things I learned in this world is that the rights of traitors don't amount to much." Sweet rubbed at his wrist as he spoke, but kept the gun pointed at Woods' head. "Lucky for you, I have no interest in you or your tribunals. In fact, I'd venture to say that your actions here are of no consequence at all. Isn't that right, Trina?"

Trina staggered to her feet and growled as she lunged at him. The soldiers grabbed her by the arms and held her back, but not fast enough to keep Sweet from stumbling backwards. Trina saw an instant of terror flash in his unbandaged eye. The gun was pointed at her now. Sweet's hand was shaking.

"Lieutenant." Woods raised his voice, but it sounded thin and woozy. "Sir. She's a civilian. It's my fault she was down there. *My* fault. She's done nothing wrong."

"Nothing wrong," Sweet echoed, his voice high and cracking. "And how would you know, exactly? This woman you've just met? If only you knew her as I know her. She's done so much more wrong than you could ever understand."

They'd been noticed now, and a few wary soldiers were sidling their way, careful to keep their distance. Out beyond the fence, people were shouting, and a truck pulling a trailer with a hand pump on top was trundling over the bridge toward the blaze. The fire was out of control, and all Trina could do was hope that Colin wasn't in it. Sweet shoved his revolver back into its holster and leaned in close to whisper in her ear.

"How is it that you inspire such loyalty so quickly? Did you make him this way? Was it because you wanted someone you could control? Maybe even a pet?"

He grabbed her chin and forced her to look up at him. The gauze at the side of his head had soaked through in shades of reddish-brown, and was starting to droop. The scalp beneath was cracked and oozing.

"And this place?" he said. "Why would you create a world where I had power and you didn't. Is it guilt? Or is it something deep in your subconscious, crying out for someone to stop you? I have so many questions. If only we had more time."

The growing crowd parted, and through the gap came two more soldiers dragging someone between them. Trina's heart leapt when she saw that it was Colin, limp but still alive. His glasses fell into the dirt when the soldiers threw him to the ground. He picked them up with trembling hands that were tied together at the wrists.

"We caught him trying to sneak in through the south gate," the soldier told Sweet, speaking to him as a superior officer, speaking to him as if all of this was perfectly sane. "No weapons. Nothing on him but some papers and a few old books."

Trina tried to get up, but the soldiers kept their grip on her. She wanted to shake Colin for not running far away from this place when he could. More than that, she wanted to touch him, just to convince herself he was real.

"Why did you come back here?" she hissed.

There was a gash on Colin's head where the blood had crusted over and the look on his face was pained, as if he were trying to understand exactly where <u>here</u> was. When his eyes met hers, they snapped back into focus and he smiled a sheepish little smile. "I didn't want to lose you again," he said.

"I invoke my right to tribunal," Woods said, his voice stronger now. "Section twelve. Paragraph three."

Sweet spun on him, his fists clenched and shaking. "Shut your mouth, Corporal. That is an order!"

"Sweet, look." Trina tried again to stand but the soldiers forced her back down. "What's been happening to me—to us—it isn't what you think it is. There's something down there, under the building, I swear. Just let Colin and Woods go and I'll show you. Please."

There came a distant crash, like the snapping of bundled twigs, loud enough to turn the heads of the gathering crowd. The distant orange light flared. Beyond the tall church steeple, cinders rose into the sky. Colin let out a little cry of mourning as he began to rock back and forth on his knees.

"Sweet," Trina said. "Philip. Just talk to Colin. He'll tell you everything he told me. About the basement. They did experiments down there. Whatever's causing all this is still there! Just let him tell you!"

Sweet pressed his hands to the sides of his head and squeezed his eye shut, as if her very words were causing him pain. "There is nothing down there! Nothing that *you* didn't put there. None of this matters. Nothing in this entire *world* matters. Nothing but you. And me.

You're all I have left. You're the only one who can set all this right."

Colin fell to the ground and curled in on himself as the crowd drew in closer. There were dozens of them now, and the guards with the beaded armbands spread out to keep them back.

"If you want me to fix it, then let me go back down there!"

She knew as soon as she said the words that they wouldn't make any difference. She'd tried the same plea on their way up from the pit. Sweet hadn't listened, hadn't even bothered to look back. But she had seen the glow of the electric bulbs brightening in those dark depths, and knew that something was coming alive.

"No more lies!" Sweet stepped in close and rested his hand on the gun at his hip. "I won't let you trick me again. You can give me back my world. You can give me back my face. I know you can. You just need to stop playing games with me and *do it*."

Trina looked at Colin, balled up like a child in the dirt, at Woods, swaying, struggling to his feet. "I... I don't know how."

"Oh, but you do," Sweet whispered. "I've seen you do it before, remember?" His unbandaged eye was wild now as the edges of his mouth curled upward. His face was shadowed and sinister in the firelight.

"All you need is a little motivation."

He turned to the crowd, raising his voice so that they could hear. "You heard the Corporal's confession. He admits he allowed a civilian into a restricted area to which he himself had no prior authorization. This, by itself is a subversive act, an act of treason."

A few murmurs traveled like waves through the crowd. Woods dared not move. They had made up their mind about his guilt the moment they had seen him on his knees. They had come here to see an execution, and only the presence of the guards with the armbands was holding them back.

"By itself, this one action would be enough," Sweet said, pacing now. "But the two of them also conspired with yet another civilian to unlawfully enter this base for the purpose of committing of sabotage."

The guards forced Woods down until his face was in the dirt. Sweet fixed Trina with his one good eye, watching her from the center of the crowd's ire, as if he were daring her to stop him.

"Of course, being civilians they'll have their own judgment at the courthouse." A rumble worked its way through the crowd at this, a smattering of laughter punctuated with hoots of excitement. Sweet strode to where Woods was kneeling and pushed him over with his foot. "But we have been betrayed by one of our own. Our justice must be swift, and we must not hesitate to carry it out."

The crowd grew louder as Sweet placed his hand on the butt of his gun. Trina could feel the sound of them vibrating the ground, a jumble of voices building to a roar. But beneath it all was another sound, something low and mechanical, a hum whose steady rhythm tugged at the edges of her hearing and penetrated to her very bones.

The guards stepped back even before Sweet drew his pistol, as if this was something they had witnessed a hundred times before, as if such madness happened every day in this place. Sweet leveled the gun and pointed the barrel at Woods' forehead. The whole while, he watched Trina with his one eye narrowed, knowing that she could put a stop to this any time she wanted. But Sweet was wrong. She couldn't stop it. She couldn't stop any of it.

"What in the good goddamn is the meaning of all this?"

The crowd grew hushed. Edie stormed into the circle, red ponytail bobbing beneath her camouflage cap. Janowski was with her, along with a worried-looking Briggs and a few others Trina didn't recognize. They made a barrier with their bodies as they moved in and squared off with the guards. Edie stepped up to Sweet and put herself between him and Woods before she clasped her hands behind her back and stood at ease.

"Sir, this soldier is under my command," she said. "May I know why you're pointing a gun to his head?"

Sweet lowered his arm at the sound of her voice. All his cruelty seemed to melt into wonder as he turned around to face her. When he spoke, his voice was low, almost a whisper. "Edie. You don't remember me at all, do you?"

Edie's brows furrowed. "Sir?"

"The old hotel," Sweet said softly. "The home for girls. Right there in that very building. You spent your entire childhood there, I remember you telling me. Or the hospital? You were head nurse, in charge of the entire lunatic wing. You don't remember one bit of it, do you?"

Edie tensed as Sweet stepped toward her, but she held her ground. The gun was still in Sweet's hand, and all around them that strange hum was building, rising up from the earth, resonating deep in Trina's bones.

"The first day I met you I was ten minutes late," Sweet said, "and it was almost a year before you let me live it down. Or was it that I was on time and you kept me waiting? I remember you were wearing a green dress. And a red one.”

He moved closer and brought his hand up, as if to touch her cheek. He stopped himself when he saw the confusion on Edie's face, the hint of fear.

“Both of these things are as clear to me as if they'd happened yesterday, but you never lived either one.” Sweet spread his arms wide. The crowd flinched back as the barrel of the gun swept over them. “To you, this world is your reality, but it's not real at all. It's just an illusion. An illusion conjured by a selfish, ridiculous little girl.”

Colin was rocking back and forth on the ground, squeezing his eyes shut. The hum was louder now, loud enough to drown out the shouts of the firefighters, the distant crackling of flames. The soldiers in the crowd had begun to notice it too, and they exchanged confused looks, not knowing what to make of it. Trina knew exactly what that sound was. She'd been struck by its absence ever since she'd arrived in this place, that low background murmur that could only come from live electrical wires.

“But I can show you,” Sweet turned toward Trina and leveled the gun at her forehead. “I'll make her put it all back. Back to the world where you knew me. The real world. A world without this stupid, petty war and everything that came with it. A world that makes sense. A world where you'll remember me.”

Woods was shouting something, trying to get Sweet's attention. Trina could barely hear him. All her thought was fixed on the end of the gun barrel, at Sweet's finger, tightening down on the trigger. Behind him, the windows of the building that was once Ms. Dixon's Home began to glow pale yellow. The lights were coming back on.

"Just put it back, Trina. Put it back and all of this goes away. You can stop running. Don't you want to stop running?"

Trina squeezed her eyes shut and tried to wish the gun away, tried to wish it all away. "I can't!"

"You can. And you will." He swung the gun away and pointed it at Woods' head. Sweet smiled but his good eye was full of tears. "You have to."

Woods clenched his jaw, determined to not look away. Trina closed her eyes. She didn't want to see. She didn't want the gun to be there at all. She thought of the flowers and tried to turn them blue, tried to turn the whole world. She heard a shout somewhere off in the distance, then a sharp pop as the gun went off.

When she opened her eyes again, Woods was on his feet, patting at his chest, searching for a wound that wasn't there. Sweet was on the ground, rolling with Edie, struggling in the dirt. Colin watched them wide-eyed, frozen on the ground, his hands pressed against his ears.

Edie forced Sweet onto his back. His bandages unspooled from his face as she pinned him down and fumbled for the gun. There was another sharp pop, hollow, like a breaking window. Edie stopped struggling then, and slumped away into the grass. Her hands clutched at her stomach, and there was blood between her fingers.

Trina screamed. Colin screamed too, and the wind around them changed.

For an instant Trina felt as if she was falling. She held her breath and fought the sick feeling that rose up from her stomach. When she opened her eyes again, the base was gone. The sun was high and the sky was a deep and cloudless blue. A cracked blacktop road stretched out to the horizon, alive and rippling with the shimmering heat of the desert. Colin was there with her. He was on his knees with the heels of his palms pressed against his eyes.

Sweet was there, too. He clawed at the sand in the spot where Edie had lain bleeding just an instant before. But Edie was gone. Woods was gone. The crowd was gone. There was only Colin and Trina and Sweet, alone beneath the desert sun.

Not like this, Trina thought. *Edie can't be dead. She can't be dead.*

Over and over, she whispered the words. She tried again to think of the flowers, but the only color she could see was the red that had poured out of Edie's stomach. The bandages on Sweet's head hung loose, and as he turned to face her she could see his scabbed and reddened scalp, the deep cracks where the skin had split and begun to fill with blood.

"My God! What have you done to me?" Sweet clenched his fists and the sand poured from between his fingers. His whole body was shaking. "All those lives you made me live. I remember them now. How could you create so many places, make me do so many terrible things? Oh, God. I remember them. I remember them all!"

Colin rocked frantically on the sand, his arms wrapped around himself, his mouth open in a silent scream. This new world was a wasteland. In the distance, Trina could see the outlines of familiar stone buildings, their roofs shorn away, their walls pitted and crumbling. Half of a bridge rose up over the sandy ground. A carriage was wedged against the broken railing, its leather harnesses empty and frayed, swinging loose in the hot wind.

Not like this, she thought. *Not like this.*

"You have to put it back," Sweet cried. "You have to put it all back!"

Trina closed her eyes, squeezing them tight until the pressure of it felt like a vise around her skull. She felt Sweet grab her by the shoulders, heard his mad laughter taken by the wind. The ground fell away beneath her feet. New ground rose up to take its place. All around her were shouts and confusion, and through her eyelids, Trina could see that the sky had gone dark again.

Sweet was back on the ground. Edie was on top of him, then beneath him as they rolled in the dirt. Edie forced Sweet onto his back. His bandages unspooled from his face as she pinned him down and fumbled for the gun. There was a sharp pop, hollow, like a breaking window. Edie stopped struggling then, and slumped away into the grass. Her hands clutched at her stomach, and there was blood between her fingers.

All was quiet, all but for the steady hum that vibrated along the old electrical wires strung above their heads. The lights in the old hotel were brighter now. Old streetlamps were coming to life all down Main Street. Everywhere lights were shining. The people stared up at them in wonder. Trina barely noticed. She was too busy looking for Colin, but Colin was gone.

Sweet scrambled to his knees. The sound of his hitching laughter rose into the still of the night sky, only to be drowned away by the rising drone of the camp sirens as they spiraled to life, first one, then another, until the air was filled with a steady, mournful wail.

The crowd around them moved like a colony of ants, dispersing all at once to their assigned posts. They threw panicked glances over their shoulders as they ran, pointing at something in the distance, something far away beyond the trees.

High up on the water tower, the Blinker was uncoiling itself, its long tentacles feeling their way toward the ground. At the center of its bulbous head, a glowing red eye opened.

19

There were screams, but the sirens drowned them. Bodies rushed past her, blurs of green and grey, but all Trina could see was Edie lying lifeless on the ground, a dark patch spreading out from the hole that Sweet's bullet had made in her stomach. Edie had died once, then died again, right here in this same spot. Both times, Trina had been unable to do anything but watch.

Something behind her exploded with a sharp pop, and she turned to see sparks rain from a broken streetlamp like fireworks falling to the ground. All along the street, the electric lights were blazing to life. As they pulsed with newfound energy, they too began to explode, one by one. High above, the angry red eye of the Blinker began to shimmer, gathering energy as the thing lurched toward them on the tips of its rubbery tentacles.

Woods grabbed Trina by the hand and pulled. "Come on! We have to go!" Before she could stop him, they were running.

Sweet's guards had been swept up in the chaos. Soldiers ran in all directions. Some had taken up their rifles and their pistols and were firing them at the advancing Blinker. Trina looked back, searching, but Colin was nowhere to be found. There was only Doctor Sweet, his bandages unspooled, standing frozen amid the chaos, oblivious to everything but the dead woman at his feet.

Truck engines roared to life as the soldiers worked their starter cranks. Mounted guns swiveled toward the Blinker. Bullets sparked as they bounced off its jet-black hide. The thing turned its gaze to one of the trucks. The red eye flared, and at once the truck was on fire. The beam had drilled a hole the size of a volleyball through its hood, a perfect circle beneath the windshield where the engine had just ceased to be.

Woods and Trina wove their way through the crowd, tripping through the gap in the high fence, running for the old hotel. The light from its windows was so bright now that the very brickwork seemed to swell with it. Gunfire was all around them. Bullets whizzed like angry insects over their heads. A soldier knelt in their path, a long metal launching tube balanced on one shoulder. Woods spun around to shield her, and she collided with him just as the mouth of the tube breathed fire and sent a rocket sailing out into the night.

"Is this you?" Woods had to yell just to be heard over the chaos. Trina watched the rocket, trailing flame as it soared toward the Blinker's head. It bounced off some invisible barrier and burned out as it spiraled away.

"Colin's gone," Trina said. "We have to go back. We have to find him!"

Woods took her face in his hands and forced her to look him in the eyes. "Was the L.T. right? Are you making this happen?" Somewhere in the distance the rocket exploded. The soldier who fired it screamed and fell to the ground. The launcher was gone and there was only a semicircle of charred flesh where his shoulder had been.

"Can you make it stop?"

"I don't know!" Trina put her hands to her ears but her heart was beating too fast and she could still hear the screams as more soldiers fell all around them. She tried to picture the flowers, but all she could see was red. "Maybe. I don't know, but I need to get to that basement."

He let go of her then, and as he did, his face became grim, like something carved out of stone. He nodded. "Okay. Come with me."

Beyond the fence, the townspeople were pouring out of their doorways. They gathered their robes and their hastily-donned coats around them, pointing skyward, scattering as the Blinker's tentacles whipped across the rooftops and sent shingles raining down on their heads. Woods and Trina wound their way past the soldiers, ducking low, trying to stay behind the gunfire. All around them, men and women fell with gaping holes drilled through their torsos, their legs taken off at the knees.

Another Blinker appeared over the rows of houses, lumbering on its stilt-like appendages. Trina wondered if it was the same one she had seen wrapped around the dome of the courthouse. More gunfire sounded from the far side of the old hotel. More Blinkers, and they were all coming this way.

Trina pulled free of Woods' hand as they reached the steps leading up to the doors. Two soldiers lay dead on those steps, one on top of the other. She recognized Janowski's face right away. His eyes were open and the corners of his mouth were curled into the barest hint of a smile. Briggs lay on top of him, her face against his shoulder. Trina couldn't tell if she had been trying to protect him or he had been trying to protect her. A single hole had been bored through both of their chests. Woods wouldn't look at them. He stepped over their bodies and held the door open for Trina to follow.

Inside, the electric light was almost blinding. Woods pulled Trina past the long front desk, past the chandelier that glowed white-hot above their heads. The sounds of gunfire echoed from the windows of the offices above. Those lights had been on too, and they made easy targets of the soldiers in the windows. Plaster rained down as great holes punched through the walls ahead and behind. With each one, another gun fell silent.

They found the stairway at the end of the atrium and took the steps two at a time. The sounds of gunfire grew muffled, and the light no longer hurt her eyes. Overhead bulbs flickered in dusty wire cages. The whole place smelled faintly of baking dust.

"How is this happening?" Woods' words echoed in the empty hallway, and though he hadn't slowed, she was finally able to keep up with him. "The lights haven't worked in over twenty years. It's like magic."

Trina pushed past him. She already knew where they were going, and she didn't want to have to look at him. "You keep acting like I have answers, but I don't know any more than you do."

"But you found something down there. In that pit. Didn't you?"

"Something. Maybe." She was angry and she wasn't sure why. When she looked at him, all she could see was Briggs and Janowski on the steps, the perfect, bloodless circle where their hearts should have been. "You don't have to stay. I'm good from here."

"I couldn't have done anything for them," Woods said, and Trina couldn't be sure if he was saying it to her or to himself. "They were dead. If we'd stayed up there, we'd be dead, too."

He was right. He couldn't have done anything for them. The only one who could do anything for them now was her. She'd gone back once, but all she'd managed to do was get Edie killed twice. Maybe she could go back again. Maybe she could save them if she went back far enough. She just had to figure out how.

The steel door marked AUTHORIZED PERSONNEL ONLY was wide open. The faint scent of burning oil drifted up from the pit as they descended the creaking metal staircase. There was no need for lamps now. The whole place was bathed in blue light, more light than the electric bulbs could account for alone. Something was moving in that light, deep down in the pit. Its reflection danced on the walls, liquid and shimmering.

Trina felt the Shadows before she saw them, a vibration in the air deeper than the hum of any electrical wire, deeper even than the beating of her own heart. They stood arranged along the edge of the pit, all seven of them, spaced evenly, like the numbers on a clock. She recognized them by their shapes, by the names she had given them. The Hound. The Tall Man. The Kid. The Burnout. The Cheerleader. The Goddess. The Crone. Their outlines danced in the bright light, their borders seething and changing, almost daring her eyes to define them.

Trina stepped forward, wary but no longer afraid. The Shadows did not move as she approached. Though they had no faces, Trina could tell that they had their backs to the pit, standing at attention like wooden soldiers. If they were here to catch her, they would have done it by now. Instead, they seemed to be waiting for something. Waiting for whatever was happening down in the pit. Waiting for her to arrive.

"What the hell is this place?" Woods blinked against the light as he edged up to the pit and looked carefully down over the rail. He didn't seem to notice that the Shadows were there, but still he managed to step around them as he moved, avoiding the spaces where they stood as if by instinct.

"You can't see them, can you?"

"See what?" He put his hands on the railing and tested it before he leaned out. "There's nothing down there."

He was standing right next to the one that Trina had named The Goddess. She was thin and regal, her outline flowing behind her like a dress caught by the wind. She'd been frightening to Trina once, but now she was almost beautiful. Woods couldn't see them, not like Colin had. Trina realized then that she had been hoping that Woods was like Colin, that he would remember her in the next world, when the next world came. But he would forget her. Whatever happened next, she would lose him, just as she had lost everyone else.

The sounds of gunfire were growing louder. Trina could hear shouting from somewhere up the stairs. It wouldn't be long before the soldiers found their way down here, searching for shelter. She stepped in next to Woods, but kept her eyes on the Shadows. They'd lost their menace, but she didn't want to get too close to them, to risk the feel of their cold-fire touch against her skin. This whole time, she'd been trying so hard not to let them catch her. Maybe all along, they had only been trying to bring her to this place.

The light rippled at the bottom of the pit, alive, like the surface of a lake at sunrise. It covered the entire floor, and yet it churned with the same inner darkness that seemed to make up the Shadows. Trina stared at it, stared into it, and saw that it was rising.

"I suppose you don't see that either," she said.

Woods seemed not to hear her. By the time she turned around, he was already inside the little control room testing the switches. "One of these has to shut the power down. Come here and give me a hand, willya?"

She didn't want to tell him that none of those controls would make a difference anymore, if they ever had at all. Whatever had been set in motion here, whatever had brought the Blinkers to this world, it was long gone. Whatever was happening at the bottom of that pit, it was something else entirely.

More voices floated down the stairwell, raised shouts cut off in mid-cry. The shimmering liquid was higher now. She watched it engulf one rung of the ladder, then two. She looked to the Tall Man, who stood next to her, seemingly oblivious to her presence. Before she could stop herself, she reached out to touch him. Her fingers brushed his outline and she felt a little pull, a change in pressure like opening a door. She felt the cold like a winter wind, but it no longer burned her. She watched the shape of her hand change, warping as if she were seeing it through the surface of still water. And yet, as her fingers pushed past the emptiness, they brushed against something soft and solid. Trina rolled it against her thumb. It was the hem of a wool coat.

"Would you get away from there and help me?" Woods burst out of the control room and began pulling at the metal piping on the wall, looking for a weakness. "There has to be a way to stop this."

"No. There isn't."

Trina pulled her hand back as the Shadows turned in unison toward the sound of this new voice. Their outlines rippled with a new intensity as Doctor Sweet stepped off the stairs and onto the circular catwalk. The bandages around his head were gone now, and Trina could see cracked and bleeding bits of scalp where his hair had burned away. The filmy white of his dead eye stared out blindly from inside a ruin of red flesh. His gun hung heavy at the end of his arm.

"There never was a way to stop it," Sweet said. "This world—all of it—was doomed before it was ever even made."

The Shadows' vibrations grew more urgent as Sweet moved closer. From the level above them came the muffled sound of an explosion. Trina could hear the distant fall of plaster and brick, like the patter of a soft spring rain.

Woods stepped in front of Trina, shielding her body with his own. "Sir, stand down." When Sweet didn't stop, Woods drew his pistol. "Lieutenant, I need you to stand down."

With the pistol leveled at his heart, Sweet paused. He smiled, his own gun forgotten, his dead eye fixed on Trina. He nodded toward the pit. "Tell me what you see."

Trina glanced down over the railing. The shimmering liquid was halfway up the pit walls now. It seemed to beckon to her as it rolled and undulated, and she had to fight the sudden urge to jump in.

"Do you see it too?" she asked.

Sweet took a step closer. Woods tightened his grip on his gun, but Sweet seemed to barely notice he was there. "Tell me," Sweet whispered. "Tell me what you see!"

Something was moving in the pit, just below the surface, dark shapes coalescing at the center of the wavering mass.

"I don't know!"

"You *have* to know!" He was close enough now that she could see the blind eye leaking, weeping yellow-white onto his cheek. "The Others have stopped speaking to me. They won't tell me what to do. Why won't you tell me what to do?"

Another explosion overhead. Dust rained down around them. Sweet stepped closer to the pit, trying to see down to the bottom. The Shadows moved then, converging to block his path.

"Whatever it is," Sweet said through clenched teeth, "they've put it there for you. Not for me. Never for me. Only for you!"

The shapes beneath the surface resolved, their outlines distorted in the teeming liquid. Trina could see two figures there, two people with their arms outstretched. They were reaching out for each other, but they were too far apart to touch.

"Every possibility. Past and future. All of it waiting to be coaxed and molded." Sweet limped closer. The Shadows turned to face him as he moved toward her but they gave no sign of stopping him. "All of it at the whim of a stupid, selfish little girl."

"Sir." Woods was between them now, both hands on his pistol. "You need to stop right there or I *will* shoot you."

"Everything you've broken, just begging for you to fix it," Sweet said, ignoring Woods, ignoring the sounds of screams coming from above, ignoring the Shadows and their inscrutable stares. "You made this place, but it knows it's not right. It wants to be unmade. It *needs* to be unmade."

There came a crash from the end of the little hallway, the sounds of a metal door bending and shearing away.

"Sir!" Woods' voice boomed, and Trina started at the sound of it.

Sweet turned to him then, his smile awful and full of knowing. "Go ahead and shoot, Corporal. Protect your creator. Then ask yourself if she'd ever do the same for you."

Woods' eyes darted toward Trina, and his gun wavered. It was only an instant, but it was enough for Sweet to raise his own gun and swing it in Woods' direction. Woods fired, the sound of it like a whipcrack reverberating through the metal catwalk. Sweet's body jerked, his shoulder driven back as the bullet opened a hole in his uniform. He barely seemed to notice. His maniac smile never wavered as he pulled the trigger. Woods fell back against Trina. She tried to catch him, but he was too heavy. Together, they went sprawling to the floor.

"It doesn't matter." Sweet said, still smiling as he tossed the gun over his shoulder. "Nothing in this festering miscarriage of a world makes any difference when you can change it with a thought! I know you can put it back but you just. Won't. Do it!"

Woods gasped. There was a hole in his chest just below his shoulder. A pool of blood was forming there, too fast, faster than Trina would have ever thought possible. She pressed her hands down on it, trying to stop the flow, but all it did was make Woods cry out.

"What I saw in that other world…" Chunks of ceiling began to rain down around them, but Sweet barely seemed to notice. "The things I've done there. They can't be real. It's impossible."

Another explosion, close enough this time to vibrate through the metal walkway beneath them. The hole in Woods' chest was bubbling now, and when her hands pressed against the wound she could feel it pulling in air. There was blood in his mouth, and it rattled as he tried to breathe.

"I still remember them. I remember everything I did, everything you made me do. Every patient. Every barbaric, backward <u>cure</u>!" Sweet tried to step closer, but the Shadows were converging on him now, their vibrations so insistent that they'd become almost musical.

"I won't let you make me into a monster!"

Woods' eyes went wide as his breath began to slow. The blood was barely a trickle now, but it had already soaked through his shirt and made a pool beneath him on the floor. Tears were streaming down Trina's face. Woods reached up as if to brush them away, but his hand only fell back to the dusty catwalk.

Another crash came from the top of the stairs, and with it the sound of breaking concrete. A long tendril, shining and black, emerged from the stairwell and began to grope its way along the wall.

"Put it all back," Sweet cried.

The black tentacle was joined by another, then another, until a great mass of them filled the stairwell, wedging apart the concrete walls. Woods shuddered beneath Trina's hands, let out a last breath, then grew still.

With a great lurch, the tentacles flexed forward and tore back a section of the concrete ceiling. At their center, the great eye of the Blinker glowed, relentless and red. One of the tentacles lashed out and caught Sweet around the waist. It snatched him off his feet and yanked him back through the broken wall. Trina could hear his screams as he disappeared into the darkness.

"Put it back!"

The shimmering liquid was almost up to the edge of the pit now. The Shadows turned back in unison to face it, almost too fast for her to see. They were humming now, a singular high tone that Trina felt all the way down to her bones. The liquid hummed with them, matching their vibrations until the surface seemed to grow solid, frozen into shimmering concentric waves.

The great eye of the Blinker was upon her, the thing's tentacles probing in her direction. Woods' blood was wet and sticky on her hands. His body was still. She backed away from him and felt the rusty railing against her back. The Shadows had all turned to face her. As she looked down at the wavering liquid, she felt their eager stares. She knew at once that they would not try to stop her. All at once, she was afraid to find out why.

A tentacle whipped out to catch her foot, but she was already over the side. As the ceiling came down around her, all she could feel was the cold.

20

She should have been falling, but she no longer knew which way was down. Direction had lost all meaning. Weightless, she floated, buoyed by the darkness until, at last, she felt herself begin to rise. She could see the distant light of some shimmering surface, faint and impossibly far away. She had the sense of something below her, something large, receding into the darkness. She had the mad urge to swim down, to try to reach it, but her lungs were burning and when she looked down she could see nothing but the black.

Her body took over where her mind could not, and she kicked, moving her limbs even as her mind gave in to the panic of not being able to breathe. The light above her grew brighter. Her chest convulsed and drew in the muddy water. It tasted of dirt and rot, the decay of a whole world, of maybe more than one.

Sputtering, she broke the surface and coughed the muck from her lungs. Her frantic splashing gave way to treading water as she caught her breath. The space she floated in was bordered in brick and lined with half-submerged wooden doors. A wide glass skylight hung above her head, cracked and clouded over with grime. The air was thick with the smell of mold and decay.

She swam for the wooden railing. The handrail barely broke the surface of the water, but once she was on the other side of it she found a floor that her feet could touch. One of the doors was half off its hinges. She waded toward it, but she already knew what she would find on the other side. There was enough light coming in through an open window that she could see the pictures that still hung on the wall. Mold had filled in the spaces where their corners had curled away from their frames. And yet the bed was still there, its posts standing defiant above the water. The odd wheel was gone from the wall, but the wallpaper had faded in a perfect circle where it had once hung. The armchair where she'd once sat listed sideways, sodden, but still unmistakable.

Somewhere beyond the railing, beneath the dark and swirling water, lay the atrium she had looked over with Edie, the atrium where she'd last seen Janowski alive. Far below that, in depths now lost to her, lay the basement and its pit full of shadows. She remembered the pulsing shape that had lain at the bottom of that pit, the feel of wet skin beneath its buzzing surface. She wondered if Woods' body was still down there. Had the waters risen up around him, or had he simply ceased to be?

She worked her way down the flooded hallway, brushing aside bits of floating debris and waterlogged furniture. Every movement she made sent little waves lapping against swollen wood and sodden plaster. Tarnished wall sconces hung low over the surface of the water, and she used them to pull herself along toward the end of the hall, toward the stairs that would take her up and out of the wet.

She climbed the steps and sat upon a dry landing. Dirty water dripped from her clothes onto carpet that was loose and curling away from the rotting floorboards. She had the mad thought that Edie would rush down the stairs at any moment, and that it would be up to Trina to try to explain what had happened to her hotel, her home. Trina smiled a little at this, but the smile didn't last. Edie wasn't coming, because Edie was dead.

Her hands were dirty from the water, but all the blood had been washed away. She tried not to think about Woods, about that awful rattle that had come from his throat. She tried not to think about what might have happened to Colin. The memory of him curled up like a child beneath Sweet's gun had its hooks in her and would not let go.

She was sitting beneath a window, but it was too clouded and dirt-streaked to see out of. Pairs of initials had been carved into the wall beneath it, deep gouges in the crumbling plaster. Trina ran her fingers along their edges. They were sharp enough to have been made with a knife point, and fresh enough that they might have been made only yesterday. They made her wonder if there really had been a yesterday in this place.

She muscled the window open, and the swollen wood protested with a sharp squeal. The outside air brought with it a spray of rain and the thick, earthy smell of the swamp. The street below was completely flooded, but she could still see make out the shape of it, snaking between the tall buildings that rose from the surface of the water. A few once-stately structures of brick and stone stood solid despite the broken glass in their windows. Others sagged with time and neglect, little more than crumbled shells, now silent and empty but for the few birds' nests that dotted their high ledges.

Woods had died to bring her to this place. So had Edie. Maybe Colin had, too. For all she knew, the Blinkers had killed him in that other world, the same way they'd killed Briggs and Janowski. Trina still held onto a sliver of hope that he was out there somewhere, looking for her even now. She didn't know that dying in one world meant dying in all of them, not for sure. But Colin was like her, the same way that Sweet was like her. If there were rules to the Turnings, if there was any order to them at all, then that had to count for something.

The rain fell in lazy sheets from the steel-gray sky and made ripples in the still water. Trina thought of the empty hospital, of the flood that had carried her away down the very street she was looking over now. Perhaps this Turning had brought her back to that world, or at least to the world that those rising waters had left behind. She didn't think so. That city had been active and alive. This place seemed as if it had been empty forever, as silent and neglected as an overgrown grave.

It struck her then that she would have to find her own way out of this place. She could swim, but she wouldn't be able to swim for long. She had no food, and no means to catch it, assuming there were any fish in those impenetrable, muddy waters. Still, she might be able to last until the next Turning, assuming the next Turning came at all. She held a cupped hand out of the window and tested the rain. It tasted faintly of smoke, but it was clean, and as long as it kept up it would keep her from having to risk drinking the stagnant muck below.

She watched the rain and tried to rub some warmth into her arms as she thought of that strange pit, now drowned and completely out of reach. She wondered if there was a way to get down there, a way to turn all of it back the way it was, the way she'd turned it back when she'd watched Edie die. She'd gone back in time, if only for a moment. If she really had made this world, maybe she could unmake it too.

Colin would know. If not, he'd at least have something to say that would make her feel better. He was good at that, making her feel better. He was still out there, somewhere. She was becoming more sure of it by the moment. If she squinted, she could see far enough past the rain to make out the silhouette of a building that might just be the library. She could picture him there, carrying stacks of books to the upper floors, salvaging what he could as the waters rose. It was a needy thought, maybe even a silly one, but still she clung to it like a life raft.

Gradually, so slowly that she could hardly be sure of it at first, she became aware of another silhouette, distant and small, barely more than a dark spot upon the water. As it drew closer, the spot resolved itself into a little boat. It was just wide enough for two people to sit abreast, and what paint there was left on its weathered hull was faded and flaked with age. At its prow sat a hunched figure, facing backward, working the oars with long, measured strokes.

Trina leaned out the window as far as she dared, waving frantically with one hand. She knew immediately that it was a bad idea, that she had no idea if the person in the boat would want to help her or hurt her. Still, she had the crazy thought that somehow it might be Colin in that boat, that he was rowing out to save her.

The little boat drew closer. When the hunched figure gave no sign of having seen her, she called out to him. Her voice echoed against the crumbling buildings, and she was surprised at how strong it sounded, despite the way it cracked as it rose, despite the clenching soreness in her throat.

When the figure in the boat didn't react, she called out again. Her voice was weaker this time, and she could hear the pleading in it. Still, she called out once more, waving with both arms, no longer caring if she fell.

"All right, all right. I hear yez." The voice was not Colin's. This voice was lower, gruff and world-weary. The man was close enough now that Trina could see bushy tufts of gray beard sticking out beneath his rain hat. "How in Hell'd ye get all the way up there anyway?"

"I... I don't know." It was the truth, and she didn't think that saying more would explain it any better anyway. The old man let go of the oars and let the boat drift as he looked up at her, squinting as if the sun was at her back, making up his mind.

"There's a fire escape around back," he said at last. Trina didn't have to ask him which way because he was already rowing off in that direction. "If you can get to it, I'll pick you up there."

21

Trina sat in silence as the old man guided the little boat through the flooded canyons of the city. His arms bulged against his heavy oilskin jacket as he pulled at the oars with a steady rhythm, never slowing or tiring, as if he had been doing it his entire life. When he saw that she was shivering, he tossed her a dry blanket made of coarse wool. She thanked him as she wrapped it around her shoulders, but his only response was an indifferent grunt. If her presence in his boat held any concern or novelty for him, he didn't let it show. He kept his eyes hidden as he rowed, shadowed by the hood of his jacket.

They kept to the widest roads, rowing straight down the center, never straying too close to the broken buildings that rose like teeth out of the dark water. The old man seemed to negotiate by memory the hazards that lay just below the surface. Trina could see their outlines beneath the murk as they slid past. Sometimes, she would see black shapes, slick and leathery, slithering among the ruins, but they would disappear as quickly as they came.

The old man pulled the oars smoothly, and the only noise they made was the faint dripping as they rose out of the water between strokes. Some of the buildings were painted with crude, black markings. Upside-down triangles and clusters of dots wrapped in hastily-sprayed rectangles. Signals in a language she could not understand. Makeshift wooden docks jutted from broken-out windows, and the metal boats lashed to them hinted at people within. The old man kept a wary eye on those places as they passed, holding the oars out of the water, letting their momentum carry them so they would not make a sound.

Trina wanted to tell him that they were going in the wrong direction, that the distant silhouette that she'd taken for a library was further behind them now. She wanted to tell him about the pit beneath Ms. Dixon's Home, and how they had to go back, to be close in case the Turning came, in case the next world might allow her to go down there again. She wanted to tell him, but couldn't bring herself to speak.

Hours seemed to pass before they saw another person. They were on the outskirts of the city, where the buildings sat so low that only their sagging, cratered roofs peeked out of the water. A rusted car with high tailfins drifted by them. Clusters of blue barrels had been strapped to its sides to keep it afloat. The dark-haired woman crouched on the hood paid them no mind as she stabbed at the water with a paddle made from a street sign. Two children sat on the trunk with their feet dangling in the water. They were little girls, though it was hard to tell for sure beneath the grime and their threadbare lifejackets. They watched Trina suspiciously, staring back at her until the fog and the rain swallowed them up, as if they'd never been there at all.

One by one, new shapes began to materialize out of the fog: ramshackle houses on high stilts, canvas tents perched on top of flat tarred roofs and held up by bent light poles.

The old man rowed the little boat near to a rusty water tower. A raft made of sheet metal and innertubes bumped against a makeshift dock lashed to one of the tower's legs. Trina could just make out the high windows cut into the side of the tank, and the plastic sheeting that had been hung there to keep out the rain.

A voice called out to them through the fog, and the old man took his hand off the oar long enough to wave in its direction. They were rowing toward a great, shadowy island, still shrouded in mist. Trina could hear the sounds of distant voices, the sharp metal-on-metal sounds of people at work. As they drew closer, she could make out the little lights of fires set in upright oil drums and people moving among the jumbled, angled structures that seemed to cover the place from one end to the other.

They tied off to a sturdy wooden pier amid a rag-tag cluster of boats and rafts. Somewhere in the distance, a tin bell sounded, and a dog barked as if in answer. The old man pointed, and Trina passed up a heavy duffel bag before he reached down to help her out of the boat. He took her weight easily, and once again she was impressed with how strong he was, how easily he slung the heavy bag over his shoulder when it had taken all of her strength just to lift it.

He didn't ask her to follow, but she understood that he meant for her to do it anyway. He led her up a rickety set of stairs, squeezing wordlessly past pale men in oilskin coats and bent-backed women hauling carts piled high with crawfish traps. Trina followed him through narrow alleyways, and beneath curtains of hanging clothes that were sodden from the rain. They wound through a market where ribbons of dried kelp hung above buckets of mussels. Black eels hung on hooks from curtain rods and rows of skinny rodents lay spitted on sticks to roast over hot coals. The smell reached her, spicy and rich, and it was enough to set her stomach to growling.

They worked their way toward the center of the island, farther and farther from that library she had seen, farther and farther from the familiar brick of Ms. Dixon's Home. Makeshift dwellings jutted above their heads. They seemed to be cobbled together from whatever these people had been able to find, a piece of rusted metal here, bits of driftwood there. One of the doorways had part of a wooden sign lashed across it with rope, the lettering faded and unreadable.

All around them, she saw a world that was crumbling, a world that had given up, a world that was waiting to die. The unraveling that the Turnings brought with them was worse here, worse than she had ever seen it before. As they climbed above the fog, she found cracked solar panels lashed to the high roofs with bungee cords. Satellite dishes and TV aerials jutted from the walls at all angles. Trina wondered if any of them still worked, if they'd ever worked at all.

She watched the old man as he climbed, the heavy bag slung over his shoulder, the hood drawn low over his eyes. She searched his shape and his movements, wanting desperately to find something there that might ring in her memory the way that bell had rung on the dock. She thought of her grandfather, of his hands, the skin stretched paper-thin over his bones. This man's hands were large and meaty. They were hands made for rough work, and there was nothing in them that she recognized.

When they reached the far end of the little island, the old man paused before a little garage-sized shack set against the side of a corrugated steel tower. Its roof was a patchwork of asphalt and wooden shingles, and its siding was made from sheets of metal that had been hammered smooth and oiled to keep the rust away. He shouldered the door aside, and Trina wondered for a moment if it was all right for her to follow. But he held the door open behind him and managed to look annoyed at the time it took her to make up her mind. The air inside was dry and warm. There was a fire burning in a little pot-belly stove, and she rushed to kneel in front of it, feeling its heat against her chest and rubbing feeling back into her stiffened fingers.

"Darlene," the old man called. His voice was loud in the enclosed space, and it startled Trina back to her feet. "I've brought in a stray."

"It'd best not be another cat," came a call from behind a curtain in the back room, "or you can put it back outside right now and I don't care how much it gives you the sad-eyes."

Trina perked up as the woman spoke. Her voice was familiar, and for a moment Trina imagined that it could be Edie, older somehow, but her all the same. But as the old woman trundled in, drying her hands on a towel, she saw that this wasn't Edie at all. This woman was thick around the middle. Her gray hair was piled up on top of her head in a hasty bun, with long strands that hung loose around her ears. But her eyes were kind like Edie's had been, and when she saw Trina standing by the stove, trembling despite the heat, she threw the towel up over her shoulder and rushed to her side.

"Oh, you poor thing. Let's have a look at ye." She took Trina's hands in her own, and as she pressed down on the girl's fingers, her eyes went wide.

"Ach, dear, you're as cold as the grave." She turned back to the old man, who stood watching them from the doorway. "Well, don't just stand there like a great lump o' blubber. Get this poor girl a blanket and put the kettle on the fire so's I can make her some tea."

The old man gave a derisive snort, but trundled off to do as he was told. When he came back with the blanket, Darlene took her time arranging it around Trina's shoulders and gave a satisfied little nod once it was done.

"Get caught out in the rain, didya? Those squalls come up out of nowhere if'n ye don't keep a tight watch on how the breeze is shiftin'. Easy enough to get swamped and stuck out there. Happens to the best of us."

"I found her up top of the old hotel," the old man called from the kitchen, his words punctuated by the hollow banging of metal pans. "Outside the border waters over down Main Street."

"Main Street?" Her eyes told Trina that the old hotel might as well have been on the far side of the moon, as far as she was concerned. "What were you doing all the way out there?"

She raised her voice and called back to the kitchen. "And you, John Bishop. Where do you get off rowing so far out in the first place? You know it's nothing but smugglers and bottom trawlers between here and there who'd just as soon kill you for the hat on your head as trade one-for-one like decent folk."

She laid a hand on Trina's cheek, and the gentle concern warmed her more than even the fire. "Who was it? Some boy, I'd wager. I know their type. See 'em every day in the market, making promises to sweet, young things like yourself. They take what they want and go on their way, and if they don't get what they think is their due, so much the worse for the one who put her trust in 'em."

"No, it wasn't like that at all. I just..." Trina shook her head, every explanation she could think of dying before she could get it out of her mouth. "I just got lost."

The old man clomped his way back into the room, shedding his hat and overcoat, hanging them neatly on a tarnished brass hook. "Didn't have no boat to speak of, neither," he said. "Else I would have towed 'er in."

The little woman nodded knowingly. "Went straight to the bottom. And took your whole kit with it, by the look of things. Poor dear. The water's deep out that way. Not much chance of getting it back. You got people hereabouts?"

"No, ma'am." She thought of Sweet, of how he might still be alive in this world despite everything, and pulled the blanket tight around her shoulders.

"Just a drifter, drifting with the tides," the woman said knowingly. "I was young once too, hard as it might be to tell by the look o' me." She smiled and Trina smiled back, though inside she didn't feel like smiling at all. For all she knew, everyone she knew—everyone she'd cared about—had drowned away in that deep water. Everyone she hadn't already managed to get killed.

"You got a name, little one?"

"Trina. Trina Bell."

The old woman gave a solemn nod, as if the name imparted a depth of knowledge that only she understood. "Well, you're welcome to stay with us until you're back on your feet. Provided, that is, that you ain't in no trouble. Ain't my business to ask, but if you are, just see to it that you don't bring any of it to our doorstep, hear?"

The old man settled into rocking chair in the corner, seemingly uninterested, but the little woman stared into Trina's eyes and held that stare for long enough that Trina began to wither beneath it. In time, the woman's face softened, and she nodded, satisfied.

"My name's Darlene, but most folks call me Dar, or Lena, or just about any other damn thing they think I'll answer to. The big lunk over there who can't ever remember to take off his shoes in the front room, his name's John."

John had a little tin box in his lap and was pulling out what looked like a hand-rolled cigar. He looked down at the shoes on his feet with the barest shift of his eyes and went right back to rocking.

They sat together in the front room after that, sipping the tea that Dar brought in from the kitchen. It was bitter and smelled faintly of fish, but it was warm and Trina drank it anyway. John filled the room with smoke from his cigar. It had a pleasant, almost earthy smell that left her feeling a little giddy. Between the smoke and the warmth of the little stove, Trina felt her spirits begin to lighten. She listened to Dar and her stories about being short-changed at the sundry store, about scolding a group of kids who ran too fast and almost knocked her over outside the cooper's shack. For a little while, she almost forgot that none of it was real, that it was just a place that her imagination had made. A place that was running out of time.

Her clothes were dry and the squish had gone out of her shoes by the time Dar stopped talking. There was something in the silence that seemed to weigh heavy on the place, as if a shadow had fallen over all of them. It took Trina a moment to realize that she had been staring at a photograph that sat on a low shelf in the corner of the room. It was a portrait of a young boy with blond hair, seated stiff-backed in a wooden chair, framed in hammered tin. The picture was blurry and sepia-toned, the kind of photo she that might have been taken with an old-timey box camera on top of a wooden tripod. Trina knew at once that Dar had caught her looking, because the old woman's eyes lost their focus, as if they were searching for something far away.

"That's our Nathan," Dar said at last as she folded her hands in her lap. "We lost him in a squall gone about, oh, twelve years ago now. Wind came up out of the south, like the wind'll sometimes do, but this time it caught the sails aback and the boat tipped over as quick as you please. By the time we got it back to rights, the waves had already taken him. Ain't naught left to remember him by, 'cept for that picture."

Trina stiffened at the sound of the boy's name. John took the cigar out of his mouth to regard her with a wary eye. How had she not seen it before? The curve of the boy's nose, those wide, impatient eyes. The picture was faded, so posed and awkward that there was nothing in it to suggest the man he might become. Even so, now that she'd seen it, there was no denying it. She was looking at a picture of Woods.

"Time was, I wanted nothing so much as to follow him right down to the bottom. But after a while you get used to all the empty spaces that people leave behind. Even the big ones. I wanted to try for another, after a time, but, well…"

She looked to John, who had gone back to sucking on his cigar, staring out at the same spot on the wall he'd been watching for almost an hour. Trina turned away from the photo but still felt its eyes upon her. If Sweet was right, she was the reason that Woods had died in that other world. If Sweet was right, she was the one who had killed him here too.

"But fate's fate, and we've accepted it. And of course, we've contented ourselves over the years with what you might call a large extended family." The dark cloud seemed to lift, and Dar smiled as if there had never been anything wrong. "Folks 'round here been good to us, and we do what we can do be good right back."

"You know everyone on this island?" Trina asked, grateful for the change of subject.

"Near enough, yes," Dar said. "There someone here you're looking for?"

"I don't know. Maybe." Trina hesitated, but Dar let her take her time getting the words out, and that made Trina want to trust her. "Have you seen a man with scars on the side of his head? You know, like a burn? Maybe a doctor, or something like that?"

"He the one who left you out where John found you? Out in the middle of nowhere with no way home?"

"No." She hesitated again. John shifted in his chair as he pulled another draw from his cigar. "I mean, not exactly."

"Well, someone like that, I'd imagine I'd like to have seen him." Dar leaned in close and lowered her voice to a whisper. "But if you're in need, sweetie, I can see you over to Granny Larson down on East Quay. She's got herbs might help if we caught it in time. Quick as a jiff and so much safer than the needle."

Trina shook her head. "No, it's not like that... What about an older man? Tall? Thin? His name's Colin. Colin Williams. He'd be a librarian or a teacher, maybe."

"Librarian?" Dar sat upright in her chair. "Well, there ain't been a library 'round these parts since before the flood. Books don't last in the weather and there's not much call for readin' these days."

"Never mind," Trina said. "It was just a dumb thought." She gathered the blanket around her shoulders and looked down at the floor. There was no way for her to know how much time had passed since the Turning or if Colin was even here at all.

"Well, don't be givin' up so easy, now. It's just that tall and skinny could be near about any man on this island. But don't you worry yourself. If these friends of yours, if friends they be, are anywhere to be found, then John'll be the one to find 'em. Ain't that right, John?"

John let out a long breath that sent a fresh wave of white smoke billowing into the air.

"John knows nearabouts everyone on the island from the docks to the stacks, and if he doesn't, then it's a near guarantee he knows someone who does. We'll reunite you with your friend soon enough."

"Less a'course," the old man said, addressing no one in particular, "she don't want to be reunited." He cut the ash from his cigar with a knife before he tucked it back into the box and levered himself up to his feet.

"Well, there's not much chance of that, is there?" Dar said. "This place ain't small, but it ain't that big either. If she's gonna stay, she's bound to cross paths with 'em sooner or later."

Dar turned to Trina and placed a gentle hand on her shoulder. "Assuming a'course that you're plannin' on stayin'. I don't mean to speak for ye, but it didn't seem like you were long on options, if you'll forgive me for sayin' so."

There was something in the way the old woman nodded as she spoke that told Trina she wasn't going to take no for an answer. A part of her had already decided that would be all right. She had become so accustomed to the Turnings that she could never get attached to a place for too long, but if she ended up back here in this room tomorrow with a warm fire and a cup of Dar's tea in her hands, then that would be just fine.

Dar must have read some of that on her face because she rocked back in her chair and nodded, satisfied. "That settles it then. We ain't got much for comforts, but I can make you a nice spot for sleepin' right here by the fire. And you're welcome to stay, as long as you pull your weight and as long as you can stand my old John here and his prattling on."

"Pull my weight? How?"

John harrumphed as he slapped his hat down onto his head. "Won't know 'til we see what you're good at. For now, just follow along and be where I need you. Long as you can learn, you'll find your place soon enough." He took a rain slick down from a hook by the door and tossed it to her. It was worn thin and far too big, but she managed to shrug it on and work a few of the buttons together.

"No better way of getting to know the place than helping John on his rounds," Dar said, helping her get the jacket done up. The old woman stepped back to admire her, like a mother on the first day of school. "If'n your friend's here, you're sure to come across him sooner or later. And best to be at it 'fore the storm hits and drives us all indoors."

"Ain't gonna be no storm," John said.

"I already told you," Dar said. "And I'd tell ya again if I thought you'd listen."

"Ain't no sign of it."

"Well, you can tell that to the ache in my bones, and these bones have never made a liar of me yet." She turned back to Trina with a conspiratorial wink. "Just stick close to the old grump here and you'll be fine. I'll have supper waitin' by the time you get back."

John looked her up and down and gave a little grunt of approval. "How are ye with yer hands?"

22

The island had been built up on a high patch of land where the borders of old roads could still be seen in the largest of the thoroughfares. Cracked blacktop and bits of crumbling concrete formed the foundations of makeshift shacks and lean-tos made from sheets of salvaged metal. Now that they were farther inland, the structures seemed less jumbled and more deliberate. Or maybe it was only that Trina was starting to get the lay of the place. The people were the same, though, their backs bent in their shining oiled coats. They leaned in the doorways of the makeshift buildings that crowded the road and trundled by, balancing heavy sacks on their shoulders. A few of them nodded at John as he passed. He acknowledged them with a faint grunt and the barest inclination of his head.

Trina quickly realized that no one seemed to be taking any notice of her. She imagined that they must be used to seeing new faces come and go here in what seemed to be the center of their civilization. Or maybe it was just her borrowed coat that allowed her to blend in. Still, she kept her eyes open as she moved among them, searching each face as she passed. Searching for Colin. Searching for Doctor Sweet.

John led her down narrow alleyways, some of them barely wide enough for two people to squeeze past at once. Here the roads had given way to rough cobblestones made from old patio pavers and worn wooden boards set down as bridges over muddy ground. The ramshackle buildings crowded so close that they often converged above their heads, blotting out the hazy sun and making dry patches in the road where the misting rain could not reach.

There was a music to this place, strange harmonies that rose with the tinkle of makeshift windchimes and the distant ringing of brass bells. It was there in the steady flap of plastic tarps and linen sheets as they caught the wind. Beneath it all, the low hum of voices in the marketplace, the steady churning of gas motors reverberated through the metal structures until she could feel their vibrations beneath her very feet. No matter which way she turned, there was some new sound, some new scent upon the air. It was almost enough for her to believe that it really had grown together piece by piece, year over year, that there was no way all of it could have come from her imagination alone.

Every so often they would duck beneath the narrow awnings and John would knock upon doors that only revealed themselves as doors when they were slid open from the inside. The people who lived there would usher them into their cramped spaces and, by the dim light of candles and oil lamps, they would hand John old motors and bits of machinery. He would unshoulder his bag and tinker with them, telling Trina to hand him tools, frowning at her until she found the right ones. He pulled the motors apart and put them back together again. After a time, he would hand them back to their owners, and they would press coins into his hands that he disappeared into the depths of his coat.

They went on this way through the rest of the morning and well into the afternoon, as they wound their way through the heart of the sprawl. They called on tiny hovels with packed-earth floors, and on two-room dwellings, luxurious by comparison with their doors on hinges and separate rooms for sleeping. Every time, someone would hand John something to fix, and Trina would watch the deft motions of his large fingers as they turned the screws and coaxed pieces away from each other. She'd watch as he placed each part, almost lovingly, on the oily cloth he brought with him, spacing them out, taking note of how each piece interacted with the whole. Soon, she was able to anticipate which tools he would need, and had them in her hand and ready before he could ask for them. When this happened, the old man would grunt in approval, but he would never look up from his work.

When he found something he could not fix, he would put the pieces back together, bind it up in cloth, and stuff it deep into his bag. Promises were made and heads nodded, all of it transacted with a few words and a firm handshake before he and Trina were on their way again. Other times, he would pull finished projects from his pack, whole and made new, and their grateful owners would receive their battery lamps and water pumps with barely a word spoken between them. Trina marveled at how simple it all was, courtesy reduced to the bare necessities by the very fact of their hardscrabble existence. Despite its haphazard appearance, the island moved like a well-tuned machine, and the two of them were only pieces of the whole. For the time being, that was enough, and it served to put her jumbled thoughts at ease.

She followed John up a swaying metal scaffold to a point on one of the high rooftops, a flat expanse of cracked tar paper with a metal tower perched on one side. The worst of the fog had lifted, but the sun was still shrouded in a gauzy haze that made it a weak and distant thing. An angry gray patch of sky loomed over the horizon. Trina could see the sheets of rain falling beneath it as it churned, slowly drawing closer. Dar had been right about the storm. John stared out at it in silence, perhaps thinking the same thing, before he harrumphed and shook his head.

The old man knelt before a control panel and set to work among the wires. His fingers moved faster than she could follow, untwisting the ends of wires and pulling out circuit boards to brush the rust off their contact points. When Trina was sure that he wasn't going to ask anything from her, she drifted toward the roof's edge. From there, she could see almost the whole island spread out beneath her, and some of the stilted houses and barge-like structures that lay beyond.

Three statues loomed along the distant shoreline, each one three stories high and welded together from odd bits of junk metal, facing the horizon as if they had frozen there. In the folds of bent and rusted steel, Trina could see familiar outlines: the flowing gown of The Goddess, the bent back of The Crone. Between them stood the Tall Man with his wide and rusted hat, his hands outstretched before him, as if to welcome the coming storm.

Trina stared at them for a long time, long enough to be sure that they were only statues, that they would not turn and come for her. Deep down, she knew that the Shadows no longer had a reason to chase her, now that she was no longer running. Their angles were worn smooth by age and the sea wind, and there were birds nesting on their shoulders. She wondered if this was what she had made of them, or if they had simply frozen at the water's edge and the metal had been bent around them like a prison. Like a tomb.

Out on the rooftops, metal pipes rose alongside brick chimneys. The smoke that billowed from them smelled of wood and coal, but also of herbs and something like burning leaves. Crude jetties jutted over the distant water, spiraling around the steel lattice of electrical towers. Boats drifted past each other, laden with cargo strapped down with ropes and netting. One of them was built from what looked like a tanker trailer that had been cut in half, the other from an old billboard floating on plastic water jugs. None of it made sense, and yet it all made sense. Everything was familiar and unfamiliar all at once. The world was full of details that she could never have conceived of, let alone created.

Sweet had to have been wrong about her, or at least about her part in creating this place. If that were true, it meant that she could put aside the guilt she'd been carrying ever since Dar had told her the story of their son. It meant that this place and all the places that came before were already there, laying alongside each other like pages in a book. Turning those pages didn't mean she was writing the words. Even if, in arriving there, she did manage to alter some of the specifics, their histories were still their histories, the same as if she had been there or not. She hadn't caused Woods to drown in this world any more than she had built those boats in the distance, or the wooden battlements that rose around the half-sunken grain silo, or the platforms that jutted from the water tower like mushrooms on a tree trunk.

And yet, her guilt remained. She had carried it with her as far back as she could remember, maybe even all the way back to that hazy point in the distant past when the Turnings began. It gripped her at odd times, when she passed a homeless person on a city street or watched a child stumble and fall on the sidewalk. Always, there was the sense that she could have prevented these things, or at least that she should have been able to fix them, the way that John fixed things with barely more than his own hands. This place made her want to let go of all that, but she knew in her heart that she couldn't. If there never was another Turning, she might find a way to feel safe here, but she knew deep down that she would never feel right.

Even if Woods' death in this world wasn't her fault, his death in the last world was. When she looked at her hands, she could still see flecks of his blood dried beneath her fingernails. She had made Doctor Sweet, or at the very least she had caused him to be made. Whatever the Shadows had done to him, whatever had allowed him to persist through the Turnings, he was her responsibility. Every person he hurt was a black mark against her own conscience. Even if they never met again, those black marks would be with her forever.

She looked back at the antenna tower to see if the old man needed her, but the old man wasn't there. The control panel was closed and his bag of tools was gone. She ran to the stairs, and through the gaps in the steps she could see the hood of his heavy coat bobbing along as he made his way down. When she called after him, he didn't look back.

She called out again, louder this time, but John wouldn't look up at her. His steps quickened. A sinking sensation wormed its way into her gut as she realized she was being left behind. She took the narrow stairs two at a time, gripping the rail, trying to ignore the way they creaked and swayed beneath her weight. By the time she reached the ground, the old man was gone.

23

Trina snaked her way through the turns and switchbacks of the alleyways, trying to remember the way she had come, trying to retrace her steps. Nothing seemed familiar and every turn seemed to lead her to another dead end. When she finally found her way back to one of the wide thoroughfares, it was in a completely different spot from where she'd started. The street was bustling with a heightened, nervous energy. The storm was getting closer, and the old man was nowhere to be found.

Her heartbeat quickened as she pushed through the crowd, hoping for a glimpse of John's coat, for a flash of his long, white beard. When she couldn't find him, she called out to the passersby, taking them by the arms to force them to look at her instead of hurrying past. Most of them just shook their heads, but every now and then, someone would point down some new byway, some crooked alley, and she'd be off running to the next dead end.

She balled her fists and stomped up the lane. If the old man had wanted to get rid of her, he could have just said so. He could have just left her back in the drowned hotel and never had to bother with her at all. And it wasn't as if she wouldn't be able to find him again. The island wasn't that big. She knew where he lived, even if she didn't exactly know how to get back there. She'd find it eventually, and she could only imagine what Dar would have to say about it when she did.

Trina's anger gave way to a new feeling, a sinking feeling that only brought new questions. If John had wanted to be rid of her, he wouldn't have asked her to come out with him at all. He could have left her with Dar, or just sent her on an errand and just not been there when she came back. But he'd left her on a rooftop at the end of a maze of alleyways, almost as if he'd been counting on her to lose her way. He had to know that she'd catch up with him sooner or later. It was as if he didn't really want to get rid of her, but only wanted her out of the way for a while. That could only mean one of two things: either he was in trouble, or she was.

She thought of his little boat, tied off at the dock. If she was going to find him anywhere, it would be there. But the whole island was surrounded by docks and she doubted she could remember which one was the right one. The rain had begun to fall. Trina raised her face to it and closed her eyes, waiting for something, anything, that might tell her which way to go. The rain was driving most of the people indoors, and as the street grew hushed she could hear the distant ringing of a bell. She couldn't be sure it was the same one she had heard when they'd had pulled up to the dock in the fog, but she had no better ideas, so she set off in its direction.

She followed the sound through winding streets out to the edge of the island, where the rat's warren of shaded passageways opened onto a wide expanse of mismatched wooden piers. Rows of rusted boats rocked and strained at their mooring lines as the wind blew the rain and the sea spray into her face. The storm was closer now, a black wall of cloud and sheeting rain that stretched across the entire horizon. Trina shaded her eyes with her arm, searching for John, searching for his boat, but she could tell at once that she had never been to this place.

She could see the junk-metal statue of The Hound perched on a plinth of mortared brick just up shore. Further off stood The Goddess, her arms outstretched, her flowing hair laid out in lengths of bent copper pipe. They stood facing the water, facing the oncoming storm. Though they gave no sign of moving, Trina did not want to turn her back on them.

The bell rang out again, three times, urgent and quick. It was ringing out a warning, for the rain was falling heavy now and the whole sky was growing dark. A lone fisherman hurried along the wooden docks that stretched like broken fingers over the water, shouldering a net full of his still-wriggling catch. Trina ran among the boats and makeshift rafts, fighting the urge to shout out John's name, knowing that he wouldn't answer her anyway.

A gust of wind caught her unprepared and blew her sideways. She set her shoulder against it as she worked her way across the dock, peering into every open hatch and port hole she could find. Anxious eyes stared back at her from behind rain-streaked windows and beneath makeshift battens, people who had no choice but to ride out the storm. Their nervousness was a bad sign. She would find no shelter among them, but she would need to find shelter soon.

It wasn't until she saw the old fishing boat tied at the end of the pier that she knew she had found what she was looking for. It sat tall in the water, with a high mast that looked like it might once have held a sail. A short smokestack rose above a squat wheelhouse with a corrugated steel door and windows so dirty it was impossible to see inside. Old tires in odd sizes hung from its hull, which had been painted blue once, but had since faded to the dull gray of a stormy sky. But it was the boat's name that caught her eye, spelled out on the transom in chipped lettering so faded that Trina almost couldn't read it at all. But now that she'd seen it, there was no mistaking it.

The boat's name was *Edie's Pride*.

There was a tug at her elbow. A wide hand closed over her arm and pulled her back. When she turned around she saw John there, his face red and huffing, his hat tilted against the rain.

"Ye got no business bein' down here," he growled low in her ear. "Now come along 'fore someone sees."

Trina yanked her arm free. "No way." John's hands were strong, and she could tell that he could have kept hold of her if he'd really wanted to. "Not until you tell me what's going on. Why did you leave me?"

"Never mind that now. Just come along."

"And that boat. Whose boat is that?"

"Ain't nothin' in that place for you," he said. "Should never have come here myself, so let's be on." It was the most he'd said to her at one time since she'd met him, and though the gruff sound of his voice was enough to cut through some of the excitement she felt at seeing Edie's name on the boat, it did nothing to discourage her.

Edie's Pride had been written in a looping scroll, so much at odds with the rest of the boat that it seemed as if it had been painted there just for her to find. Her name was bookended with painted roses. Roses painted in blue and white.

"Come on away, girl." John's voice was gruff, but Trina could hear the note of pleading beneath his words. She paid them no mind, but took hold of the metal ladder and climbed it to the deck. The old man didn't follow. He only hunched against the sheeting winds and watched her from the dock.

The deck swayed beneath Trina's feet as the lapping waves pushed and tugged, stretching and slackening the mooring lines. Through the rain, she could see all the way to the bow where the ropes had been coiled next to stacks of boxy crawfish traps. The tall mast rocked with the wind, swaying from side to side above her head like a pendulum. There was no one else on deck. She was all alone.

The junk-metal statues loomed in the distant, gathering dark. Lightning flashed, and in that instant the statues disappeared. In their places were black shapes that swallowed the light, shimmering outlines that seethed and writhed in the rain. When the light was gone, the statues returned. Only now, they were no longer facing the storm. They had turned to face the boat, turned to face *her*. They stared down at her watching. Waiting.

All at once, Trina wanted nothing more than to turn back. But there were stairs leading down from the deck to the cabin below. At the bottom of those stairs was an open door, practically calling out for her to go through. John's warning was like an alarm bell in her mind. *Ain't nothin' in that place for you.* And yet, this place had to be for her. It could only be for her.

She took the steps slowly as the wind and the boat creaked around her. She heard a hollow thump as the waves pushed the boat against the dock, and felt her stomach lurch as she fought to keep her footing. She listened for voices, for some sign that she wasn't alone, before she pulled open the little door.

The cabin was dark, and as her eyes adjusted she could just make out a little table bolted to the deck and a sleeping berth set against the hull. In the berth was a narrow bed with a bare mattress that was old and covered with water stains. Upon it lay a man with his back to the door. He was snoring softly despite the thunder, and as Trina drew closer she caught the smell of him, old fish and salt air. There were holes in his weather-beaten coat and sweat soaked into his collar, but Trina knew him, even without his glasses. As his eyes fluttered open, she let out a little laugh because she could scarcely believe that she had found him again.

"Colin."

Colin's mouth fell open. He stared at her, his eyes searching, as if there was something about her that he could not quite place. He lingered there for a moment, but every time that he seemed on the verge of understanding, his eyes would lose focus. At last he seemed to come back to himself, and as recognition spread across his face, so did his smile.

"Trina," he said, though his voice was little more than a croaking whisper. "Trina Bell."

She laughed again and realized that there were tears running down her cheeks. She gathered him up and pulled him close. Beneath the sea-scent that clung to him, she still caught the hint of soap, the faint ghost of laundered linen.

"Bell. The bell. The bell rings when the boats come in. I hear it in my sleep."

She held him out at arm's length so she could look at him. There was blood on the collar of his shirt, and more dried against the corner of his mouth. His eyes were dim and distant, and she couldn't be sure that he was still seeing her at all.

"I had the strangest dream just a moment ago," he said, looking out over her shoulder. "You were there. I remember that. I was in a war, of all things. Or was I? It's so hard to recall a dream after waking, you know. You have to write it down just at that moment or it's gone. Just gone forever, like it was never there at all."

The boat lurched beneath them. Trina had a dim notion that the boards beneath her were vibrating, but she barely noticed them for the desperate, heavy feeling that had begun to weigh at her insides.

"I was in the desert," Colin said, as if it had just occurred to him. "I almost drowned. But that makes no sense. How could anyone drown in the desert?"

At last, his eyes focused on her, wide and full of horror. "The flowers in the desert are always white. I can see them under the water!"

He scrambled back against the hull and pulled his legs up to his chest. Trina put a hand on his shoulder, and felt his body tremble as he began to cry. The boat rocked again as something scraped against the hull. Only then did she become aware of the sound of footsteps on the stairs, and the presence of someone behind her in the doorway.

"John, come here," she called over her shoulder. "Quick. He needs help." As soon as the words were out of her mouth, she knew that the footsteps were too light, too careful to belong to the old man.

The boat swayed. Trina rose to her feet, her heart hammering in her chest as she turned around. Doctor Sweet was there, filling up the doorway. The bandages on his head were gone. The burns on his face had pulled tight as they'd healed, and they'd left the corner of his mouth curled up in a permanent sneer. A hammer dangled at the end of his arm, its head rusted and heavy.

"You're right, Trina. He does." His smile was patient, almost triumphant. "It seems we're just in time."

Trina stepped forward, putting her body between Colin and Sweet, between Colin and the hammer. "Don't you dare hurt him."

"I wouldn't dream of it," Sweet said, his words slurred ever so slightly by his upturned lip. "In fact, he's only in danger because of you. Take a good look. See what you've done to him. He barely understands what's real anymore, because what's real is always changing. You've broken his mind, and every time you change the world around us it breaks a little more."

From the corner of her eye, Trina could see Colin on the dirty mattress, rocking himself, his hands in front of his eyes. "And what about you?" she asked Sweet. "I suppose murdering people is your idea of reasonable?"

"I have perfect clarity. I have a purpose!" The hammer bounced against his thigh as he spoke, punctuating his words. "Everything I have done has been to undo the damage you have caused, to put right everything you have destroyed!"

"Is that what you told Woods? What about Edie?"

She knew at once that the words were a mistake. His eyes went wide, the rage in one only made worse by the milky-white blankness in the other. "Losing Edie was unfortunate, even if you did drive me to it." He tightened his grip on the hammer as he edged toward her, blocking the doorway, leaving her nowhere to run. "But your boyfriend? That one's all on you."

Something moved in the shadows behind him, quick and catlike. Sweet must have sensed it because he turned and brought the hammer up, an instant too late. A fist connected with his jaw and snapped his head back. The hammer fell to the deck, and Sweet followed as his legs crumpled beneath him.

John Bishop looked down at Sweet disapprovingly, as if he had only just found him there. He nodded once, certain that it was done, and turned back to the stairs.

"A'right then," he said to her. "Now that we're here, there's work to do."

24

Trina got Colin to his feet and did her best to maneuver him around Sweet's body and up the stairs. The boat lurched sideways with a sound of crunching wood, and she had to fight to keep upright. The gray sky above her was in motion, the rain falling in sheets now. As the hum of the engine grew louder, she realized that the boat was no longer at the dock.

From the deck, she could see the little island disappearing into the distance, swallowed whole by the rain. Pieces of a raft bobbed, half-sunken, in the boat's wake, its cargo thrown overboard, its pilot left to drown. The boat hit a wave and the bounce lifted Trina off her feet. They were driving into the storm and picking up speed. She lowered Colin to the deck in a corner near the railing where she thought he'd be safe. He curled back into himself, as if he had never moved, as if he hadn't seen her at all.

John was already in the wheelhouse. He paid her no mind as she stepped in alongside him. He was standing at the place where the wheel should have been, the place where now there was only a bent metal post jutting from a wooden dashboard full of smashed dials and broken indicators. The wheel lay in pieces on the ground. The old man stared down at it and frowned.

"Snapped off the throttle, too," he said. "Fix'n for a one-way trip and didn't care where."

The boat crested another wave and pitched Trina against the doorframe. The old man barely moved.

"Can you fix it?"

He shook his head. "Could maybe stop 'er if I had a set o' pliers, but I left my tools back on the dock when you jumped aboard."

Trina had picked up John's hammer and tucked it into her belt. Her thumb brushed nervously against its handle. "What were you doing here anyway?" She didn't think that he meant her any harm, but she hadn't expected to find him in the same place as Sweet either. "You knew he was going to be here, didn't you?"

"Wouldn't've been a problem if you'd stayed put instead of stickin' your nose in." John dropped to one knee and felt along the underside of the dash. "I came to tell 'im I was done with this business, and to leave you be. But you went along and handed yerself over to him like ye was all wrapped up in a bow."

"Done with..." Her mouth hung open as she realized what he was saying. "You mean, you were helping him?"

John got his fingers around the end of the wooden panel and pulled. It cracked under the strain and came away in one piece. "I said that I was done with it."

"But why? Why would you do that?"

"Because he told me you could bring him back!"

He paused to steady himself, his hands on his knees, trembling. "He came to me two months ago, talkin' all kinds of nonsense 'bout what's real and what's not. Worlds on top of worlds, he said. But he knew I had an eye on all the comin's and goin's on the island, so he told me what you look like and gave me some coins to watch out for ye. He told me it was you who made it so my boy died."

He nudged the dashboard panel aside and began to poke his fingers into the mess of wires and broken controls. "Didn't think much of it 'til I found ye out on that building. I figgered out pretty quick that he didn't mean anything good by gettin' hold o' ye, so I told him I was done, and damn me for a fool."

His hands grew still and when he turned to her, his eyes were shining. "I *was* a fool, wasn't I?"

His jaw was set, but his look was pleading and she knew he wasn't going to let her turn away until she answered him.

"He told me things," John said. "Things I don't rightly understand. But ye didn't make my boy dead, and you can't bring him back. Not you, nor anyone else. Can you?"

Her hands were shaking, and she rubbed them against her jeans. She wanted to tell this man that she hadn't killed his son. More than that, she wanted to tell him that she hadn't been responsible for his dying either. She wanted to say these things, but she couldn't, not with him looking her in the eye. She wanted to believe that they were true, but she couldn't do that either.

"No," she said softly. "No, I can't bring him back."

John nodded once and turned back to the dashboard. Through the rain-streaked windows, Trina watched more boats scatter as they approached. They were leaving the island behind, heading out toward the border settlements, and they were picking up speed.

"Fuel line's beneath the hold," John said finally. "We cut the line, she'll stop soon enough."

"What do I do?"

"Ain't nothin' *to* do." He got back to his feet and frowned out the window at the open water ahead. "See to your friend." He pulled himself along the handrail to the prow, found a hatch in the deck there, and just like that, he was gone.

Trina tried to keep her footing as the boat jolted and swayed. Colin was still where she'd left him. His clothes were starting to soak through. He'd curled one of the ropes around himself and was holding onto it as if his life depended on it, but he didn't seem to notice that the other end wasn't tied to anything. But he was safe for now, and he would stay safe up here for a few more minutes at least.

Sweet was still down in the little cabin where she'd left him. Her hand strayed to the hammer at her belt, but she picked up a coil of rope instead and started down the stairs. She felt every creak and shudder the boat made as if they were happening in her very bones. Once she had the ropes around Sweet, once she was sure that he couldn't hurt anyone else, she could talk to him. She could look him in the eye and make him tell her everything he knew, about the Turnings, about the Shadows. But when she reached the bottom stair and pushed the door to the cabin aside, Sweet was gone.

She dropped the rope and pulled the hammer from her belt as she raced up the stairs. The boat jolted across the waves and sent her staggering against the rail. Colin still cowered, wrapped in his tangle of rope. Trina looked back at the boat's wake, hoping that Sweet had gone overboard, that she'd see his head bobbing among the frothing waves.

But there was no one out there. Apart from Colin, she was alone on the deck, but the deck seemed so much bigger now, with plenty of places to hide.

She knelt next to Colin and took his face in her hands. His skin was cold, his glasses fogged over. "Did you see him? Which way did he go?"

His eyes focused on her for an instant before he faded away again. "Ugly lamp," he said, so softly that she could barely hear him through the rain. "Flower blanket."

She left him there and crept toward the bow, one hand on the wooden rail, the other gripping the hammer. She called out for John, but she could barely hear herself above the roar of the boat's engine and the steady hiss of sheeting rain.

The door to the wheelhouse hung open, flapping against the doorframe like a bird with a broken wing. Trina didn't think that she had left it open, but she couldn't be sure. Sweet could be in there. Sweet could be anywhere, just waiting for her to let her guard down. She swallowed hard and felt the weight of the hammer in her hand. If he tried to get the jump on her again, she was going to make sure he paid for it.

The boat leapt once more and sent her staggering against the bulkhead. She tried to look inside the wheelhouse, but it was too dark, the windows too streaked with rain. She brought the hammer up and readied herself to swing. When the door banged again she leapt inside. But there was no one there. The wheelhouse was empty.

Out on the water, a rickety wooden shack held up on pylons slid past. The rain swallowed it back up again, quick enough for Trina to see that the boat was moving too fast and still picking up speed. Another wave hit the bow and sent her staggering, shoulder-first, into the wall. The sky was dark, and the water seemed to go on forever. She couldn't see beyond the rain to know which way they were headed.

Something moved at the front of the boat, someone coming up from below deck. Trina ducked down behind the windows because she could see at once that it wasn't the old man. The side of Sweet's scalp was red and glistening. He used his arm to shade his eyes against the rain, and his lips were drawn back in a grimace.

Trina pressed herself against the wall and held the hammer close with both hands. Her chest was heaving, and she fought to control her breath. She tried not to think about John, still somewhere below decks. She tried not to think about what Sweet might have done to him.

Sweet's shadow fell across the wheelhouse window. Trina's heart was beating so fast that she was sure that he could hear it too. She pulled the hammer back, ready to bring it down on his head, ready to slam the door against his chest the moment he stepped inside.

But Sweet's shadow moved away, gliding toward the rear of the boat. Trina felt herself relax, but only for an instant, because she remembered then that Colin was still back there.

She bolted to her feet, the hammer raised above her head. When she burst from the wheelhouse, Sweet was ready for her, his dead eye milky and wide with rage. Trina swung the hammer, but Sweet raised his arm to block it. He cried out in pain as the claw end raked through his skin. Trina could see Colin at the back of the boat, gathering the coils of rope around him in a protective blanket, his feet scrambling to push him against the railing.

Sweet swung his fist and missed Trina by inches as she stumbled back to catch herself against the doorway. The boat lurched and slammed Sweet into the rail. As he gathered himself, something at the front of the boat caught his eye. Trina saw it too, looming out of the rain like a thicket of metal trees. It was the water tower, standing tall on its wide stilt legs, standing right in the boat's path.

Trina had just enough time to brace herself before the boat and the tower collided with a scream of tearing metal. The boat skipped along one of the tower's legs, crumpling the steel railing as if it were made out of paper. The boat lurched sideways. Trina fell back into the wheelhouse, and Sweet fell with her. His head collided with the metal doorframe with a sharp ringing sound. He collapsed at Trina's side and lay still.

Trina fought to her feet as water began to rush in through the open doorway. The boat was listing, starting to sink. As she sloshed her way up the sloping deck, she glanced back at Sweet. His head was above water, but she couldn't tell if he was still breathing. Now that he was helpless, she felt a pang of sympathy for him, a pang that went away when she remembered the feel of his hands around her throat. Still, she didn't want him dead, especially not if there was still a chance that he could help her.

The boat's motor foundered, then sputtered to a stop. Trina could hear distant shouts of alarm through the sheeting rain. She remembered Colin. The thought that he might have gone overboard put her into a panic. She slogged out onto the deck. The boat was sinking in earnest now, and the spot where Colin had been was completely underwater. Coils of rope floated like water snakes, but Colin was gone.

Trina's heart sank, but a moment later she heard a wailing cry from above and turned to see Colin hanging from the boat's mast. He clung to it with all four limbs, inching his way higher like a frightened cat in a tree. Voices were calling out to them from the high wooden platforms, from the windows cut into the skin of the tank. A wooden dock had been turned to splinters, but the ladder up to the tower was still there. It might take her and Colin to safety, if only they could get to it.

She'd left Sweet in the still-flooding wheelhouse. She wasn't about to let him drown, not again. She slogged back to the wheelhouse, but Sweet wasn't where she had left him. She kicked around, searching, but couldn't see him crouched behind her, so low in the water that only the hairless ruin of his burned scalp and the filmy circle of his dead eye rose above the surface.

He grabbed hold of her leg and she tumbled back, thrashing. In an instant she felt his weight on top of her, pinning her beneath the water. She had lost the hammer in the crash, so she pounded at his chest with her fists. His hands were on her shoulders, forcing her under, and she could not move him.

"You remember me, don't you?" Sweet's voice was a distant thing. The water between them had made the sound of it low and almost comforting. "You remember what I was, before all of this. You know what you did to me."

She tried to kick him off, but her legs only flailed uselessly against the deck. Her arms were weak, and every time she struck out with them they became weaker. When she couldn't hold her breath any longer, her lungs pulled in water. Her vision began to darken, until all she could see the white circle of Sweet's ruined eye, a bright point of light receding into darkness. She heard his voice, loud, the way a whisper is loud, next to her ear.

Remember.

25

T rina's eyes snapped open. The weight was gone from her chest, along with the deck and the boat and everything around her. There was only the water. Panic ran loose in her mind like a wild animal as she worked her legs and flailed her arms. She could see the surface in the distance above her, a far-away shimmer of pale light, but even as her failing lungs urged her upward, an even greater urging told her that she must go down. That urge pushed all her panic aside. It became a voice, screaming past the pain in her chest and the tingling in her arms, growing louder by the instant.

Below her, everything was dark, but still she kicked out with her legs and tried to drive herself back down. Her lungs burned. Something glinted down there in the black, two points of light falling away, sinking deeper. She reached out for them, but they were too far away. She tried to follow them, but the water buoyed her up, and each stroke of her arms was weaker than the last.

Her body convulsed as the last of her strength left her. Still, the voice screamed at her to swim, to fight to reach those sinking lights. They were paler now, or was it only that her vision was failing? The darkness buoyed her up, and as she rose, she thought of Colin, of Edie, of her grandfather. As the last spark of consciousness flared within her, she thought of the flowers.

26

Trina sputtered, and coughed the water from her lungs. She could breathe again, and as she gasped she could feel the wooden deck beneath her once more She could see Sweet's dead eye leering down at her, his hands clenched around her throat.

"Is this what you wanted?" he growled. "Is this what you brought me here to do?"

He hauled her up by her shirt. The rain had stopped. In its place was a bright and cloudless sky. The water tower was gone and the old fishing boat had become a crumpled sailboat, run aground on sharp rocks that stabbed like stunted fingers from the water. The boat was sinking fast.

"Look at me!" Sweet's muffled voice was almost lost among the sounds of her thrashing. "Look at what you've made me into!"

Colin clung to the top of the mast, sails billowing beneath him. He cried out in a mindless, mournful wail, calling out with his eyes closed, calling for help, calling for his mother. The sound pierced straight through to Trina's heart. He was calling out the mantra. *Small room. Pink rock. Ugly lamp. Flower blanket.* She tried to answer him, but Sweet pushed her back down beneath the water.

"It's not enough for you to destroy world after world. You had to destroy me too."

Again, the water filled her lungs. She reached up and found Sweet's face. She dug at his burns and raked her fingernails against his cheeks. He howled, but he would not let go.

"I was a doctor!" he growled, though his voice seemed so far away. "I healed people! But you took all of that away from me. You made me into a monster!"

He pulled her up again, and this time the water she coughed from her lungs tasted of salt and ocean air. They were still sinking, but now they were on a raft no bigger than the hood of a car. It was kept afloat by two great, wooden outriggers, but they were listing sideways and one of the outriggers had risen into the air. Colin clung to the end of it, his feet dangling as he struggled to keep hold. In the churning water around them, sharks had begun to circle.

Colin tried to grab onto a loose rope, but the sudden movement caused him to lose his grip and fall into the water. Trina called out to him, but he didn't answer. As the sharks drew closer, their fins sank beneath the frothing waves. The sky was black with storm clouds, and when the lightning flashed, they picked out dark silhouettes high in the sky, great Shadows that loomed over them, watching.

"I won't let you," Sweet whispered, his voice rasping in her ear. "I won't let you take anything more from me!" He pulled her from the raft and let his weight carry them down. Trina pounded at his shoulders and tried to kick free. A shark knifed past them through the water. Above the shimmering surface, the silhouettes stared down at her from inside the darkening sky.

Her fingers found the wound in Sweet's shoulder, the wound that Woods' bullet had made. She gouged at it with her thumb, and dug deep until she heard Sweet's howl of pain. Trina gasped, and found that there was air. The water was shallow now, a square pool lined in marble, surrounded by tall, fluted columns that rose up into the clouds.

With Sweet's grip on her gone, she turned on him, and used her weight to force him under the surface of the shallow pool. She blinked, and at once the columns were gone, replaced by a river bed with stands of tall grass and bushy tufts of cattail reeds. She bore down on him, her hands at his throat, her knees on his chest. His breath came out in fat bubbles that broke upon the surface of the churning water. He was trying to speak, but she could not hear him. He tried to push her away, but she only squeezed down harder.

The world around them had become a riot, a new Turning with every thrash of Sweet's limbs. The leathery wings of featherless birds blotted out the sun. Skyscrapers rose and toppled to the ground. The sun climbed over snowy mountains and set over a vast and endless plain. Fire rained down from a starless sky. Great beasts strode above them, balanced on the tips of their stilt-like legs. But always, there was the water. The water was a torrent. The water was a still pool. The water was a sphere where they floated without gravity.

Sweet's hands were at her shoulders, his strength fading as he tried one last time to pull her down with him. He'd stopped thrashing but that only made Trina clench down harder on his throat. She held him under until the last of the air escaped from his mouth, and his body went limp. His dead eye stared up at her, wide and milky-white. When she finally let him go, she saw that he was smiling.

Trina looked for Colin, but Colin was gone. The water rose above her head, and she let it take her. It drew her down and down until she became one with the cold and the deep, until she no longer knew where she stopped and the water began. Everything she was sank away, all identity, all memory, until there was nothing left of her at all, until

27

Two lights blossomed out of the endless darkness, two lights that seemed to illuminate an entire world. Clouds had turned the midday sky a pale steel-gray. Great splats of icy rain fell against the windshield, and the lights became starbursts. They turned everything ahead into a kaleidoscope that the wipers could not sweep away.

The lights were closer now, and getting nearer with every instant. They were too close, and drifting across the centerline of the two-lane road. Trina pulled hard on the wheel and felt her tires start to slide. The wipers swept out an arc, and for an instant she could see the driver of the other car, his arms stiff, face frozen as if she were seeing him in a photograph.

Trina turned the wheel again but the car would not follow. It slid sideways, tires spinning uselessly. Her brakes failed. Everything slowed as pavement gave way to snow-covered grass that sloped down and down, toward the concrete embankment and the sharp drop to the river below. She had time to wonder why there had been no guardrail, time to notice the jogger out running with her dog on the riverwalk below. The car would miss them both, she remembered even as it was happening, but it would not stop at the water's edge.

A sharp cry came from the back seat, another memory snapping into place, as the tires slid along the embankment and out over open air. The car tilted forward, like a roller-coaster about to drop, and all Trina could see through the windshield was a vast sheet of ice. It filled her vision, coming closer and closer, until at last the wall shattered and everything went dark. Her body jerked against the seat belt and her face hit the steering wheel. She heard the cry from the back seat once more, but the darkness closed over her before she could turn to find it.

···•·•···

She came to with a start. Her breath clouded the windshield as she pulled in great gulps of air, like a fish stranded at the edge of a pond. The icy cold of the water had brought her around. It was up to her knees and rising fast. There was blood on her face, blood in her eyes, and from the way her hair hung down she could tell that the seatbelt was the only thing keeping her in her seat. With trembling fingers, she felt for the latch. It clicked open, and she fell against the steering wheel. She cried out, because something in her chest was broken. She could feel it grinding with every motion she made. Still, she tried to turn around, had to turn around, because the child in the back seat was screaming.

The little boy sat red-faced, his arms stretched out to her, his eyes full of tears. The booster seat had held him with its straps still tight against his chest. He howled again, and the anguish in that sound was enough to get her moving. The water was at her waist now. She tried the door, but it wouldn't budge. Water sloshed outside the window, chunks of ice bobbing against the glass as the car sank deeper.

She shifted her weight as she tried to climb into the back seat. The car tilted. Her wet shoes slipped, and fresh waves of pain shot through her chest like lightning as she slid back down. The boy was above her now. She could feel his hot tears as they fell against her face. She reached for him again, but her wet fingers could not undo the plastic buckle at his chest.

The water was all around her now, and the cold of it made each breath feel as if her lungs were bound with iron bands. Already the car was growing dark, and darker still as the water closed over the top of it. Trina reached up again as the cold crept its way along her neck. As the water covered her ears, she heard the child's muffled cry. She reached out once more, straining, her shoulder popping. Her fingers were numb, and they only brushed against the buckle. The water rose over her head, and enfolded her in darkness.

She kicked against the dashboard, and the water buoyed her up enough that this time she caught the buckle in her hand. The water hadn't reached the child, not yet. That meant there was still time.

She fumbled, trying to squeeze the buckle open, but her fingers were too numb to move. She tried to pull herself up to get a breath, but her foot was caught on something and she could not shake it free. Her lungs ached for air. The buckle slipped from her hand, and she no longer knew which way was up. Panic took her like a sapling in a windstorm. She pounded against the glass. She threw her shoulder at the door. All thought had been shoved aside, all memory. She forgot about the boy. She forgot her own name. There was only the water, and the water was endless.

At last, the door gave way with a distant thunk, and she was floating. She rose in the darkness, dimly aware of something important falling away beneath her. Something precious. It rang in her mind like an alarm bell. She was going up, but she needed to go down. She couldn't remember why. She only knew it was important, that it was the Most Important Thing. If only the memory of it could push past the ache in her limbs, past the pain in her chest that threatened to consume her.

She was almost to the surface now. The light above was growing brighter. It glinted off the bumper of the car below, so close, so impossibly far. She kicked toward that surface. One breath. One breath was all she needed, and she could go back down. There was air in the back of the car still. It wasn't too late. She had time enough for one breath.

She kicked again and her head struck something solid. She pressed her hands to it but it would not move. Snow swirled above her. Through it she could see the concrete edge of the river bank, and the silhouettes that had begun to gather there. The sheet of ice had made their edges fuzzy and indistinct, but she could still make out their shapes. A tall man. A girl with a high ponytail and her lanky boyfriend. A hunched old woman with a child. A slender woman and her dog.

Trina tried to call out to them, but she had no air in her lungs, no strength in her left to pound against the ice. She looked down but she couldn't see the car anymore. A realization came to her then, colder than the ice, colder than the water around her. She would die here. Both of them would die here, and there was nothing she could do to stop it.

On the riverbank, seven figures in silhouette were watching her through the ice, watching her die. She closed her eyes and remembered a kindly old man. The memory was so clear that she could see his face as if he was right there beside her. He knelt with her next to a cluster of flowers, and the flowers were white.

Think of the flowers, he said. *Hold them in your mind and let them be any color you want them to be.*

She felt her body go limp, felt herself float and flatten against the ice until her body melted away to nothing and there was only the cold. Until she could feel nothing at all.

Hold them in your mind, the old man said, *and know that the color you want them to be is the color they have always been.*

Her body was gone. She could no longer feel it. There was only the cold, the distant murmur of shouts somewhere beyond the ice, the lapping sound of the water. There was only the car, sinking into the deep. There was only the child inside it, frightened and alone.

Trina wanted to go back for him. She wished that she still had arms so she could gather him up and take him somewhere far away from here, somewhere where it wasn't so cold, where they could kneel by the flowers the way she had knelt there with her grandfather, where together they could feel the warmth of the sun on their faces and see those flowers the way the flowers had always been. She thought of these things until she could no longer think, until there was nothing left of her to float in that inky darkness.

And the world turned blue.

28

Trina bolted upright and coughed the icy water from her lungs. It fell onto the hot ground with a hiss and disappeared down the cracks in the dry earth. The sun was high and already she could feel it driving the cold from her wet skin, from her sodden clothes. They weren't the clothes she remembered, the worn jeans, the gray t-shirt that Edie had given her at the base, back when Edie had been alive. She looked down at the waterlogged wool coat, at the sweater with the red stripe across the middle, and wondered who this person was who had dressed herself this way.

She left the coat at the side of the long blacktop road. She had the vague idea that she might need it when the night came, but she didn't feel strong enough to carry it. A mile later she left the sweater too, grateful for the t-shirt underneath. She liked to dress in layers, this person that Trina had been. With each layer she left behind, she felt farther away from that woman in the car. But that child in the back seat was closer than ever.

She walked down the center of the dusty blacktop, careful to keep her feet on the cracked and faded yellow line. Putting one foot in front of the other left no room for remembering. It left no room for any of the swirling thoughts that threatened to rise up and finally unravel her once and for all.

On the horizon, the great hulls of crashed airships showed their rounded backs to the sun. Their coverings flapped in the wind and their metal ribs poked skyward like the bones of a bleached whale, left to rot, forgotten. She didn't allow herself to look too long, or think about how they had gotten there. She didn't let herself wonder why she was the only one on the road, because she already knew the answer.

Her boots were dry by the time she came to the boat. It sat listing in the sand at a fork in the road. The tall mast leaned out over the pavement, and a rusted cage swayed beneath it like a traffic light. The cage looked like it had been bent out of a piece of wrought-iron fence and held together with chains. Inside it was a skeleton, its hands still wrapped around the bars, its bones bleached white. The side of its skull was capped in black metal. From the depths of one eye socket glowed a bright red light.

There was no mistaking which boat it was. The door had fallen off of the wheelhouse, but its side was still crumpled where it had struck the water tower. Years of rust had opened a great mouth in its side that seemed to sneer at her as she drew closer. Its stern was buried in the sand but she knew that Edie's name would still be written on the transom. Trina didn't look too long at the skeleton for fear that she might find something familiar in the bones of its face. The red eye clicked in its socket and moved to track her as she passed by.

The desert went on in all directions, so vast and so featureless that she could hardly be sure she was getting anywhere at all. And yet, here and there, she passed waypoints sticking out of the sand. The wheel of a carriage. A half-buried hover taxi. The rear end of a bus rising skyward, rusted hollow like an enormous empty beer can. She didn't need to wonder how they had gotten there. She had made this place as surely as she had made the others. Only, this one, she had made for herself.

This was her reality now. She would live whatever days she had left under the scorching sun. Her throat was dry, and it struck her that not long ago she'd been drowning. One reality had been subsumed by another. This one was as real as the next, and it meant no more than any of the others. The car and the ice had been just another Turning, another construction from the wilds of her subconscious mind, and there would never be another one. She told herself this over and over with every step she took, and still she could not convince herself that it was true.

She didn't notice the town until she was almost upon it. It sat in a low spot in the road, its outlines shimmering and indistinct in the midday heat, so small that she could see from one end of it to the next. As she approached, the wind sent a spray of dry weeds skipping across the road. They gathered at the bases of rusted-out trailers and sprouted from the grilles of abandoned military trucks that lay crooked and broken, as if they had fallen from the sky.

Wooden fences leaned away from the empty shells of broken houses where abandoned cars sat on rotted tires in overgrown driveways. As she shuffled along the cracked sidewalks, Trina could feel eyes at her back. Someone was watching her from behind the crumbling walls and beneath the tented remains of collapsed roofs. When she turned around, she heard the scattering of dust even when there was no breeze.

There was a little motel at the crossroads. She'd been there before, but she couldn't remember when. She squinted up at the rusted sign, but its painted letters were so cracked and faded that she could not make out the name. The words NO VACANCY were spelled out in white lettering streaked with rust and grime. The neon glass had broken away from the first two letters, but the rest still stood out in dusty loops, as if they were only waiting for the power to come back on.

The diner across the street had wide windows with rounded corners. Beside it sat a little gas station. An awning had fallen away from a set of oddly-shaped pumps, and it left them looking like tombstones leaning against a graveyard fence. The door to the diner swung lazily in the wind, but it was dark inside and she couldn't see anything beyond the threshold. Again, she had the sense of being watched, and wondered for a moment who might be waiting for her inside.

The place was empty. Trina realized that, deep down, she had known it would be. It was in better shape than the outside would have suggested, without so much as a tear in the seat of a barstool or a single dent in the stainless-steel countertop. None of the windows were broken. Apart from a layer of dust and some weeds gathered in the doorway, the place was perfectly preserved, like something out of a museum, like something out of a memory.

The vinyl booth squeaked beneath her as she sat down. The air was cool, and she noticed a noticed a ceiling fan spinning lazily above the counter. She listened to the steady hum of its electric motor and wondered where the power was coming from. She wondered if it might just keep going, on and on, until the end of this world, this last world. There would be no others. She had accomplished that much, at least. The world had already ended. The fan had just forgotten.

There was a button on the table, a big, red plastic thing set into a square plate of stainless steel with the words CALL FOR SERVICE painted in a looping yellow script. Trina looked at it for a long time before she pushed the button. At once there came a loud crash from the other side of the kitchen door, followed by the high-pitched whirr of electric motors. The door burst open, and in rolled a shiny steel robot. It was balanced on its single wheel like a unicyclist, and wobbled from side to side, steadying itself with its spindly arms. It rocked to a halt next to Trina's booth and held up a yellowed notepad to take her order, though it had no pen to write with.

"Well, hi there, Sweetie. Hot one out there today, ain't it? Now, what can I get for ya?"

The words were distant and tinny, and they came from a slotted speaker in the thing's tarnished chest, because it had no head and no mouth. Still, there was no mistaking the voice. It was light and welcoming, a voice she had thought that she would never hear again.

There was a plaque bolted next to the speaker. The lettering was faded, but she could still make it out.

**Electronic Diner Interaction Expert
Model 8311D
Inverness Ambitronics, Ltd.
Rockford, Illinois**

"We got coffee, iced tea, lemonade. There's a mean pot pie on the dinner menu tonight. Fresh mushrooms. Cook brings 'em in spe—."

The contraption froze, and Trina stared at it for a moment, wondering if maybe its ancient mechanisms had strained too far and given way. The voice had caught her off guard. As she sat, watching the thing in silence, she could almost convince herself that she'd only imagined it.

"You need a minute, hun? I can see to some of the other customers and come back when you're ready." The thing tapped its metal finger against the notepad, as if to hurry her along.

"I... No, um... Just, could I have a glass of water, please?"

The voice from the speaker let out a derisive little huff as the machine went through the motions of making a note on the pad with the pen that wasn't there. Motors whirred as the contraption made a show of turning around and teetering its way back into the kitchen. It returned a moment later with a little glass clutched in its hand. It was dusty and there was no water in it.

"Anything else I can get for you, hun?" The robot drew up its arms and put its hands on its sides, right where a person's hips would be. "I don't mean to chase you off, sweetie, but if you don't mean to order, we could sure use the table back for the lunch rush."

"No. Um...thank you," Trina said. The robot turned away with a dismissive air and began to trundle back toward the kitchen. "Wait, I..."

The robot wheeled back. "Yeah, sweetie?"

"Do you know about, you know, other stuff? Can you tell me about this place?"

"You talking 'bout the diner or the town?"

"The town."

"Well, sure, darlin'." The machine leaned in conspiratorially, and when it spoke again, it was in a whisper. "I know just about everyone in this place, comin' or goin'. Could tell you some stories too, believe you me. If you get caught repeatin' it though, you didn't hear it from me. I have to keep up my reputation, after all."

"I'm looking for someone," Trina said. "A man. His name's Colin Williams."

The thing straightened and raised one hand to stroke a chin that wasn't there. Motors whirred behind the slotted speaker. "Can't say I've heard the name," it said. "Had a salesman come through a ways back by the name of Walton. Tried to sell us a contraption for puttin' foam on coffee. Can you imagine? 'Course, this is goin' on eighty, ninety years ago, so I don't believe he's the one you're lookin' for."

"What about a place? Ms. Dixon's Home for the Dispossessed? Have you heard of it?"

Again, the motors spun, but only for a moment before something sprung loose inside the thing with a sound like a snapping guitar string. Its arms froze in their places and the machine tilted sideways a little before the rest of it froze too. Trina stared at the speaker in its chest for a long time before she finally got up to leave.

29

They were waiting for her outside the diner, eight figures, clad all in black. They had arranged themselves in a row near the fallen awning and the gas pumps. The tallest of them stood at their center, one spindly hand resting on the shoulder of the one next to him, who was small enough to be a child. They all wore black hats on their heads and long gloves on their hands, and there were black masks over their faces that jutted out like the beaks of giant crows. A black dog, as big as a mastiff, lay panting in the dust. It wore its own pointed mask, this one a muzzle woven out of twigs and wire.

Trina watched them from the doorway. Their outlines didn't shimmer, and when the wind blew it tugged the edges of their long black coats. They did not approach her. They did not move at all, but only stared at her from behind the holes in their masks, like carrion birds waiting for their meal to die.

"Well, go on then," Trina said at last. "If you're here for me, then just get on with it."

The only answer was the wind. Trina found strength in the silence, and the longer it passed, the taller she stood. These people—if they were people—had no hold over her. There was nothing more that they could do to hurt her. The longer they stood watching her, the more she realized that it was because they were the ones who were afraid. They had finally revealed themselves to her, and still they had to wear masks.

"I'm not running. So, if you think I've got something else you can take from me, then go right ahead."

The Tall Man looked down at the Crone, who stood at his opposite side. The beak of her mask tilted up to him in answer. Then, as if with one mind, they all turned their heads toward the figure at the end of their line. He stood apart from the others. His shoulders were slumped in submission, his mask a flattened cage of woven twigs that hid his features. His hat drooped where the others were crisp, and his gloves seemed too big for his hands.

He shuffled forward. Trina's first instinct was to back away, but she held her ground. She could see that she no longer had anything to fear from this man. His hands were empty, and he dragged one leg behind him, kicking up dust as he drew closer.

He stopped just out of arm's reach, as if he were waiting to see what Trina might do. She only crossed her arms over her chest and narrowed her eyes. She didn't want to look at him, but she would not let herself turn away.

After a moment, he straightened himself and reached a gloved hand inside his long coat. It emerged holding something black, something that glinted in the sun. He knelt down, moving slowly, as if every moment caused him pain, and set the shining rectangle upon the ground.

It was a phone. It was *her* phone. She'd given it up for lost in that flooded basement beneath Ms. Dixon's home, in that place where Sweet had strapped her down and held an ice pick to her eye. It seemed so long ago. He'd worn a different mask then, but she knew him all the same.

He took his time standing up. Trina could feel him staring at her, but whether he was expecting a question or a thank you or something else entirely, she could not tell. She offered him none of those things, and after a time he turned away without a word. As he did, Trina saw the burned skin, the puckered scars peeking out beneath the edges of the mask, and almost felt sorry for him.

He took his place in line, but the others had already turned away. They walked single file to the road, their heads down, as if they were marching to a funeral. Trina stood in the doorway of the diner and watched them go. They crested a small rise and disappeared into the shimmer of heat rising up from the baking asphalt.

Trina stared at the phone for a long time. There was nothing distinguishing about it, but she knew absolutely that it was hers. It was the last artifact of the life she had lived before this one, her *real* life, before the Turnings, before the car and the river, and the rest of it. She had thought that it was gone forever. Now that it had returned to her, she could almost dare to hope that everything else she'd lost could return as well. But she couldn't bring herself to cross the dust to pick it up. If that hope was a lie, she did not want it.

A muffled buzzing cut through the silence, and a tiny cloud of dust rose up around the little glass rectangle. The phone buzzed again, and as it vibrated in the dirt its screen began to glow. Trina dove for it and scooped it up. It buzzed once more as she stared at it, dumbstruck. On the screen was a name she had forgotten until now. The caller was there on the other end of the line. All she had to do was answer.

She touched the name with her finger and brought the phone to her ear. There was no one there. The screen had gone black. She pressed it again and again, but the name was gone. The phone was dead.

· · · · ● ● · ● ● · ·

Trina fell to her knees in the dirt and felt the heat begin to rise in her cheeks. Of all the tricks that had been played upon her, of all the tricks she had played on herself, this one seemed the most cruel. She'd been given a key that she couldn't turn. She'd been thrown a lifeline that could never be grasped. She'd made her own Hell, and as she knelt in the dirt with hot tears running down her face, she wanted a way out of it.

The door to the diner opened with a hollow bang, and the little serving robot trundled out into the sun. It wheeled past her without a word, bouncing along the cracked pavement toward the fallen awning as if she wasn't even there. It stopped alongside one of the narrow pumps, reached out with its spindly arm and found a sagging black cord. With practiced ease, it plugged the end of the cord into its undercarriage before it slumped forward and grew still.

Trina looked over the gas pumps again and realized that they weren't gas pumps at all. There were six of them, and at least three of them were broken, their painted-metal cowlings dented, their innards rusted through. The one next to the robot was almost intact, and sported an unruly tangle of cords, at least two dozen of them. Most were just frayed and broken wires, but a few sported connectors, each of a different shape and width. She tested each one to see if any of them would fit her phone. None of them did.

She squeezed her fist and bit down on her tongue until the pain brought tears to her eyes. She was close. So close. The key was in her hand. She only had to allow herself to use it. She closed her eyes and breathed deep. The air tasted of smoke and metal. When she opened her eyes, she searched through the cords again. There, hidden behind the rest, was one that she had missed. When she pushed it into the bottom of her phone, it connected with a satisfying snap.

The phone lit up immediately, and Trina watched the battery indicator work its way up to full in the space of a few seconds. There were two alerts on the screen. One was a voicemail, the other a text message. When she thumbed the screen, the phone unlocked, and she paused when she saw the picture beneath all the icons. It was a picture of a little boy.

He was squinting against the sun. There was grass beneath his feet and trees in the distance, and he was smiling. It was the boy she had left to drown in the sinking car. His eyes were blue, shot through with greens and browns. They seemed to be looking right at her. Her heart clenched, for she could not bear to look back at him, and yet she could not bear to look away. Looking away felt like losing him all over again.

When she finally forced herself to click on the message icon, there was only a single line of text, along with an address. She found a brittle old phone book under the register in the diner with a map on the inside of its cover. She tore it off and used it to get her bearings before she started walking. The voicemail, she decided, would keep until she got there.

30

The map led her to a vacant lot bordered by the remnants of a chain link fence. The ground there was stony, and had given rise to tall stalks of thistle and knee-high patches of tufted grass. Trina checked the map again. She'd followed what street signs were left, checked her movements against the angles and directions on the torn sheet of paper. There was no doubt that she'd come to the right place, but the place was crumbled and gone.

Three narrow stone steps jutted up from a weed-choked walkway, but there were no wooden doors at their summit, no balcony of wrought iron. Those steps were all that was left of the hospital, of the military base, of the old hotel. They were all that was left of Ms. Dixon's Home for the Dispossessed. It was the last cruel joke in a long series of cruel jokes that it should be denied to her, here, at the end, when she finally understood everything except why she kept coming to this place.

She sat in the dirt and pulled weeds from the ground. In the distance she could see the outline of a building that might have been a courthouse, though its dome had long-since collapsed and gone to rust inside its crumpled walls. There was no gallows there, no sign at all that anyone still lived in this world. A bookstore stood on one side of the street. There was a broken cart leaning next to its faded green door, and all its windows were smashed in. Someone had scrawled graffiti across its brick face, but the letters were too faded to read. Whoever had written them must have died a long time ago, assuming that someone had written them at all. And yet, she could not shake the feeling that there were still eyes out there, watching her from every shaded corner, from behind every broken window.

Next to the bookstore was a movie theater. The light bulbs in the marquee were all broken out, but a yellowed letter T still clung crookedly to its mounting wires. She wondered how long it had been since the last film had been shown there. She pictured the little boy from the tintype photograph, young Woods sitting in the front row, staring up at the screen with his eyes wide open. Had that little boy ever lived in this place? She wanted to believe that he had, that he had lived a long life all the way to a peaceful end, long before this world rotted away.

Trina looked at her phone and thought again about playing the voicemail. She let her finger hover over the icon for a full minute before she finally put the phone back in her pocket. It wasn't that she knew for sure what the message would say. It was only that she feared what it might be. She didn't think that she could bear to hear the child's voice again. If this Hell was of her own making, then surely all she would find on that message was the sound of a little boy screaming.

After a while, she got up and walked the edges of the lot. She watched the ground, taking care to avoid the great clumps of sticker-seeds and the tall, thorny thistles that grew almost as tall as she was. Grasshoppers, some as long as her hand, scattered before her feet, flinging themselves into the air, only to drift back down on fluttering wings.

She traced the edges of the foundation, and as she walked, she could just about picture where the walls should have been. If she closed her eyes, she could see the curving staircase and the front desk where Edie had first smiled at her. She could see the overstuffed chair where Colin had sat waiting. She saw these things when she closed her eyes, but no matter how hard she tried, when she opened them again, all that was there was dirt and weeds.

Her shadow had grown long before she finally gave up. The sun was setting and soon it would start to get cold. She was hungry, and she wondered if there was any food left in that old diner, something in a can tucked away somewhere the little robot could not reach. Out beyond the movie theater, the eight figures in black stood at the crest in the road. They had been there, watching her, since she stared pacing, but whether they were expecting something from her or were merely curious, she could not tell.

Trina stared back at them, waiting for them to do something, to do anything but watch over her like vultures waiting on a wounded animal. Her hand went to her pocket and absently traced the edges of her phone. Maybe they weren't just waiting but trying to tell her something. Maybe they were here because they already knew that she was exactly where she was meant to be.

She closed her eyes and breathed deep, and as she breathed she caught the smell of the place again, all metal and rot and dust. If she had really made this world, then there had to be more to it than this, more reason for it than this. She pulled the phone from her pocket. If this truly was the end for her, if this truly was the last place at the end of the last Turning, then she would make the last decision she had left. She stood with her face to the setting sun, swallowed her fear, and made her choice.

····•••••··

The phone crackled as Trina held it to her ear and heard the faraway sound of static, of wind blowing against the speaker. When the voice finally spoke, it was distant and tinny, as she were hearing a recording of an old phonograph record. And yet, the voice itself was clear and strong, and the sound of it hit her like a punch to the heart.

It's all right, her grandfather said. *If it was easy, then everyone would do it. The key is in the knowing, you see? If you think you are changing the flower, then of course you will fail. Who could do such a thing? But if you hold that flower in your mind and know in your heart that the way you see it is the only way it could ever have been, then that is exactly what it will be.*

Her lip trembled and hot tears rolled down her cheeks. She remembered his face now. When she closed her eyes, she could see him smiling down at her. This was the last thing he had said to her, on that day before he died. She knew the rest, and mouthed the words along with him.

You're not changing it into something new. You're only remembering it the way it always was.

A distant voice called out in the background. They'd been summoned to dinner, she remembered, and her grandfather had taken her by the hand as they walked back to the house. They'd found him dead in his room the next morning. She'd spent all that day crying next to the flowers, begging them to change, begging her grandfather to come back to her, but in the end the flowers were still white, and her grandfather was still gone.

The recording hissed, then stopped, but Trina did not open her eyes. She knelt on the ground and listened to the buzzing of the grasshoppers in the weeds, the slow ticking of gravel being blown by the wind. It hadn't always been that way. This place was new and it was not right. If it wasn't right, all she had to do was remember it the way that it was. All she had to do was remember it the way it always had been.

She folded her hands in her lap and breathed deep. The air was wrong too, with its smell of rust undershot with burning oil. She knew what it should smell like. Neatly potted plants, carnations and day lilies. The air, cool and clean drifting out from beyond the lobby doors. She breathed again and could almost smell it, this scent she had thought lost forever, this place she thought she would never see again. How strange that she should think that, because the place was never lost. It had always been right here.

The wind had changed and the air told her everything she needed to know. When at last she opened her eyes again, she was not surprised. Still, she smiled as she saw the stone steps leading up to the double doors, the columns flanking the entrance of the stone and brick building looming, impossibly and inevitably, above her. She stepped off the sidewalk, and there was grass beneath her feet, green and alive and wet with dew.

She ran up the steps but paused in the doorway to look back up the street. The windows weren't broken, because they had never been broken, and the lights in the theater marquee had just begun to shine. The sidewalks were empty and the blacktop was new, and at the end of it, the eight figures in black still stood. She watched them as they turned away, moving in unison as they shuffled out of sight. The last of them paused a moment to look at her once more. When he turned away, his head was bowed as if the weight of the cage on his head was dragging him down. Then he too was gone.

31

S he found Colin sitting in the same overstuffed green armchair where she'd left him when they'd first come to this place. His knees were pulled up to his chest and his head hung low between them. Her footsteps clipped against the checkered marble floor as she went to him, and as she drew close she could hear him muttering softly to himself. She knelt beside to him and put her hand on his shoulder. He lifted his head and as he looked up at her, recognition dawned on his face.

"The water," he whispered. "We were sinking."

"It's all right," she told him. "We're safe now."

She took his hands in her own. They were cold and they were trembling, but as she rubbed her warmth into them, he sat up a little straighter, relaxing by degrees.

"You left me."

"I know," she said, and felt fresh tears making tracks down her cheeks. "But I'm here now, and I'll never leave you again."

She crawled into his lap and cradled his head against her shoulder. He stared up at her, recognition giving way to something like wonder. "I was so frightened," he said.

"So was I," she said.

She smoothed down his hair. His eyes were deep pools of blue, flecked with color like tiny stars, and they tracked her every movement as if he was afraid she might disappear if he looked away.

"Small room," he said quietly, like a child drifting off to sleep. "Pink rock."

She laughed, and as she laughed a tear fell onto his forehead. "Ugly lamp," she said as she wiped it away. "Flower blanket."

"I waited for you," he said. "I waited for you so long. I forgot. I forgot all about you. I forgot everything. Can you forgive me?"

She tried to answer, but could not speak for the lump in her throat. "It was my fault," she said. "I got scared and I did everything wrong. But I'm not scared anymore. I know how to fix it."

He smiled at this, but it was a distant smile, a sad smile, and in it she could see that he was slipping away from her. She could see that she might lose him all over again.

"Do you want me to fix it?"

He nodded. It was the nod of someone half asleep, who had no interest in waking.

"Everything will change," she said softly. "It'll be just like starting over. But I'll do it better this time. I'll get it right."

She held his hand. His knuckles were bony, his skin paper-thin over bulging veins. She smoothed the wrinkles beneath her thumbs until he looked up at her again. There was trust in his eyes, more trust than she deserved, but she knew all the same that he understood.

"All right, then," she said. "Close your eyes."

32

She came to with a start as she pulled in great gulps of air, like a child newly born. Her breath frosted the air. The icy water was up to her knees, and rising fast. There was blood on her face, blood in her eyes, and as her hair hung down she remembered that the seatbelt was the only thing keeping her in her seat. She felt for the latch, her fingers already numb from the cold. It clicked open, and she caught herself against the steering wheel. She put a hand to her chest. Nothing was broken this time, because it had never been broken. Still, she knew she had to work fast, because the child in the back seat was screaming.

"It's okay, sweetie," she said as she turned to face the boy. "It's okay." He sat red-faced, his arms outstretched and his eyes full of tears. The booster seat held him with its straps still tight against his chest. He cried out again, but she was already moving.

The water was at her waist now. She didn't bother with the door, because she knew it wouldn't budge. She ignored the water sloshing against the glass, the chunks of ice bobbing as they followed the sinking car down.

The car tilted when she shifted her weight, but she was prepared for it. She planted her feet, and was careful not to let them slip as she climbed into the back seat. She braced herself and squeezed down on the buckle. It came loose, just as she had known it would, and the boy fell into her arms. She pressed his face against hers and felt his hot tears on her cheek as his breathing slowed and his crying ebbed away. He clung to her with all four limbs, squeezing her tight. Already it was growing dark inside the car, and darker still as the water rose over it. They did not have much time.

"Okay, listen to me," she said as she took the boy's face in her hands. "I know this is scary, but we're going to be okay."

He looked back at her, his blue eyes wide and rimmed with red, searching her face to see if it was true. But it was true. She knew it down deep, as if it had been written in her very bones.

"You're stuck with me, right? I'm not going anywhere."

The boy nodded. She kissed him on the head and held him tight against her body. "Okay. The water's getting higher, so it's going to get really cold in a couple seconds." In fact, the water was already up around her hips, and the bottoms of the boy's pants were soaked through. "So we're just going to have to be brave, all right?"

She felt the boy nod as he started to shiver. She held him tighter, and as she did, his fear became her own. In that fear she felt an instant of doubt, and she squeezed her eyes shut to push it away before it could take hold.

"Now, when I say go, we're going to take a big deep breath. And we're going to hold it as long as we can. And I want you to look at me, okay? I want you to keep your eyes on me and don't look away. Can you do that for me?"

Again, the boy nodded. The water was up to their chests now, and his chin was beginning to tremble. She felt beneath the water for the door latch as the water rose around their throats.

"Are you ready?"

The boy didn't nod this time. He didn't speak, but she saw the trust in his deep blue eyes, and she saw the love there, too. It made a warmth in her that not even the cold of the water could draw away.

"Okay," she said. "Go."

They rose in darkness. She watched his face, only dimly aware of the car falling away beneath them. He held his eyes on hers as she kicked, his cheeks puffed, his body shaking. She tried to tell him without speaking not to be afraid, that she would protect him, that she would not lose him again.

They were almost to the surface now. She could see the light above growing brighter. She thought of the ice above her head, but it did not worry her. It would not stop her, because she knew it could not stop her. Bubbles rose from the child's mouth. He thrashed and went limp in her arms, but she did not fear. The ice at the surface was thin and they would break through it at any moment. She would shake him awake and he would cough the water from his lungs and he would breathe. Just one breath and everything would be just as it was meant to be.

33

They made a chain with their bodies, descending the slippery boat ramp hand in hand, spreading out across the cracking ice. The girl with the high ponytail reached out and took Trina by her flailing hand. Her fuzzy boots slipped and the teenage kid with the long hair steadied her as they pulled.

Trina let them draw her across the ice and up the ramp. The whole way, she clutched the child to her chest. He was cold and he wasn't moving, but she knew that he would be all right. They had come all this way, and this world had not been made to destroy them.

As they slid onto the snowy ground, she turned the boy on his side and pressed at his chest until the water drained from his lungs. The people stood in a circle around them. As she worked the boy's arms the big dog crouched low and whimpered. When at last the boy began to cough, the hunched old woman crossed herself and the little kid behind her pumped his fist in the air.

They closed in around Trina and the boy and covered them with their coats. Smiling with relief, they rubbed the warmth back into their arms as they led her to a park bench, where she sat with the boy pressed against her chest until his crying ebbed away. The tallest of them sat next to her and held her hand as the wide brim of his hat shielded them from the snow.

When the ambulance came with its flashing lights, they sat on its bumper with heavy blankets around their shoulders and chemical heating packs in their laps. The men in their uniforms shined flashlights in their eyes and made them both count backward from twenty, checking off boxes on their clipboards as they went. She told them that they were fine, both of them, and she smiled because she knew it was true.

She watched the tall man in the hat, silhouetted in red, then blue, talking to the police, talking with his hands and pointing to the bridge as he told his story. The woman with the dog had already left. So had the kid and the old woman, the pretty girl with the high ponytail and her boyfriend. She hadn't even had a chance to thank them.

She answered all the questions, then answered them again at the hospital. Doctors felt along their bones and nurses took their blood. They found the old scars on her arms, found the old bruises on the boy's ribs. They asked her more questions then, and she answered them all because she remembered it all. The boy slept against her side as she spoke. She held him close and smoothed his hair, and listened to the gentle rhythm of his breathing.

An hour later, when the social workers came, they took the boy into another room. He didn't want to go, but Trina looked him in the eyes and told him that it would be okay. He looked at her for a long time before he believed it, and though she could see the fear in his eyes, he did not cry. By the time they brought him back, she had told them about the other car and the ice on the bridge. She told them why they'd been on the road in the first place.

She told them about the bruises and the scars, but she did not tell them the rest. Already, the memories of all those fractured worlds were starting to fade. There was only this world, just as it had always been.

When they brought the boy back, he had a small teddy bear tucked under his arm. Everything she'd packed for him—his pajamas, his changes of clothes, his little toy cars—were at the bottom of the river with all the rest. Her backpack was down there too, with her phone tucked into the outside pocket. She didn't think she'd ever miss it.

There was a smile on the boy's face now, but his eyes were tired. He clambered up into her lap, and the warmth of his body against hers made Trina feel tired, too. The social worker watched the two of them for a few minutes and asked her if they had some place to stay.

Trina nodded, and told her the address.

· · • • • ؛ • • · · ·

They rode in the back of a police car with the lights off. The boy slept the whole way with his head in her lap, lulled by the rhythmic thumping of the wipers as they swept away the wet splats of late-spring snow that splashed against the windshield. Trina didn't speak to the officer in the front seat, nor did she say any more to the social worker who sat next to them with her hands folded in her lap. They were all out of questions, and now that they were, they seemed as eager as Trina was to move on.

The lights of the red brick and limestone building were on when the car pulled up to the curb. The curtains were open and she could see into the lobby through the narrow windows, all the way to the long wooden counter and the first steps of the winding staircase. She didn't know how late it was, but she imagined that the place was always lit up this way at night, with bright sconces flanking the doors that threw the shadow of the wrought-iron balcony all the way up to the wide cornice of its roof. Like a beacon. Like a lighthouse in a storm.

She held the boy's hand as they climbed the freshly-salted steps. The door opened almost as soon as she knocked, as if it too had been waiting for them. A tall woman in a plain green dress was there to usher them inside. She waved to the social worker and the policeman on the sidewalk. They waved back and smiled in a knowing way that told Trina they had been there before, and would be back again.

The woman took Trina by the hand and led her to an overstuffed green armchair. She sat down and let herself sink into the cushions as the boy clambered up to sit by her side. The woman was thin and regal, with her red hair pulled back in a no-nonsense bun. She balanced herself on her black heels as she crouched down next to the armchair. Her expression was warm, her smile pleasant and inviting.

"I'm Trina," Trina said, her arm protective around the boy. "Well, Katrina. Katrina Bellamy."

"I know. We've been expecting you." The woman held out her hand. "I'm Edie. It's nice to meet you, Katrina Bellamy."

Trina took her hand and marveled at the sound of her own name, her whole name, the one she'd forgotten for so long. She'd heard it from the mouths of the medics, from the police officers who'd spoken to her back at the river, but it hadn't seemed real until this moment. Hearing it now felt like planting a flag in new soil, knowing that it had belonged to her all along.

"And who might this be?"

"I'm Colin," the boy said. His voice was eager now, and it seemed to explode out of him like a shaken bottle that couldn't help but burst. Katrina remembered that it had always been that way, and hearing it now was like the sun breaking through after a rainstorm.

The woman held out her hand for Colin to shake. "I'm very pleased to meet you, Colin."

The little boy shook her hand, his ordeal nearly forgotten, his face solemn and serious beyond his years. "Are we going to live here now?"

"Well, that's something your mother and I need to talk about, but you're both welcome to stay here as long as you like."

Her eyes were on Trina, taking stock, asking permission. Trina smiled back at her and ran a hand through Colin's hair. "What do you say, kiddo? Do you want to stay a while?"

"Do you have books?"

Edie leaned in close, as if she were sharing a secret. "Oh, yes. We have lots of books. A whole room full of them, in fact, along with a few children who are just about your age."

"I packed all my books in my suitcase," he said, almost absently. "But my suitcase got drowned."

Edie flicked her gaze to Trina, who nodded solemnly.

"I almost got drowned, too. But Mommy saved me."

Trina had to look away, then. A tear spilled down her cheek as she kissed the top of his head. Edie watched them both, giving them room, allowing the moment to be theirs alone.

"It sounds like your mommy is very brave." She said at last. Colin nodded. He fell back against his mother and pulled her arms around him like a blanket. He was tired. Trina was tired, too, but now, at long last, she thought she might be able to rest.

"Come with me," Edie said, and took her by the hand. "I'll give you the tour."

34

The room Edie led her to was the same one where the two of them had sat together in that other world where the smoke from coal fires belched up around electrical wires and airships floated like great whales across the sky. The dark wood trim was a little more faded than she remembered, and the wallpaper was gone in favor of deep green paint, but it still felt the same. It still felt like home.

Two of the other girls brought in a little bed for Colin and set it up near the bathroom door. It would have fit better at the foot of the bed with the tall wooden posts, but the girls seemed to know that Trina would want to be able to see the boy from where she slept. They showed her how to lock her door from the inside, and took pains to tell her that Edie was the only one with the key. They told her when breakfast could be gotten in the morning, and offered them sandwiches in case they were hungry. Trina shook her head and thanked them again, and didn't bother locking the door behind them when they'd gone.

Colin was asleep on her shoulder. Trina lowered him onto the big bed and curled in beside him. Their clothes were dry, but they still smelled of river water. There would be time enough to clean up in the morning. For now, it was enough that she could hold her son, that he was safe now, after all of it. She watched his chest rise and fall, and as she drew her fingers through his hair, she tried to picture the man that he had been, the man that he might still become. She remembered the way he pushed his glasses up onto the bridge of his nose, the light in his eyes as he pored through old papers, but she didn't want to remember too long. If she did, she feared that the memory might return them to that place. But she didn't want to forget either. Forgetting would be worse.

········

It took three days of waking in the same bed for Trina to be sure that the Turnings had stopped. For three days she startled the boy out of his sleep, grasping frantically to make sure he was still there. Each morning she threw open the blinds and took inventory of the street below. Each morning she counted the streetlights she could see from her window and made sure the fire hydrant and the little newspaper box on the corner were still in their places. She ran down the hall and pressed her palms to the solid curve of the wooden railing. It was only when she saw the great stone fireplace in the atrium and heard the low chatter of the place beginning to come alive that she finally allowed herself to breathe.

And yet, there were still nights when she was sure that this world was slipping away, nights where she was almost certain the waters were still rising around them and the boy was crying, just out of reach. Those were the nights when she feared to open her eyes, because in opening them, she might cause it to be true.

Colin took to the place so quickly that after a few days it seemed as if he had lived there for years. He and the other children—there were four, all older, but by no more than a few years—tore noisily through the halls together. They argued and laughed and crowded around a video game system so ancient that Trina thought that it might have been older than she was. Colin made the place his home. In turn, it became her home.

The rules of Ms. Dixon's were few, and Edie laid them out to Trina with a gentle insistence that made it clear they were not to be breached. "No drinking and no drugs. No men, no romantic entanglements of any kind. That means the other girls too. I don't judge, mind you, but we've had a few couples here in the house make a go of it over the years and it always ends badly. Last, everyone pulls their own weight, with the exception of the little ones. We give them a pass, as long as they keep up with their schoolwork." That last bit she said with a little wink, and Trina couldn't help but smile a little as she nodded her agreement. Now that she was here, she might have agreed to anything.

It took a while for the other girls to accept her. It was Phoebe who told her later about two girls who had come to the place within a few months of each other. Neither of them had thought much about the first two rules, and both of them were prone to stealing anything that they thought they could sell later. Both times, Edie had taken care of it and found new places for the girls to live. But it had left the others suspicious of newcomers, and that ice took longer to thaw.

Phoebe was the exception. She had taken to Trina right away, and set about showing her all the ins and outs of the place. Together they folded laundry and pulled weeds and took inventory in the storeroom. The routine took hold, and soon enough each day began to feel the same as the last. Still, Trina often caught herself staring into the shadows of the place, expecting them to change, expecting them to be different from one day to the next. It was as if the place were haunted by memories of things that might have been, and things that never were.

· · · • • · • • · · ·

Philip came looking for them twice in the week that followed. The first time, she had seen his Audi parked along the street and heard the threats and the shouting from the sidewalk below when they would not let him inside. The second time, he was on foot, and she could see him from her bedroom window. As he looked up from the sidewalk, she was almost sure that he could see her, too. His hair was swept back and his eyes were clear, and she wondered for a moment why she hadn't left him with his scars, the way he'd left her with scars. His scars were not a part of this world, though, the world where she had her son back. She couldn't have one without giving up the other. Still, as he stood in the cold on the sidewalk she could see the echo of that broken creature in the mask that had looked back at her in the desert. She knew now that that creature had been a part of him all along, and would be a part of him still, no matter what path this world might set before him.

· · · · **·** **·** **·** · · ·

Snowy spring gave way to summer so quickly that it seemed as if a switch had been thrown. Afternoons spent in the atrium in front of the fireplace were abandoned in favor of afternoons in the courtyard, where the residents of Ms. Dixon's were able to relax in the shade afforded them by the high walls that stood like sentinels on all sides.

New girls came, and a few went just as quickly. Before long, Trina was one of the veterans of the house, the one that the others would come to with their troubles, with their doubts. Phoebe became a familiar presence, one that was never too far from her side. Trina hadn't recognized her at first, with her long, black hair framing her face. Nor had she recognized the deep brown eyes that had once stared at her from behind a metal hospital door. It was almost two months before Phoebe told her that her last name was Briggs.

35

Trina agreed to meet Philip at the little coffee shop around the corner on a weekend in July. He was waiting for her by the time she got there, newspaper folded in his lap, a showy-looking pen gleaming as it danced impatiently between his fingers. He didn't look up as she slid into the chair across the table from him, but she could tell that he was watching her all the same.

"The car's a total loss," he said. "Though you probably knew that already."

"It's insured," she said.

"Yeah, that should just about cover what it cost to get it towed out of the river. I should be thankful you at least took the Honda. No great loss there."

He looked up at her then, and his hard expression softened a bit. "You look good, Kat."

He stared at her, waiting for a reaction. She gave him none. She'd made two rules for herself before she came to meet him: don't say thank you and don't agree with him, about anything. She knew from experience that either one was just the first step down a very short and slippery slope. Still, she hated when he called her Kat, and knew that he remembered it.

"What were you even doing out there, anyway?"

Phoebe was sitting at the next table, staring at him over the top of a cappuccino mug as if she could set the back of his head on fire. Trina had told her that she was going to be all right, but Phoebe had insisted on coming anyway.

"You know exactly what I was doing out there," Trina said.

"Yeah, I suppose I do." He dropped the paper on the table and laid the pen down on top of it. There was a square filled with letters on the page, and he'd made black lines on it where the words were, so deep that they'd almost ripped through.

A teenage kid came by, rummaging in his apron while he asked them about their order. Philip waved him away. "It's not all my fault, you know," Philip said, leaning in close when the server was gone. "You just... Sometimes you just get so..."

He scratched at the side of his face. The burns were gone, but the skin around his eye still looked red, like it was breaking out in a rash.

"Look, I'm sorry, all right? That's what you want me to say, right? Well, okay. I'm sorry."

He reached out to her, wanting to take her hand. She pulled away.

"You don't have to be like that," he said. "I don't know why you always have to be like that." Over his shoulder she could see Phoebe tensing, ready to jump in. Trina gave a little shake of her head to let her know it was still all right. Philip didn't notice.

"I'm doing my best here, okay? It's not like I haven't been hurt, too. Did you ever think how I would have felt if they didn't find you? If you didn't get out of that car in time? You left without a word. Not one word."

Trina fought hard to not cross her arms, to not rub at all the places that still had the memories of bruises. "You would have tried to stop me."

"Of course I would have tried to stop you. I love you." He smiled at her then, but she had seen that smile a hundred times before. It was the same smile he had worn when she had met him in that other world, before he'd strapped her to a table and tried to kill her. But this wasn't that Philip, nor was he that cowed and shrinking creature she'd left behind in the wasteland. He was neither of those men, and both of them. More, and somehow less.

"So, when are you coming back?"

"I'm not," she said.

"What do you mean you're not?"

"That's what I mean. I'm not coming back."

He closed his eyes and breathed deep, as if he were praying for patience. When he opened them again, the warmth of his smile was gone. In its place was a stony cold, a jaw clenched beneath narrowed eyes.

"And you think I'm just going to let you go?"

"I do."

"And you're sure about that?"

"I am."

"And why is that?"

"Because you're afraid of me."

She saw the way his eyes widened at this, and knew at once that it was true.

"You're afraid of me and you don't know why. You never used to be. Before the crash, it never would have occurred to you. But I can tell by the way you're looking at me now. You know that things are different. You just can't put your finger on it."

He stared at her, and rubbed at his face, so red on one side that it looked as if he had fallen asleep in the sun. Trina could see by the way he moved that his shoulder was hurting too.

"And the funny thing about it is, you know exactly why. You just don't remember."

He crossed his arms and watched her, measuring, evaluating this new Trina, this woman he had followed through world after world, this woman he had never known until this moment. She met his gaze, her chin high, her hands folded in her lap. It wasn't long before the caution fled from his eyes, and his lips pressed into a hard, thin line.

"You know," he said at last, "I think you did it on purpose. I think you did it just so you could take something away from me."

"His name is Colin. And no, that wasn't why."

He stood up, so quick that he made the chair squeal against the tile floor. Phoebe stood up too, her fists balled. Trina didn't move. The other people in the coffee shop were looking at them now. Philip saw that they were looking, and his shoulders seemed to droop, so that he no longer loomed but merely stood, and not quite as tall as she remembered.

He reached into the pocket of his coat and started to pull something out. Phoebe tensed again, but Trina already knew that he had nothing that could hurt her.

"I was going to give you this," he said. "It was in the car. I'm amazed it still works. I was going to say you should call me, but now I'm thinking it's better if you don't."

He slid it across to the table and she caught it before it could land in her lap. The screen had a crack running right down the middle, but she knew there would still be a message waiting for her when she powered it on. She turned it over in her hands as she watched him go, watched him slam the door behind him.

"Yes," she whispered to no one in particular. "It is better."

36

There were times in the days that followed when Trina would watch Colin, sitting by himself with his toy cars, or laid out across an armchair with a book balanced on his chest. It was in these times that she could most see the adult that he had been. She saw echoes of her grandfather there too, in the way his brows furrowed when he was concentrating, in the way he scratched at the back of his neck, in the way he sighed when he was tired.

She asked him about that other life, at least insofar as she could ask about such a thing. She asked him if he ever dreamed about being older. She asked him if he ever thought about what it would be like if cars could fly, or if the world were covered in water. Mostly, he just shook his head and went back to his books and his games. Those were the times when she felt most like a thief. He had lived and grown old. Perhaps he'd had friends. Perhaps he'd even loved. He had sculpted a life for himself, living in the eye of the hurricane that she'd forced upon him, and she had taken it all away from him. She'd shown him what she had done to him, and it had almost driven him mad. It had almost destroyed him.

Only once did he show any hint of remembering their time in those other worlds. He was sitting on the floor in the atrium of Ms. Dixon's Home, arranging toy cars in a circle. It was just before the dinner hour and the two of them were alone with only the sounds of the little wheels against the stone floor. Trina had been watching him over the top of a book, a book whose pages she'd been turning without really seeing the words. He was playing just as absently, his mind somewhere far away, and before she knew what she was saying, the words were out of her mouth.

"Small room. Pink Rock."

He gave no sign that he had heard her, and as he pushed his cars along the floor she held her breath. "Ugly lamp," he said softly, to no one in particular. "Flower blanket."

·········

Summer was almost over by the time she decided to move on. She talked it over with Colin first. He had grown two inches since the accident and though he protested she knew he was eager to have a bedroom to himself. Edie had helped her get a resume together, and she'd found a job as a data analyst less than a mile away. Phoebe drove her back and forth those first few weeks, but before long Trina was driving on her own again and even walking when her courage was up and the weather was nice. The world seemed so much smaller now that she had a place in it. Still, she didn't stop looking over her shoulder when the air grew still and the street grew quiet. She didn't stop wondering if it was all too good to be true.

She told Edie in the courtyard, after she'd already packed their things and gotten the new apartment set up with furniture. She wanted to make sure she wasn't giving herself a chance to back out. Edie pulled her in close and held her like a sister and told her that she could come back any time she wanted to. Trina said that she would, but there was something in Edie's eyes that said that she didn't believe it. Trina wasn't sure that she believed it herself.

She found Colin in the courtyard at one of the flowerbeds, making a track for his toy cars in the mulch. She crouched in the grass beside him, but he would not look at her.

"I don't wanna go," he said, pouting. Trina gathered him up in her arms and tickled him playfully until his squirms of protest gave way to little squeals of delight. She had hoped to distract him, but when she put him down, he looked up at her, his face solemn and full of resolve.

"We have to, kiddo," she told him at last. "We were never meant to stay in this place forever."

"Why not?"

"Well," she said, considering, "we have a new place now. A place just for you and me. You'll have your own room and your own books. And school's starting soon. You'll have all kinds of new friends there. Doesn't that sound nice?"

He perked up a little at this, but he still looked doubtful. "Can my room be green, like our room here."

"Absolutely." She reached out and took his little hands in her own. "It belongs to us, so it can be whatever we want it to be."

She believed it, too. She had wanted to see Briggs again, even if she hadn't known it until it happened. If Briggs was a part of this world, then maybe Janowski was too. And if Janowski was out there, maybe Woods was somewhere out there, waiting to meet her again.

"I want green walls, and a green floor, and…" Colin trailed off and looked to his green toy car lying in the mulch.

"And green windows?" she asked.

A smile spread across his entire face and all the way up to his eyes. She remembered that smile. She had seen it once before, in his office in the town library. Seeing it again put a lump in her throat, and she had to fight to hold back her tears.

"Can we get green flowers, too?"

A little breeze danced across her shoulders and stirred the asters in the flowerbed. "Green like those?" she asked.

Colin looked at her doubtfully. "Those ones aren't green."

"Aren't they?" She pulled him close and kissed the tops of his hands. "We'll see about that. Close your eyes."

If you or someone you know is experiencing domestic violence or the threat of domestic violence, call the National Domestic Violence Hotline at 1-800-799-SAFE (7233), or visit www.thehotline.org

Acknowledgements

The road that *I Contain Multitudes* took from inception
to the book that you currently hold in your hands
(or on your e-reader or phone) was a long one.
Not long, perhaps, in publishing industry terms, but
in-real-world terms it often felt like an uphill slog filled
with switchbacks, traffic jams, and potholes, with no
real destination in sight. I would never have been able
to navigate that road without the guidance and steady
support of the people closest to me. I will always be
grateful for their encouragement and assistance.

Thanks go, first and foremost, to my wife Kris for
helping me to hone and shape this book through its
various incarnations and edits over the course of six years,
and for weathering all the complaints, self-doubt, and
obsessing over plot points that came with it. I may have
written *I Contain Multitudes*, but it exists because of her.

Thank you to my sons, Tim and Ben, for always
being the reason I keep writing and for putting up with
my endless dad jokes. They grew from children into
exceptional young men during the writing of this book,
and I couldn't be prouder of both of them.

To Charlotte Bunce, Katie Bunce, and Alan
Matsumura for reading those early drafts when I thought
I was finished but still had so much work left to do.

To J.A.W. McCarthy and Brian Pinkerton for their feedback and support. To Scott Kehoe for his invaluable eye for detail in squashing typos and helping to make this book fit for print.

To Alan Lastufka for lending his considerable talents and even more considerable patience to the creation of the cover for this book. To Emily Kardamis for her help with additional layout and design.

Thank you to the Chicago Writers Association and the folks at the Killer Nashville conference for recognizing this book's potential before it was even properly finished.

Last, but not least, I want to thank the members of the Chicagoland Chapter of the Horror Writers Association, who have given me endless motivation, lasting friendships, and a purpose beyond the page. You guys rock.

Christopher Hawkins, February 2025.

About the Author

Born and raised near the shores of Lake Michigan, Christopher Hawkins has been writing and telling stories for as long as he can remember. A dyed-in-the-wool geek, he is an avid collector of books, roleplaying games and curiosities. When he's not writing, he spends his time exploring old cemeteries, lurking in museums, and searching for a decent cup of tea.

Christopher is the multi-award-winning author of Downpour and Suburban Monsters. He is the former editor of the One Buck Horror anthology series and the co-chair of the Chicagoland chapter of the Horror Writers Association. His works of short fiction have been published in numerous magazines and anthologies, including Cosmic Horror Monthly, Underland Arcana, Fusion Fragment, Read By Dawn vol 2, and The Big Book of New Short Horror.

An expatriate Hoosier, Christopher currently lives in a suburb of Chicago with his wife and two sons.